BLOOD SICK
VAMPIRE

J. E. Serrano

This book is dedicated to my friend Duffy

Blood Sick Vampire

ISBN 978-1-955531-50-4 (paperback)

PROLOGUE

Genesis 4:10–15

(v. 10) And the Lord said unto Cain. "What have you done? The voice of your brother's blood cries out to me from the ground.

(v. 11) Now, you are cursed from the ground which has opened its mouth to receive your brother's blood from your hand.

(v. 12) When you work the ground, it shall no longer yield to you its strength. You shall be a fugitive and a wanderer on the earth."

(v. 13) Cain said to the Lord, "My punishment is greater than I can bear".

(v. 14) Behold, you have driven me away from the ground, and from your face, I shall be hidden. I shall be a fugitive and a wanderer on the earth, and whoever finds me will kill me."

(v. 15a) Then the Lord said to him, "Not so! If anyone kills Cain, vengeance shall be taken on him sevenfold."

CONTENTS

CHAPTER 1

DESTINY AWAKENED

The sun rose over the horizon casting its light, awakening the villagers of Cadiz. Roosters crowed, dogs barked and the villagers went about their morning routine. Sunlight pierced the window awakening its sleeping occupant. Diego Sat up abruptly, a headache throbbed between his temples from the previous night of revelry that was his going away party. Diego shielded his eyes, moaned aloud, and sank back into bed. Feeling a stirring beside him Diego looked down to see a mass of black hair draped across a slender back and a foot peeking out from the bear-skin blanket. "Master Diego it is time to rise, you have a busy day". Pablo, his servant reminded him as he entered his young masters' bedroom. Diego looked over at Pablo. "What would I do without you, Pablo"? Diego asked for the hundredth time while rubbing his eyes. Pablo laughed gently responding. "I shudder to think Master," Pablo answered somewhat snidely. Diego peered up at Pablo through his slowly diminishing hangover. "Perhaps it is the wine or the earliness of the morning but do I hear an edge to your voice," Diego asked detecting sarcasm in his usually jovial man-servant. Pablo stopped folding Diego's clothes for a moment and took a breath, leaned over the bed, and looked his young charge in the face. "Today is the day." He simply said. Diego smiled, warmly and put his hand on Pablos' shoulder. "How long have you served our house old friend" Pablo looked at Diego. "My Family has faithfully served the house of Torrolisimo since my grand-fathers time and if I'm lucky my sons and theirs shall do likewise, now, enough banter unless you intend to spend all day in bed and miss your fire well party I suggest you get up because this my dear boy is the day you've been waiting for". Pablo prompted. Diego looked at the young lady lying next to him still asleep. Catching Diego's meaning Pablo smiled. "Do not worry master Diego I will make sure she is properly fed and I shall send your condolence that you were not there to greet her this morning but you have business to be about". Pablo prompted Diego who excitedly jumped out of his luxurious feathered bed onto a cold stone floor. Standing a modest five foot nine inches, with a medium build, short, black curly hair. He quickly got dressed while Pablo hurried his female company out of bed. In playful protest, she complained. "But Diego, Can't we sleep in"? Diego laughed, kissed her gently. "I apologize Rosa but I thank you for a wonderful night, Pablo will see you out". Diego announced in departure looking amorously at the curvature of her waist while waving goodbye.

This was the day he would set forth to the French countryside to meet other knights of varying orders to ride to the city of Genoa where he would rendezvous with King Richard of England and from there to the port of Tyre. Diego had trained all of his life for a moment such as this, to do something of great significance and what could be more significant than the liberation of Jerusalem from the hands of unbelievers. Diego thought fondly of his silver-maned grandfather Rodrigo who did what was necessary to secure his grandsons' passage on the flagship of the English despite the objections of Carlos, Diego's father who for reasons of his own did not want Diego to go at all. When Carlos heard that the French King, Phillip II was going the objections of Carlos grew stronger as The Spanish Duke did not trust his motives. It was only after Rodrigo secured passage on an English ship did Carlos recant his objections and give Diego his blessing. Diego ran down the stone steps to join his family for what could be his final breakfast with them. The beautiful Duchess Inez met her son with a hug and kiss. "How are you this morning my son"? The Lady of the manor asked. "I feel fine, excited. And you Mother, Did you sleep well"? Diego asked. The Duchess smiled at her only son. "How do you think I slept knowing my only son goes to do war in a faraway land"? The Duchess asked facetiously. To wrapped up in his excitement over what his day promised Diego missed the sarcastic tone of the reply. "Well, today is the day". Bellowed Don Carlos, Duke of Cadiz and Father to Diego. A well-built man with flecks of gray sprinkled throughout his hair. Carlos sported a thin mustache, ever pouting lips, brown eyes, and was equipped with a laugh that could shake the foundations. A generous man, good-natured as his laugh attested to, entered the section of the Castle Torro where they took their meals. Resplendent in his armor Carlos walked in brandishing a huge smile as he greeted his only son. "Good morning Father". Diego greeted. Carlos reached into a large bag pulling out a smaller one and threw it to Diego. "What's this for"? Diego inquired.

"Well I can't send my son away to war as a vagabond now can I"? Carlos pointed out. "You'll find fifty gold pieces inside". Diego hefted the bag in his hand hearing the tinkling of the gold inside. "Father this is far too generous". Diego disingenuously complained. "Non-sense". countered Carlos. Diego approached his Father and dropped to his knees. "Father I wish to thank you for permitting me to go forth and prove myself". Carlos put his hand on the shoulder of his son. "Rise my prince and know that while I and your Mother, are not at all happy about your departure you leave with our pride in you. That you would give yourself to such a noble cause will bring great honor to our house. We have but one command, return to us safely". The Duke said softly. Diego bowed his head. "As you command Father". Diego responded smiling. "Now, before you leave hug your Mother and go see your grandfather as he wishes to see you before you go". Carlos ordered. "Of course Father". Diego acquiesced. He stepped into his Mothers embrace. Diego looked upon her drinking in her almond-shaped eyes, hair that fell down her back like an obsidian-colored river, her tan complexion and soft voice made her one of the most beautiful women in all Espana. She whispered in his ear. "My son, many evils await you in the world and it can be savage beyond these walls. I know you are not a boy and you've seen a bit of the world but you're going into something far more dangerous. Remember your Fathers edict and come home to us". Duchess Inez said tearfully. "I shall do as you say Mother".

Diego promised. Turning to his Father the Duke clapped his son on the shoulder. "Go and do us proud my son". Carlos whispered. "I shall Father". Diego promised. Grabbing his gear Diego made his way to his GrandFathers quarters. Climbing the stairway to Rodrigo's tower (which he dubbed "El oho del Torro). Diego found the founder of their house sitting on his porch which overlooked all of Cadiz. His sword in hand, his gaze was fixed on the whetstone he slowly ran down the length of the blade. "Abuelo". Diego said aloud announcing himself. "Come come Nieto". Rodrigo called gesturing with a nod of his head, a seat beside him for the young man to take. Diego sat beside his Grandfather. "Well today is the day boy, how do you feel"? Rodrigo inquired gaze still fixed on his sword, The stone whispering the hiss of sharpening every warrior knew. Diego looked over his family's fiefdom from the spectacular view Rodrigo had built for himself. "A little nervous". Diego admitted quietly. "Good". Rodrigo responded decisively. Diego looked up baffled. "I thought you would be disappointed that I wasn't chomping at the bit to go Abuelo". Diego said surprised at his grandfathers' reaction. Rodrigo looked at Diego out of the corner of his eye. "I did not raise a family of murdering animals Diego and if you were excited about drawing blood and killing I would have you locked up in our dungeons because what you describe is an insane man and we of the house of Torro are Warriors, brave, salient but not stupid or crazy. No Diego, it comforts me that you have second thoughts about such matters it shows you are a man of conscience and that beloved grandson is far more valuable to our house than anything else I can think of, You do us proud Diego. This is my parting gift to you. Rodrigo handed Diego a long package. "Open it when you set sail and always remember your grandfather who loves you and is tremendously proud of you". Diego embraced the old man with tears in his eyes. "Always and forever Abuelo". Diego promised. Leaving his grandfather's quarters Diego navigated the many steps and turned down the hall that led to the entrance. With his head down looking at the package, which obvious to Diego was a new sword Diego looked up and saw the family and its servants lined up to the Castle gates throwing flowers and singing old songs of Cadizean valor. Diego mounted his horse Viento, a beautiful stallion, an Andalusian with a flowing black mane. Under a bright sky, Diego rode through the gates of his family estates and began the long ride that would bring him to Marseille. After a week or so of uneventful riding Diego arrived at his destination. With a week or so before the voyage Diego quickly got himself a room at a nearby inn as the town was filling up with mercenaries responding to the call that went throughout Europe for what was being called the third crusade. The ranks of the crusaders swelled as they marched to their port of call in Genoa. Flanked by his personal guard Diego held a small tight smile of pride in taking part in such a venture. Approaching the chaos that was the boarding docks Diego located the docked ship from England. Diego pointed his men to where the ship was berthed and ordered his Highlanders form in a phalanx that cut a wedge allowing Diego access. Approaching the Ship A figure stood on deck personally directing his men. "Hold". He called out. "Identify yourself". The Englishman demanded. "I am Diego Torrolisimo, here by proxy of my Grandfather Rodrigo 'El Leon de Cadiz' Torrolisimo". Diego responded with pride filling his voice. "Well met Diego, I know of your grandfathers' exploits. You are welcome". Diego smiled, nodded, and directed his men to their allocated positions. One of Diego's guards approached with a message. "My lord, the one who received us has invited us as his guest to dine with him this evening". Diego nodded. "I hope you related our sincere gratitude to his Majesty". Diego affirmed. The guards' jaw dropped to the floor after all whoever heard of a King directing troops n such a manner?

Voyage

Diego stood on the deck of the ship that served as the English flagship. The warm air of France caressed his skin as he watched the great king, Richard I of Britain, and the French king, Philip II, oversee the boarding of their troops. The waves lapped gently on the hull of the ship, and a great sense of purpose and destiny settled upon him.

He reflected on how he came to be where he was. His name was a proud one, born in Cadiz, España, in the year of our Lord 1169. Raised on the exploits of a valorous family was what focused on his aspirations. To be regarded as highly as his grandfather. Because he had been training since childhood, his talents were soon recognized. Being an heir to a ruling family severely hampered his family's desire that Diego engages in battle. Begging his grandfather's blessing—much to the dismay of his father—he loaned his skills out to various houses of nobility. His reputation grew along with his skills and he soon felt prepared to become a warrior in the Crusade of Richard Lion-heart, the king of England. Diego had become a mercenary whose abilities were well respected throughout Europe, so he was welcomed by the English to join their ranks to oust the infidels from the Holy Land.

He was twenty years old when he heard of this excursion; and though his father, Carlos, Duke of Torrolisimo, did not approve of the venture, his grandfather Rodrigo, the Lion of Cadiz, gave his blessing and a family sword to bring esteem and honor to their household. His grandfather used his many connections with the Crown to get Diego an audience with the king of England. After much dickering, his grandfather offered twenty of his cavaliers as Diego's escort and a hundred pounds of silver toward the cause.

CHAPTER 2
STAGING

With all the preparation and travel to Marseille, France To rendezvous with the English and French armies, who were staging there to board the Genoese fleet, Diego began to think that perhaps it would have been better had he stayed in bed in that sweet buxom wench's arms. What was her name again, Flora! That was it, and she smelled like flowers. Be that as it may, they sailed for the Holy Land the week after Diego joined. Diego stood on the bow watching the shoreline recede wondering if he'd ever see it again. The smell of flowers was replaced by the smell of salt. Going below decks Diego opened the package given to him by his grandfather and found a family sword. Each of the males had one made especially for them and was a passage of manhood in his family. Tearfully remembering the old man that showed him so much love Diego put the sword in a safe place and went below deck. The voyage divided the men amongst Knights and squires with the former sitting quietly sharpening weapons or cleaning armor while the squires (who would normally be the ones cleaning their lords' gear) were speaking nervously among themselves, some in fear and others in bravado. Diego sat in shadows and watched the men banter trying to evaluate who spoke well and who fought well. Diego learned early as a mercenary that serious warriors seldom spoke of battle while those that depended on good fortune or their prayers either seldom made it out alive or took to bragging. Diego sought the company of the quiet warriors. In relatively calm seas and clear skies, the fleet made its' way until they finally spotted the shoreline and they made for the port of Tyre. Disembarking the armies the generals prepared for the long march from Tyre to Damascus. Diego was invited to ride along with King Richard's cavalry. Flanked by his Cadizcan cavaliers Diego took his position in Richards company. With great fanfare, trumpets blew as if to announce their arrival. Boots stomped, horses whinnied and wheels creaked as the Army began its march.

Encounter

On their way to Damascus, bright blue skies turned an orangish tinge, the winds increased viscously pelting them with sand, pebbles, and small stones as they were overcome by a monster sandstorm. Confusion fell upon the ranks as visibility diminished to almost nothing and the only thing to be heard was the howling of the wind. Diego got detached from his company. His horse, Viento stumbled blindly about in a vain effort, Diego lost sight of his bodyguards as the wind scattered them. Diego finally dismounted his frightened horse, snatched a blanket from his saddlebag, and covered the horse's head while gently coaxing him to lay down trying to comfort him. Diego lay there listening for any sound of horse or men. There was only the howling wind and stinging sand pelting him, snatching the very moisture from his body. After what seemed an eternity Diego decided laying there was not helping his situation, the winds seeming to have calmed down a bit, he helped the horse back to his wobbly legs and urged him on. He continued not knowing if his current action was an exercise in futility but he felt a compulsion to continue the way he was going. For no explicable reason, he continued, thirsty, hungry. Viento's legs got shaky and the poor horse collapsed snorting blood from his nostrils. Diego spoke gently to the dying horse occasionally spitting out sand. Angry at himself for subjecting the poor horse to this alien environment. He watched in sadness as his equine companion died.

Unable to shed a tear (due to the dehydration he was suffering) Diego continued to stumble along until he saw what he thought to be a ridiculously large house in a very unlikely place. Without much choice, Diego continued to the house.

"Who builds such structures in such a godforsaken place?" Diego asked himself aloud, regretting his apparent stupidity of opening his mouth in such a storm.

Spitting out sand, he realized that despite the apparent incongruity, the sand and wind seemed to be pushing him toward the house, his choice appeared reduced to just one, go there or die in this uncaring maelstrom. Self-preservation being what it is, he continued to the odd house.

Upon arriving, Diego found the house empty. Of course, no one would be here, maybe when there were trade routes long ago, but not presently. He searched his shelter and was taken aback upon seeing the lavishness and relative cleanliness of the house.

"How could such a wealthy house go unmolested?" he wondered.

Without much hope, he scrounged around for food; and much to his surprise, which was quickly followed by suspicion, there was a stable built into a subfloor. There were well-tended sheep and a well of clear water. Diego did not earn his reputation by being careless, so he drew his sword and continued exploring the house for any potential threats.

After a while of reconnoitering the area, Diego finally settled down as thirst, hunger, and weariness began to assert themselves. He built a small fire, butchered a lamb, and dined on lamb chops and cool water from the well for dinner. Only now can he say that the house seemed to make everything more seductive. He got full from meat and water, and he only now allowed himself to think of his horse. While it's true Diego didn't have him for long Viento was a gift from his Grandfather. Diego sat down hard on the hard-packed earth of the subbasement. The small fire he had started to cook the lamb danced in a chaotic yet soothing manner. Diego touched his sword and fought back a sense of dread. *Everything except my sword that my Abuelo gifted me with as tokens of fortune and reminders of home is gone. My beautiful horse, my men, Oh my God my men! The storm probably has done to them what it almost did to me! What an utter failure this venture has turned out to be.* Diego mused. A bone-deep weariness settled on Diego demanding that he rest.

Diego made himself comfortable, with sword close at hand, *"It's just you and I now my friend guard me well"*. He thought before falling into a sweet, peaceful sleep. Upon awakening, Diego stretched to get whatever knots might come from the hard floor and mused aloud. "I wonder how the kings are doing?"

"they have come to terms with Saladin and have made it relatively safe for Christians to pilgrimage to the Holy City once again," a voice answered.

Diego jumped into a fighting stance his sword at the ready, looking for the intruder. "Who are you?" Diego demanded, talking to darkness and shadow. "Oh, just a friend," the voice replied.

"My friends do not hide in shadows!" Diego exclaimed.

"My, my," the voice responded, "And here I thought you Spaniards were supposed to be civilized."

"If you value your life, stranger, it would do you well not to denigrate my people," Diego warned

"My good man, I was not denigrating your people as opposed to reflecting on rumored speculation as to the level of civility displayed by your people's customs. However, since you entered my home—"

"Your home?" Diego interjected.

"Yes, my home. Uninvited! may I add". Stepping out of the shadows a short slender man, short in height, closely cropped black hair and slightly slanted eyes continued his tirade. "You slaughtered my sheep, and drank of my well. I thought the pleasant conversation was the least you owed me." Seeing the diminutive, unarmed man Diego felt less threatened but stayed on his guard.

"I apologize," Diego replied. "But the storm drove me here, such a forbidding place. How is it that you come to be here alone where none may survive?"

"Well, that is simply explained, my friend," the stranger replied.

Diego waited expectedly.

"Oh, you would like to hear my explanation?" the stranger asked, feigning surprise.

"I think that would go a long way in establishing some kind of trust," Diego responded. Well, I built this house a very long time ago when it was an active trade route but as with most things, the function of the house quickly became obsolete when the trade route dried up. Now I use it only on occasions such as this" The stranger informed Diego. "That can certainly be taken the wrong way" Diego observed.

'Whatever do you mean?" The stranger inquired. Diego eyed his host suspiciously. "You said you kept the house for moments such as this, Do you mean to imply that when you're in the area? or against this hell-wrought storm or"..." Diego let the unmentioned insinuation hang. The small, dark-haired man smiled. "Or to trap unsuspecting wanderers to accost them"? The small man chuckled. "No, I assure you that is not my reason for keeping this house". The man clarified. Then fell silent. "If you would allow me"? Diego requested. The small stranger nodded. "Your assurance means nothing to me as I don't know who you are". Diego said pointing out the obvious. The stranger bowed formally. "Rightly so". The stranger capitulated.

CHAPTER 3

SEDUCTION OF DIEGO

"I am Cain of Nod," the stranger stated calmly. Diego's face took on a look of confusion as he wondered at the name and a haunting significance associated with it.

Cain saw the look of recognition settle on Diego's face. "Your Parents named you Cain? Did they know the significance of giving you such a name"? The horror behind that name"? Diego inquired somewhat shocked.

The one who called himself Cain smiled. "At the time there was no significance, in fact, I was the only one with such a name". Cain clarified. Diego considered that for a moment. "But you are implying that..." Diego let the unfinished statement hang. "You cannot possibly mean . ." Diego stammered." Cain nodded in confirmation."Yes, I am that very same one." Cain acknowledged.

"Prove it"? Diego demanded. Cain smiled. "My birth certificate can be found in the book you call the Bible. If that does not suffice then you will learn in due time". Cain replied. Diego shook his head in denial. "You want me to believe that you are Cain of Nod firstborn of Adam and Eve and that you murdered your brother?" Diego questioned in both shock and disbelief.

"Yes, yes, I know. Wish everyone would just put that incident aside." The one calling himself Cain said dismissively.

"How can this be when this story is thousands of years old?"

"Yes. Speaking of a person's age is one of those civilities I mentioned earlier."

"But that is impossible," Diego responded, shocked.

"Improbable, perhaps. Unlikely, most assuredly, but not impossible," answered Cain.

"Look, señor, I don't know nor do I want to know what kind of craziness you're trying to spread, but I'll have no part of it."

Diego insisted. "Cain. I told you my name is Cain, and need I point out you have yet to introduce yourself?"

"Why should I give my name to a madman?"

"You think me mad, do you?" Cain asked.

"If you think you are Cain, son of Adam and Eve, brother to Abel, then yes, I think you are quite mad."

"Ahhh, there you go, insulting me again. I am a murderer many times over, and yes, I have cursed anything and everything good, but a liar, I am not."

"So you expect me to believe you're thousands of years old?"

"I do not require your belief for it to be so," Cain responded dismissively.

The menacing tone in Cain's voice put Diego on guard.

"What is it then you require?" Diego asked suspiciously. Cain smiled revealing needle-like fangs.

"Not much really, only a few drops. or perhaps a good swallow of your blood." Cain responded casually.

Diego menacingly brandished his sword. "My blood! Step but one foot forward and your taste for blood will be sated if you like your own," he threatened.

Cain clapped his hands in glee. "What a wonderful performance, but I assure you if I wanted to take it, you could not top me." Before Diego could move, Cain flashed to his left side, slapped him then to his right, slapped him again, and then returned to his previous position. Diego stumbled back, making the sign of the cross.

"Now, now, we'll have none of that," Cain admonished.

Diego looked at Cain with narrowing eyes. "What are you?" he asked.

"Oh, I've been called so many things, but the name I like the most is what the Europeans call me."

"And what's that?" Diego asked, almost afraid of the answer.

"Vampyre," Cain whispered.

"What!" Diego looked around frantically.

"Calm yourself, my friend, as I said if I just wanted to take you, I would. But I see something special about you, Diego, so I wanted to offer you the chance of immortality."

"Immortal damnation you mean! Step away from me. wait, how is it that you come to know my name"? Diego asked nervously. Cain smiled in response. "That is not important is it? besides there is no need for hostilities, is there?"

"You just told me we're going to drink my blood. I feel this is an adequate reason to be hostile, wouldn't you agree?"

"I suppose under normal conditions, you would be correct."

"I do not normally meet and converse with Vampyres."

"I imagine not, but consider what I am offering you."

"I have. The consideration is rejected," Diego shot back.

Cain looked at him shaking his head, saying, "You are a fool."

"Yes, but I'm a living fool, demon!" Diego shouted back.

"Not for long, my naive little friend," Cain whispered.

"Go ahead and end this then! You wish to drink of me, then do so and be done with it." Diego shouted.

"Oh no, my little Spanish knight. You will ask for it," Cain said, smiling slyly.

"How did you ever get so old being so stupid, Cain? I will never ask to be a hell-spawned demon!"

Cain clucked his tongue. "I know nothing of hell, knight, and as I said I am no demon". replied Cain.

Momentarily taken aback, Diego looked at Cain. "What? Are you not his servant?"

Cain looked at Diego with a stare that chilled him to his bones. "I would not serve God after he rejected me. Why would I serve one of his minions?"

"But you are evil. You drink the blood of men. You killed your brother and denounced God."

"I am not evil! Merely stubborn. And to this day, I don't understand why he chose my whiney little brother over me." He complained.

"How then," Diego asked, "came you to be this way? If you serve neither God nor the devil?"

Cain looked off into the night. "It appears you are familiar with my story."

"I am," Diego interjected. "Every good Catholic knows the story of how you slew your brother and escaped to the city of Nod."

"Yes, but what you didn't get to read about was the curse."

"Yes, yes, I know of this. 'Let those who attempt vengeance upon Cain.'"

"Yes, that one," Cain interjected tartly before continuing. "There is more to the story. I was in a village when the dark one visited me."

"You mean Satan?" Diego asked, somewhat startled.

"Do you know anyone that deserves the title more?" Cain asked sarcastically.

Diego quietly shook his head in admittance that none came to mind.

"Yes. Well, he came one night," continued Cain. "I hear you, and the big shot up there had a falling out," Satan exclaimed.

"What did you say?" Diego asked, finding himself enthralled by the tale.

"I told him to go to hell," Cain responded with a smile.

The image of this slight man telling the lord of evil to go to hell broke Diego into a fit of laughter.

"It's good to hear you laugh, my friend."

Diego gathered his wits as he realized he was beginning to like this demon in man's flesh. "I still will not join you," he defensively responded.

Cain looked at Diego. "Yes, I know. You already said that" he replied.

"Well, just in case you need reminding," Diego said.

Cain glanced at him with eyes that shone before he continued with his tale. "Well, it would seem that little horn doesn't take rejection well."

"What happened?" Diego asked curiously.

"Nothing and everything." Cain sat unexpectedly. Gracefully, preternaturally.

"Well, he gathered a coven of witches who practiced the dark arts, at his bidding they summoned a blood-drinking demon from hell that possessed me," he whispered.

Diego was stunned beyond belief. "But the promise?"

"Yes, the promise. The clever little bastard convinced God that since 'no man' lifted their hands against me, the technicality being they were women, and since I drew my brother's blood from him and defied all God's teachings, it was fit for me to be cursed so." "And God accepted that excuse?" Diego asked flabbergasted.

"It would appear so," replied Cain.

"While I may never call you friend, your story touches me," Diego replied, saddened. "Enough too . . .," Cain probed.

"No! I told you I would not willingly join you."

"Oh, but you will," replied Cain. "Why delay the inevitable? I can give you immortality!" he exclaimed.

"Yes, but at what cost? No, my blood-drinking friend, we shall part ways," Diego replied.

"A shame that. Where will you go if I may ask?"

Diego looked at Cain, feeling confused as to how he could feel compassion for an admitted murderer and blasphemer.

"It is because you are one also," Cain answered.

"What? What did you say?" To Diego's astonishment, he heard Cain's voice in his head. *I said you too have murdered and blasphemed.*

How is this . . ., Diego thought.

"Possible," Cain finished.

Diego slowly nodded his head, afraid to speak or even think.

"Very impressive, Diego. When you want to shut things out, you do so with quite a bit of strength. You would be a formidable Vampyre." Cain acknowledged aloud.

"There are others?" Diego asked.

"I've made one or two, and they've made others."

Diego was shaken to his very core. *How could such evil exist?* he wondered.

"I already told you how," replied Cain.

"I must leave now," Diego said somewhat frantically as he gathered his gear.

"Really, must you go now? There is so much I can show you," quibbled Cain.

Diego looked at Cain. "I am grateful for your hospitality, but I must leave and join my king."

"King? Your king is dead, Diego."

"What? What manner of foolishness do you speak?" Diego demanded.

"I told you, your king fought for safe passage to Jerusalem then returned to his homeland where he eventually died," Cain informed Diego. "What? That cannot be true, demon," retorted Diego.

"I do not lie, Spaniard."

"I must see this for myself," responded Diego.

"Well, there's the door. Are you sure you won't change your mind and join me?" Cain asked again.

"Yes, I'm sure," Diego answered.

"Well then, there is nothing left to say then," Cain said calmly.

"No, there isn't. Good-bye, Cain."

"Well, thank you for not calling me a monster or anything demeaning. But this is not goodbye, Diego." Cain smiled.

"What? But you said I could leave," he reminded him.

"And so you may, but you will ask for my gift before the night is over," answered Cain.

"I don't think so," Diego said. "I will die and be cursed by God twice before joining with you," he replied as he walked to the door. He turned, only to find Cain gone.

Well, I guess he doesn't handle rejection well either, he mused.

Diego walked into harsh sunlight and a majestic blue sky. checking his gear making sure he had ample provisions (Cain had given him a skin of water and some figs. Diego looked at the meager provisions. "Are you sure you can spare this?" He asked sarcastically. "Diego you know you're not going to be needing this as by the end of the day you will call to me" Cain teased. Diego shook the memory and began his march.

Temptation of Diego

As Diego got to the top of a dune, he turned to look at the strange house only to find it was gone. Staring at the spot that once contained a lovely home showed now only sand. Grunting disbelief Diego Turned and trudged onward. Before long, the sky began a familiar changing of colors as blue quickly turned a burned orange, and another sandstorm was upon him. Turning on the off chance he might glimpse the house, no such luck, Diego wondered. *Do these things spring up here?*. It may have been one or four hours later he found himself very lost and cresting yet another hill, with still no civilization in sight.

I don't understand this. I've walked the distance to the house three times over.

Seeing another dune, he thought, *Perhaps over the next one.* Exhausted and dehydrated, he crested the dune, only to see an ocean of sand. He sank to his knees as the sandstorm whipped him furiously. Diego collapsed on his side. "No, no. I don't want to die. Lord, if you would but spare me."

"Yeah, he's not listening."

Diego rolled onto his back, seeing the slender image of the one who called himself Vampyre. "Cain! I should have known," Diego said with a dry, scratchy throat.

"You did know," whispered Cain.

"Lord, hear my prayer," Diego began.

"Diego, please, I already told you. He isn't listening," said Cain.

"How would you know?" Diego rasped out of a parched throat.

"My, you sound terrible. Try not to speak. You know when the holy one is listening because you are awed by his presence to answer your question. Are you in awe?" Cain inquired facetiously.

"No," Diego snapped. "But I'm not easy to impress." He laughed, coughing up a froth of blood.

"Diego, you must rest, for though the sight of your blood is very appetizing, it does not bode well for you."

"To die so far from my homeland without even the comfort of God to whom I bid relief," cried Diego.

"You're not alone, Diego. I'll stay with you," Cain responded.

Diego laughed, coughing up more blood. "To think I'm going to be comforted by one such as you."

"Now, Diego, I know that is fear of death talking, but there is no need to be insolent," Cain complained, sounding offended.

Diego would have laughed if the pain weren't so great. "So the nightwalker has feelings?" he mocked.

"I don't appreciate the insinuation, Diego."

Diego looked up, too weak to speak.

"That I am unfeeling or a creature of the night. I have feelings and walk in the daylight same as you."

How? Diego thought, too weak to utter the word.

"I am the firstborn of my kind, and only me and my immediate converts also share this luxury to one degree or another. So I would not be damned to the night. Perhaps it is the Creator's way of showing me that I am not damned to darkness, perhaps not, I want you to Come with me Diego, and you wouldn't be damned either Diego," whispered Cain.

Diego moaned, and Cain shifted him to a more comfortable position. *I'm dying, aren't I, Cain"?* Diego thought.

"Yes, Diego, you are, but you don't have to," Cain pled. It was then Diego noticed that the storm had abated.

"What happened"? Diego thought weakly. Cain considered the question a moment before realizing what Diego meant. "You mean the storm"? Cain asked. Diego, with great effort, nodded his head. "Oh, that? It served its purpose. I sent it away". Cain remarked casually. In Diego's dying mind, he became aware that the storm was designed by Cain to lure Diego to the strange home. "Just so," Cain admitted. "When your armies disembarked, I sensed a peculiarity which turned out to be you, so I conjured the storm and urged the compulsions that led you to me," Cain concluded.

"Death is upon you, Diego; you have only to ask for my gift, and you shall live forever," Cain promised.

No, thought Diego. *I will face my death.*

"Then listen for the choir," said Cain. "They will lead you home."

As Diego lay back facing his mortality, he heard a din arise—a cacophony of moans and screams. Diego thought, *What is this?*

Diego heard a voice that sounded very distant—Cain's voice. *"Hell comes for you, Diego."*

No! Diego thought. *I will not serve Satan.*

In the background, the din grew more discordant, followed by a terrible voice ringing in Diego's head. *"You will serve me!"*

Diego frantically called out to God, *"Lord, save me,"* only to hear a bloodcurdling laugh was heard in response.

"I think not," The booming voice of doom continued in his head. *"Murderer. Lust full fool. Did you think praying would save your soul"?*A screeching voice demanded. *"You forsook your soul as a mercenary and drew blood! Your soul belongs to me"!*

Diego's thoughts turned to Cain. "You are almost there, my friend," Cain said as a warning.

Diego heard a voice that sounded like it was underwater. *"Cain! Butcher, murderer. He is mine! You have no authority here,"* the booming voice demanded.

"You have authority once he is dead. Not before then, Scrotch." Turning to Diego, Cain urged him aloud, "Tell me now what you wish, Diego, or prepare for your new master."

"I would rather walk in the sun than burn eternally," Diego rasped.

"But you will burn upon Judgment Day, and you will be mine," the booming voice condemned.

"Satan, your arrogance is astounding. You have no idea what the Lord's plans are for the end of days." Cain projected forcefully, trying to stop the unstoppable. Satan pushed his way closer to Diego's soul, feeling his authority grow.

"And you, Cain, you too shall be mine!" Satan exclaimed, feeling triumphant.

"Well, that's just fine. Until then, why don't you go find some goat you find attractive and go fornicate with it?" responded Cain in an attempt to distract Satan as Cain felt Satan's power grow because of

the legitimacy of his claim. Diego was indeed a killer, and he had slain many men during his time as a mercenary and now had to answer for the blood he's spilled. Returning his attention to Diego, Cain asked, "What is it to be, Diego? You are about to die. "God forgive me. "I would join with you," whispered Diego.

"That didn't sound very sincere," replied Cain.

Is it your wish to torture me? Diego thought to himself.

"Not at all, my friend. As I said earlier, you would have to ask." Cain responded aloud.

"Then I request that I join you," Diego coughed.

"Then prepare to join the immortals," Cain exclaimed to the howling winds and infuriated demons as he sank his fangs into Diego's neck.

CHAPTER 4

DIEGO'S CONVERSION

Diego only felt a pinch as he was so near death, then his body felt as if it were aflame. *"Cain, you lying son of a—."* Diego thought while his body spasmed. "Be still, Diego; that is only your body ridding itself of the yoke of mortality," Cain whispered.

The pain continued to increase to unbelievable levels. A white flame enveloped him searing his soul. Then as suddenly as it started, it stopped, and Diego found himself by a stream where he saw a man bathed in a white aura. He approached the man and was shocked to see blood streaming from his forehead, hands, and feet. Diego dropped to his knees.

"Master," Diego said, recognizing the Son of heaven.

"Why do you still call me that, Diego?" The one known as the Logos asked. "Because you are my Lord," Diego responded quickly.

"Then why, Diego, did you join with Cain?"

"Lord, I will never accept Satan as my master, and when I called out to you and the Father, Satan came instead."

"As was his right, Diego. Did you not kill? But instead of accepting the judgment you brought upon yourself, you sought an escape, so then, Diego Manuel Torrolisimo de Cadiz," proclaimed the Holy Son, "by your own words, will you be judged, twice cursed, Return now to your master of choice."

In an instant, Diego sat upright in his body, yet not his body. No. Yet he could feel strength flooding his veins.

Cain, I."

"I know, Diego. Each one of my converts goes through that, although to be frank, I thought.

Satan was successful, as I couldn't sense you at all."

"You mean they all go through the white fire?" Diego asked.

"White fire? What white fire?" asked Cain, intrigued.

"I went through a white-hot fire that felt as if it was burning my soul."

"It sounds as if you were cleansed by the Holy Spirit!" Cain replied, shocked.

"Is that unusual?" asked Diego.

"For those such as us, yes. Is that all that happened?"

"Well, no. I met Jesus."

"What!" exclaimed Cain.

"Yes, he questioned why I chose you instead of the judgment I chose for myself. Then he told me by my own words am I cursed."

Cain rubbed his chin thoughtfully. "Well, this can't be good. Come, let us go explore. We will feed and perhaps garner a clearer understanding of Yeshua's meaning."

Diego stood looking around as if seeing for the first time. Cain smiled, knowing what Diego was experiencing.

They walked for a bit; the sun was scorching, a gentle breeze kissed them. Diego looked to Cain. "Did you order this for me"? Diego inquired, noticing how good the sun felt on his face and how seductive the breeze felt. "As much as I would love to take credit for the beauty of Nature, I must admit it is a perfectly natural day," Cain admitted. They continued walking, allowing Diego to become accustomed to his new powers.

Approaching a tree on the outskirts of a village, Diego seemed mesmerized by his heightened senses. He looked over to ask Cain a question when he noticed him gone. "Over here," Diego heard Cain's voice whisper, but he was nowhere to be seen. "In the tree, look up." Hearing the softly spoken command, Diego looked up at the tree and was amazed by how he focused on Cain.

Well, are you going to stand there?" Cain badgered.

Diego walked over to the tree, looked up, and asked. "How did you come to be up there?"

"Same as most get in a tree—I climbed," responded Cain.

"Climbed," Diego repeated, doubt resonating in his voice.

"Well, actually, I jumped."

"Excuse me?" asked Diego in disbelief.

"You know, jump," Cain exhaled impatiently. "You know, you put both feet together, bend at the knees."

"I know what jumping is, pendeho." Diego interrupted. "I just can't believe you jumped up there," retorted Diego.

Cain floated down from the tree. "Ah yes, of course," said Cain. "Forgive me, Diego; it has been a while since I've had a youngling."

"If you weren't so damn old, I'd take offense at that, Cain."

"Of course, you would, my boy. Now, are we ready?"

Diego grunted, flexed his legs, and shot off like a bullet. High into the air, he went.

Not even the dome of Constantinople is this high," Diego thought. His thinking changed its focus when he realized he was falling. Arms flailing, When he felt a steel like grip.

"What is a pendeho?" asked Cain. Diego looked around wildly and realized they were floating gently to the ground.

"A pendeho? That's like a teacher who's a nice guy," lied Diego. Cain looked at him in disbelief. They reached the ground and touched down softly.

"Let's try this again. All you want is the top of the tree. Understand, Diego?"

But Diego had already leaped and was perched on a branch. "Hurry up, Viejo."

Cain landed gently beside him. "You know, this name-calling will stop once I assimilate your language," Cain warned.

Cain and Diego perched high in the tree, hidden by its leaves. "Que? What are we doing?" asked Diego.

"Shhh, listen," commanded Cain.
Somewhat put off by the abruptness of the demand, Diego leaned back. Much to his surprise, the small village seemed to explode with sound.

"How did I not hear this?" Diego wondered.

"Because you were not focusing on it," answered Cain, allowed to Diego's internal query.

Diego reeled, almost falling out of the tree.

Que en diablo thought Diego.

"The devil had nothing to do with it," answered Cain.

"But how?" Diego sputtered.

"Oh, blessed moon. You are dense, aren't you?"

"Hey!" Diego retorted, agitated by the derogatory remark.

"You haven't caught on to the fact that I can scan minds?" Cain asked condescendingly. Diego looked at Cain sheepishly—if such a word can be used on the undead.

"I thought, maybe but . . ."

"But not really?" Cain asked quizzically.

"Yes, but not really! You happy?" Diego snapped.

"Rarely," responded Cain.

Diego, who had been scanning the area during the argument, looked back at Cain. who had a look of curiosity on his face? "Why, may I ask, are you looking at me like that?" inquired Diego.

"I thought you wanted to feed," said Cain.

"No, ancient one, you said let's go feed and find a clue involving this curse," Diego replied.

"Yes, yes, quite correct, but are you not hungry?" queried Cain.

"No, not really," Diego answered.

Cain said, "That is simply astonishing!"

"What?" Diego asked. "What is astonishing?"

Cain stared at him. "That you're not—forget hungry—but starving right now."

Diego looked at Cain. "I had a big breakfast," he responded jokingly.

"This is no joking matter," Cain whispered fiercely. "What if the curse is that you can no longer feel when your hunger is sated?"

"Well, wouldn't that be a good thing?" Diego asked.

"I see," Cain began, "so you think it would be a good idea to starve for eternity?"

Diego grew pale—as much as the undead could. "Wh-wh-what! But I would not starve if I fed anyway." Diego tried to reason. Cain patiently explained. "But you would not know when to stop, Diego. You would bleed the country dry."

Diego looked up at the sky. "I know I've sinned, but I cannot believe my Lord would condemn me in such a fashion," a worried Diego expressed.

Cain looked at him. "Accepting this may be your fate, maybe the only thing that keeps you alive, Diego."

Diego hurled himself into the night, landing in another batch of trees, far removed from Cain.

Cain watched him soar into the night. *"He is surprisingly powerful for a new unborn,"* he silently mused.

"Cain, I see you have a new student." A voice said from below Cains vantage point

Cain looked down. "Satan, you old goat. How's it burning?" quipped Cain.

"Very amusing for a fratricide-practicing bloodsucker," Satan shot back.

"Flattery gets you nowhere with me. What do you want, worm?" Cain asked insultingly.

"A little respect. Leech. Parasite. Do not forget to whom you are speaking," Satan fumed.

Cain struck a thoughtful pose. "Let me see. The guy who had it all but wanted what wasn't his? The guy who is so insecure that when puny mortals came along, he felt threatened and was jealous? The guy evicted out of the towers, only to call the dungeons his home? You mean that guy?"

"At the end of days, you shall be mine, Cain. Then will you pay for your arrogance," fumed Satan.

"I know you like deluding yourself, Satan! However, I have no fear of you." Cain responded boldly.

Satan stared at Cain with hate flooding him, a malicious smile formed on chapped lips.

"Yes, well, perhaps your new plaything would be more receptive to my coercion," responded Satan with an expression meant to be devious. Cain chuckled.

"Go ahead, although I strongly doubt you'll get the response you desire," He dared.

"Arrogant and foolish! Say goodbye to your new plaything, Cain."

"Very well, goodbye, Satan," Cain mocked.

"Not me, you fool. "Your." Satan vanished as silently as he appeared, leaving the wretched odor of hell behind,

Cain wondered if Diego would indeed be strong enough to hold his own against the Lord of evil.

CHAPTER 5

DIEGO'S EDUCATION

Diego sat quietly, contemplating what Cain had told him. He was under a full moon hunting, Cain at his side. Recalling his last attempt to feed, it had not gone as well as he had hoped.

"Diego," Cain whispered. "What are you waiting for?" asked Cain.

Diego looked at his intended victim. "This doesn't feel right," complained Diego.

"What, Diego? What doesn't feel right? Is this is how we live."

"But they are so weak, so frail. It doesn't seem fair."

"Quite right. And your complaint would be?" Cain asked teasingly.

"At least as a man, I required skill. It was a kill or be killed scenario, This, this is butchery," Diego responded with a tone of disgust. Cain shook his head in disagreement. "Butchery is what the evil do; we drink only to survive," Cain responded. "Be that as it may, this is what we do."

Diego looked over at Cain, grunted, and flew at his victim. It was hard even for Cain to follow him. Upon landing beside him, Diego finished feeding and put his victim down gently on the ground.

"What are you doing?" Cain asked. "He still lives."

Diego looked at Cain. "My thought," began Diego, "is that if I don't require a lot of blood, taking all of it is just greed."

"But how did you . . . with, you know," Cain asked curiously.

"I closed my eyes," answered Diego.

"Not ingenious, but if it works," Cain agreed.

Diego was startled out of his reverie, somehow sensing the presence of evil.

"Is that you, horned one? Come out," said Diego. From a tree emerged an imp.

"What," laughed Diego, "are you supposed to be?"
"I have come for you, dark one," answered the imp.
"Have you?" Diego asked mockingly.

"Yes, blood drinker. My master informed me that your torture would not be severe if you but give yourself over to him."

"Well, little one, as tempting as that sounds, which I might add is not at all, I find myself in the position that I would rather embrace the open blue sky as opposed to that foul beast you call master!" Diego chided.

"But you are mistaken, dark one. My master is not Satan; curses upon him. No, no, my master is the dark high demon Mastema-Satan. He that brings dread to all he gazes upon."

Diego looked at the imp. "Let me get this straight," he began. "You are the flunky of a lackey that is a heavenly reject, thinks to frighten me with tedious threats?"

The imp looked visibly shaken. "You don't understand, blood drinker. My master does not make empty threats. It is only because Lord Satan ordered us not to damage you in your extraction that Satan sent me for you. This is the extent of Satan's mercy, and I strongly suggest you seize it before the Dark Lord unleashes Hell on you". The imp advised.

Diego looked at the imp. "Listen, tiny, you crawl back into whatever pit you crawled out of and tell both your lord and your master that the only thing they can have of mine is my contempt, and if they want my soul bad enough, not to send any more lightweight demons. We do not fear you or your foul kind. Now begone from my sight and remember to tell whomever rules you that if they continue to bother me, I might have to kick them all into a deeper part of perdition."

The imp stood amazed. The demon never heard someone speak so arrogantly against the master and certainly not about Lord Satan. "Foolish, foolish creature. I will deliver your message," said the imp, shocked beyond belief.

With that, the imp disappeared in a flash of smoke.

Ishars' Creation

In Hell, a demon belonged to one of the following classes. The fallen. These demons were once angels and knew the light of Heaven, but they were cast out with Satan in the age of the great rebellion. They held positions of power and were the kings and dukes of their own infernal fiefdoms. Another class of demons was the Ravagers. These were violent, That gave homage to the Fallen, and in their devotions of a child, blood sacrifices were cast into the pit with the fallen. Ravagers were only released once in their demonic form in the mortal world, and they almost slaughtered all of humanity. It was by direct interference by the Archangel Micheal that humanity was saved. Luckily for humanity, this occurred in the infancy of humans, so while they have no memory of the events, they still carried with them the fear of the dark, which was derived when the Ravagers attacked the early man in the darkened places. Humans who practice sorcery for selfish gain is another class of demon. (the Celestial Courts determined that people who were among the very clever and abused their gifts by manipulating people's thoughts and beliefs and coercing them to act in a manner destructive to their neighbors, environment, or communal areas also fit into this category). Those who partook in acts of genocide. Murderers. Social deviants or pariahs that purposely and with malicious intent sought to inflict suffering for their own sake. This class of demons was the evil of humanity who swore allegiance to Satan upon death and damnation. While the ravagers were the brutal warrior class, the malicious was the tacticians.

The lowest class of hell-born demons are named imps. A unique class, Imps were born in the fires of Hell. They are initially damned souls seeking reprieve from the punishment inflicted upon them. In a vain attempt, the soul may beg his tormenter for status condemnation which is a state that, while removing you from the pain of immediate torture, further condemning your soul, increases your time in Hell. Imps register very high on survival but low on courage among the craven of demons. There are those among the Imps that would allow evil to occur and, in abject cowardice, ignore whatever base thing is being perpetrated in front of them. One was created among them who, upon witnessing the slaughter of his entire family, denied the events before an authority that could have rendered justice, but because the perpetrators made his life comfortable, he kept his silence, allowing the culprit to elude justice. The soul of the coward writhed in agony as he pled. "Please master, allow me to serve you," the initiate begged. Mastema Satan (as this demon liked to be called). Stoked the flames of punishment hotter, making the foul spirit trapped inside scream in anguish. "Stop screaming coward"! Mastema demanded. "I will not allow any into my ranks that cannot suffer in silence. "He demanded. "why would I trust a spirit that cannot withstand torture"? He facetiously asked. "Did you not watch as a ravager tore your family to shreds"? The initiate remained quiet. "Fool, did you not hear me"? He asked, raising the flames. The initiate remained quiet. "It would seem this one might finally be ready, master." Mastemas' assistant demon observed. Raising the charred soul, Mastema inspected it and ordered the soul be tortured a while longer before allowing it to recuperate, then to processing for the acceptance ceremony. The assistant nodded his understanding and went back to torturing the initiate. In Hell, there is no real perception of the passage of time, so it could have been one or a thousand years before the initiated soul was brought before the throne of Satan. Alongside the initiate were Mastema and his assistant demon. "My lord, I bring before you one that has gone through the fires of damnation. I bring it here before you asking for your curse upon the initiate so that he may always do your bidding and leave your mark upon him." Mastema requested. Satan glared down at the small soul. "Are you ready to follow my directives without question or complaint"? Satan asked. The soul responded quietly. "I am my lord." The eternal flames of Hell cast light that reflected sinister shadows. "Do you swear by my infernal name that my bidding shall be a command to you"? Satan asked. "Yes, Lord." Answered the initiate. "Satan pierced the soul of the initiate with his gaze. "Know that any disobedience is met with torture, a treasonous thought with exile in the well of oblivion. Do you understand and accept this charge with all the privilege and consequences of the position you seek"? Satan questioned. The initiate nodded while responding. "I do, my lord." Satan stood. Rise then and be recognized, for you are beyond a damned soul. I dub you Ishar the lowly of the house of Imps. Go now, receive your assignments, serve me well and make your torturers proud". Satan exclaimed. Thus Ishar the imp demon came into being. In his first assignment, Ishar was sent to wound a powerful spirit that had taken a god-head of evil unto himself. He gathered many worshippers with minor miracles and dared to try to supplant the lord of evil with his figurehead of evil. Ishar cleverly convinced the Shaman of the worshippers of the faults of this minor deity that there was one who sat on the throne of true evil and that his wrath was soon coming to plague their houses if they did not stop paying homage to this false spirit and worship him instead who's name is Satan. Terrified, the people begged the Shaman to whom Ishar had warned them that they would indeed abandon this false lord of evil and beg his mercy. Later that evening, Ishar appeared before the Shaman, choking him with the smell of brimstone. "What say your people, Shaman? will it be life or tortured life"? Ishar threatened. The Shaman dropped to his knees. "We give homage to Satan and abandon praise to Adophis." The Shaman exclaimed. "You serve your people well, wise one, and I shall now return to our lord and inform him so that you may be spared his awesome wrath." Ishar promised. In another incident, Ishar was sent to stop an event which, if allowed to occur, would create a difficulty Satan surmised would come to fruition. Having no to little information, Ishar went to the assigned destination awaiting the messenger demon to deliver final orders as to the what and when of his mission. Ishar waited into the spring when the demon messenger finally arrived in a small cave that served as a staging area. The messenger appeared, quickly handed Ishar a sealed scroll, and just as quickly vanished. Ishar broke open the seal, unrolled the scroll, and read his assignment. *There is one that is giving birth to a son that our seer says shall be of great nuisance to the plots of he that you serve. Think you a way to dispose of the child quietly, Mastema.* Ishar sat still for six days, stirred, went to the back of the cave, dug a bit, and then teleported to the newborn's crib. sat beside it a moment, then snuck out of the window with the baby. Seeing a peasant in a stack of hay, Ishar laid the baby carefully beside him along with the poisonous worm he had found in the cave. Waiting for the worms to do their job, Ihar left satisfied. Upon his return, Ishar reported the events to his over-lord Mastema, who then reported it to Satan, who immediately conjured the scene. As he watched, Satan saw the villagers frantically searching the village, finding the peasant and now dead baby. The villagers ignored the man's pleas of innocence and immediately hung him. Satan was pleased by Ishar's' work. "It would seem like you have brought me a fine servant from your ovens, Mastema." Mastema bowed at the rare compliment and answered appropriately. "I exist to please you, my lord." Mastema wondered why the lord of evil had not dismissed him but wisely remained silent with his head bowed while Satan sat on his throne staring down at Mastema. "Tell me, Mastema, this creature that has been doing well. Do you think he is ready for a larger assignment"? Satan inquired. Mastema felt terror as his denial would infuriate Satan; who would ask why Mastema was bringing him the help that could not handle important assignments? Was it the fact that any failures would also be assigned Mastema for poor training and evaluation? "My lord, I beg we give Ishar the imp more assignments before we engage him in anything My lord think to be vital." Mastema responded, trying to cover his backside from the flames. Satan considered the words of Mastema. "I will allow you a session of preparation. I have an assignment that he has proven suitable. See that it is done". Satan ordered. Mastema bowed, knowing he had very little time to prepare Ishar for something that could elevate him or condemn them both. Looking up, Mastema saw he was in his office where Satan had teleported him. He immediately sent for Ishar. Appearing promptly after receiving his summons, Ishar kneeled at the feet of Mastema. Considering the knelling subject, Mastema attempted to deduce the likely outcome to the assignment he was being forced to assign this newly formed imp. While it was true, the imp performed exceedingly well in turning a belief system on its head and won lord Satan many new worshippers Mastema was either doubtful or resentful that a newly formed imp did what few demons could have bragged about doing themselves. "Ishar." Mastema began, finally acknowledging the imp, who to his credit stayed perfectly still since kneeling with his head down, never glancing up even once in curiosity, further infuriating Mastema. "Ishar." Mastema repeated. "Lord Satan has given us an assignment of importance." Ishar continued staring at the ground. "Lord Satan witnessing your ability thinks it appropriate that we prepare you for elevated status. His infernal majesty thinks he may endow you with full demon status"! Mastema proclaimed. Unable to contain the surprise, Ishar lifted his head, looking at Mastema. "my lord"? He gasped. "Yes." Mastema continued. "Lord Satan is pleased with your past performance and desires that you be endowed with teleporting abilities, unfettered. However, the full status shall not be granted until the successful completion of your new assignment". Ishar bowed his head. "What are my lords desire"? He asked. Mastema lifted his hand. "Not so quickly, little imp." Mastema watched for tensing of the body that would have shown offense in the imp revealing pride. To both his satisfaction and dismay Ishar revealed none. "Remember well who heard your pitiful pleas when you burned in the fires of damnation. Who rose you up, who provided the opportunity to please the Lord Satan and provided you now the opportunity to rise as a full demon". Mastema proclaimed. From his bowed position, Ishar responded. "You lord." Mastema raised his hands, proclaiming aloud. "Your failures become my punishments, and my punishment becomes your damnation. With this curse, you are set forth to bring back to Hell the upstart Vampyre, Diego Torrolisimo, either willing, through force or deceit. Fail me, and you will wish you never came out of the flames that were your punishment. Ishar raised his head. He felt power enter him as the power of teleportation infused him. "This power is yours until your mission is complete by Lord Satans' command so no other jealous demon might take it from you. Do not fail us, Ishar". Mastema intoned. Ishar disappeared in a cloud. Mastemas' face was that of worry.

CHAPTER 6

DIEGO'S ARGUMENT

Diego sat in the garden of Cains manor, enjoying the night and the beautiful garden Cain had cultivated. The wonderful aroma of lilacs hung in the air when suddenly he began to have that same feeling he had when the imp was watching him.

"Come out, little one. I know you're there," said Diego to the seemingly empty night.

From behind a bush, the imp stepped forward. "How is it that you knew I was here?" asked the surprised demon.

"How could I not?" asked Diego. "Evil clings to you like a cheap garment, and you smell like rotten eggs!" exclaimed Diego.

"But my master shielded me with a spell of concealment! How is this possible?" asked the unbelieving imp.

"Perhaps your master is not as powerful as you thought," Diego answered snidely.

"You must come with me," pleaded the imp. "My master does not take to failure well."

"One would think he's become familiar with it by now." retaliated Diego.

"Arrogant, insolent fool! You do not understand. I cannot return without you!" screamed the imp.

"Sorry, little one, but I must decline your somewhat rude invitation," Diego responded tartly.

Without warning, the imp screamed and threw himself at Diego. Diego caught him quickly by the scruff of his neck. The demon squealed and thrashed until he exhausted himself. The imp said, looking up at Diego, "You have defeated me, dark prince. Kill me now so that I may go face my punishment."

Diego looked at the imp, feeling a strange stirring within. "No, imp, I shall not destroy a helpless puppet. You served your master to the best of your abilities, and any lord would appreciate such a subject."

The imp looked at Diego, astonished. "Never in my existence have I received such mercy. Thank you, dark prince," said a very thankful demon.

"I am no prince. You may call me Diego."

The imp could not believe what he had just heard.

"Why do you stare at me so, imp?" asked Diego.

"For fear of me and what I represent, no man has ever freely told me his name."

"I have no fear of your master or the dog you call lord," said Diego.

"I understood that among men, names are exchanged in friendship. Is this so, my, Diego?" smiling, Diego set the imp to his feet and released him.

Diego smiled at the imp. "This is true, imp." "Confirmed, Diego. Are we to be friends then?" the demon asked sheepishly.

"If you'd like," answered Diego.

The little imp began jumping up and down in glee. "I've never had a friend before."

"You do now," Diego said, smiling.

"I am called Ishar the lowly," said the imp by way of introduction.

"Well, how about I just call you Ishar, and let's lose that lowly title."

The imp looked at Diego deeply. "You have a strange aura about you, Diego," said the imp.

"So I've been told," said a smiling Diego.

"You had best to leave now before your colleagues become suspicious," Diego warned.

Ishar stepped back. "Yes, my friend, you are correct. I shall not forget this, Diego. Thank you."

And with that, he disappeared with the usual fanfare of smoke and smell. Diego sat back, smiling. "Let's see where this takes us," mused Diego.

"You can come out now," Diego said aloud.

Cain stepped in from the shadows.

"Interesting guests you've been receiving."

Diego looked at Cain seriously. "No friend of mine," he retorted.

"Let's examine that," said Cain.

Diego let out an exhale of frustration. "Let's not and say we did," Diego answered back.

"Hmmm, let's see. You could have—and I think should have—killed him, but you didn't," began Cain ignoring Diego's attempt to deflect the subject.

"What does that prove?" growled Diego.

"Two," continued Cain as if uninterrupted, "you told him your name."

"And!" commented an increasingly frustrated Diego.

"And three, he told you his name!"

"So, what are you getting at?" Diego said forcefully.

"What I'm getting at, my young disciple, is that demons do not reveal their names and before you ask—"

Diego attempted to look offended. Cain looked at him said, "Stop it, you know you were going to ask. Demons do not share their names because it gives you power over them."

"So you think the demon was . . . trusting me?" asked Diego.

"I don't think they can do this, but they serve their masters loyally until the demon is destroyed or their master discards them," Cain answered.

"What?" asked a shocked Diego.

"Yes, my understanding is that sometimes the demon masters discard into hell's pits those that dissatisfy them and destroy those that become more powerful than they like."

"Rule through fear, and sounds right for hell," observed Diego.

"Yes, but the point I'm trying to make is that you showed pity to the demon, and while they are not trustworthy, they pine for God's mercy. And if someone comes along powerful enough to overpower them and doesn't, well, that holds great appeal to them," declared Cain.

"I did notice that when the imp returned, he smelled less, shall we say, hellish," observed Diego.

"Really?" Cain asked, somewhat surprised.

"Yes, really," Diego shot back.

"Curious," Cain said as he walked back into the house.

"Cain," Diego began, "I want to apologize for earlier if I—"

"Say no more, Diego. You are my disciple, and I think the almighty has a plan for us."

Diego followed Cain into the house, considering his words.

Ishars' Report

Ishar materialized in the chambers of his master, who was busy screaming at his staff. Noticing Ishar, he dismissed the terrified staff and summoned Ishar, who approached and slowly kneeled. "Well"? Mastema began. "Where is my prisoner"? With his head lowered, Ishar gave his report. "Master, this Vampyre has no fear. He openly reviled you and Lord Satan. He defies you or any demon of hell". Ishar reported. Mastema's eyes burned with fury. "What are you not telling me, Ishar"! slowly lifting his head, Ishar quietly whispered. "He was kind to me, my lord." Mastema stood from his seated position, unable to believe his ears. "He was what"?! He screamed. Lowering his head in terror, Ishar foolishly repeated himself. "He was kind to me and respectful."

Mastema charged and grabbed Ishar by the throat. "You ungrateful piece of pig shit." Lifting Ishar and shaking him, Mastema yelled into the imp's face. "Did your Vampyre rescue your pitifully whining soul from the flames of damnation? Did he lift you to become a servant with stature, you disloyal swine"? "No, my lord," Ishar responded. Mastema slapped Ishar repeatedly. "Didn't I clarify that your failure would also reflect upon me"? Suffering another powerful blow, Ishar slowly replied, "Yes, my lord, if you would just give me another chance but meeting this Vampyre, I do not think I or any other demon is powerful enough to defeat him." Ishar pled. "Is that so"? Mastema questioned. You will have another chance to redeem yourself but not before you receive proper motivation,". Mastema declared. Summoning another servant Mastema ordered. "See that Ishar is sent to the chamber of consequences. The servants escorted Ishar to his punishment. "Ishar," Mastema shouted. "After your reeducation, be about your duties and return with the upstart Diego in tow, or you will face Satan himself, and I assure you he will not be as merciful."

CHAPTER 7

ASYLUM

Although the sun was beginning to rise, Diego didn't need to sleep, and some mortal habits died hard. He lay in an ornate silk-lined, goose-feathered coffin that, beyond any logical explanation, delighted the sense of irony in Cain. This coffin was gifted to Diego when he moved into the Manor. Struck by the conflicting symbolism of the slight, non-imposing stature of Cain compared to the elaborate, decorative grandiosity of the coffin struck Diego as comically hypocritical. Not sure what it said about him that he liked resting in it, Diego lay in his bed of hedonism (as Cain referred to it), listening to the sounds of the morning until he fell into a restorative rest cycle. Upon awakening, Diego rose and found Cain to be gone. "He must have gone to feed," assumed Diego. Just then, a familiar feeling swept over him, though not as strongly as before. Diego walked into the courtyard, finding a badly beaten and scarred Ishar. Diego was beside him instantly.

"Ishar!" Diego said, gently lifting him to a sitting position. "What happened to you?" he probed.

Ishar looked at Diego. "I went back and reported to my master as was my duty," replied Ishar. "When he asked me why your soul wasn't among the damned, I told him that you were too powerful for me or any other demon under his command."

"And this angered him?" Diego asked.

"It infuriated him, and he began whipping me and summoned Minos, one of the judges of hell. He is second only to my master. It would help if you found a place to hide, Diego!" warned Ishar.

"No, I don't think I'll run and hide as you suggest, Ishar. If he wants me, he knows where I am."

"You are either foolish or fearless, Diego," Ishar said, praising Diego.

"Perhaps a bit of both. Now, why don't you come inside and rest," invited Diego?

If Ishar weren't a demon, Diego would swear he saw gratitude in his demonic eyes. "Thank you, Diego. I could use the rest," Ishar agreed.

With the evening, Cain returned home. Landing on the roof gently, he observed his surroundings. Satisfied there were no strangers, Diego floated to the ground and entered his home. He immediately sensed the demonic presence. He found Diego in the study, reading one of the many manuscripts in his library.

"I see we are picking up strays now," Cain asked, entering the room.

Diego looked up from his reading and told Cain of Ishar's predicament, excluding the warning about the powerful demons now hunting for him.

"I don't like getting mixed up in Satans' business." Cain protested.

CAIN, THE REJECTION

It was a hot day, blazing sun overhead as Cain collected his crops. Walking home, he ran into his brother Abel, returning from his flock of sheep with a fat one draped over his shoulder.

"Fine-looking sheep you have, brother," commented Cain.

"Your harvest looks the same, brother," replied Abel. "I hope Father likes them."

"I'm sure he will," countered Cain. "Besides, you know as long as Mother is happy," observed Cain. "True, true," Abel admitted.

The two brothers walked home together. Abel questioned his brother whether he agreed with the fine sheep he carried. "Father will love this for his meal. Do you not agree, Cain?"

Cain gave a deep sigh of resignation. "Yes, Abel, it is, as I said, a fine offering you give."

Abel smiled. "Yes, and your harvest should make for a fine side dish," Abel said half-teasing and half-condescendingly.

Spoiled brat, thought Cain.

Later that evening, Adam told his children, "Cain, Abel, go you now with your finest offerings and make a sacrifice and give thanks to the Lord."

Being loyal sons, they did as their father commanded. Cain dressed an altar with fruits, grain, and vegetables, thanks to God, and awaited him to recognize his offering. On the other side of the hill, near their home, Abel did likewise. He erected an altar, drenching it with sheep blood and sweetmeats.

Within moments the Living Spirit was beside Abel, and his offering, smelling the meat and warmblood poured on the altar. Abel looked at the heavens. "The Lord favors my sacrifice, and I am humbled," he said.

Cain sat beside his beautifully constructed alter that he dressed with sweet-smelling flowers, carpeted with lush soft grass, and housed it in a structure of twigs and vines that Cain spent several days weaving and binding.

With great anticipation, Cain sat by his Alter, awaiting the presence of the Almighty.

Cain felt the incredible presence of the Creator for a moment before it departed. Wondering at the brief visitation Cain became aware of the joys sound of celebration from the place where Able built his Alter. It appeared to Cain the revelry went on far longer than it had at his alter. Cain felt a spark of anger as he considered how much work he had put into his offering while the Alter of Able was not even constructed as opposed to placing a slab or two of wood together to act as a steeple with the offering sitting on the bare ground

HELLS PREPARATION

In the bowels of Hell, Satan felt a sense of revenge (which passed for joy in hell) as he witnessed the offerings of Cain and Able and the increasing division it was causing. Now Satan being who he was, knew that the Creator didn't engage in something that didn't have a million things happening in the background; that said, Satan felt it counter-productive to his destructive causes to not seek advantage at this opportunity to sow strife in the house of Adam who Satan blames for his expulsion from Heaven. "Let us prepare demons of influence to further the division and stoke the flames of jealousy and anger in the brothers. I want to stir the animosity and blood lust so that one might do great harm to the other, forcing one to be expelled as I was". Satan decreed. So the demons of hell gathered, and in their company was Lillith, who tried to tempt Adam into disobeying The Lord Creator; also, Nachash, the tempter of Eve at the tree of knowledge, was in attendance. The demons sat and plotted on how to despoil the innocence of the brothers. It was finally Nachash that formulated a plan likely to succeed. The serpent slithered and hissed his idea. "The first family gives tithes to the unnamed this time every second cycle of the full moon." Lillith, with her usual impatience, interrupted. "How does this benefit our plan, Nachash"? She inquired sarcastically. The snake hissed at her. "Not everything is about sex, harlot." The snake hissed in frustration. "How dare you." Lillith screeched in objection. The snake hissed. "if you would listen, the simplicity of my plan will assure success." Nachash promised. The demon Lord Asmodeus was among them to supervise the meeting and make sure the demons came up with an effective plan. "Lillith." The Demon lord ordered. "Allow Nachash to submit his plan without further interruption, or I will tell Satan of your disruptive attitude," Asmodeus warned. Lillith sat with a grunt. Asmodeus nodded to Nachash. "Continue deceiver." Nachash bobbed his head in acknowledgment. "As I was saying, during the time of offerings, we should send a low-class demon, preferably from the imp class, to soil one of the brothers' offerings with our bowel movements." The snake of temptation hissed gleefully. Lillith interrupted. "Why a low class? Why, not a demon or better yet a demon lord such as our esteemed Asmodeus"? She asked sweetly. "I think it highly unwise you to volunteer my service for anything, harlot." Asmodeus spat. Nachash interrupted. "There is a reason why Lilith's idea would fail mighty Asmodeus," Nachash explained. "First, any Demon of Asmodeus stature appearing on Earth would set off alarms in Heaven alerting them something is afoot. A low-class demon can do all we need without alerting those damned watchers who report all we do to the unnamed,". Nachash pointed out. Asmodeus stood. "Perfect. Once again, Nachash, you have proven yourself worthy in upsetting the plans of Heaven,". Asmodeus said in acknowledgment. The snake bobbed his head and vanished in a puff of smoke. Lillith objected. "we're not going to go through with this absurd plan, are we"? She inquired. Asmodeus gazed at her. "Do you have a better idea"? He asked doubtfully. "Of course I do." She exclaimed. Asmodeus sat back down. "Fine, let us hear it." Asmodeus said, doing his due diligence because if Satan found out he didn't listen to all ideas presented to him, well, the punishment would be severe. "My plan is simple, I go to Earth and seduce Able the younger into NOT offering sacrifice to the unnamed but offer it to our Lord instead, thereby fully corrupting the line of Adam." She concluded as if the matter was resolved. "Should I leave immediately?" She asked. Asmodeus shook his head. "No, Lillith, it was the same plan you had for Adam, which I, if you remember, had supported, and it backfired horribly. No, Lillith, all of your plans are based on lust, and while I more than anyone am happy to implement such devices, I cannot attempt a second time that which has already failed,". Asmodeus decreed. "You shame us, Asmodeus," Lillith murmured. "It's Lord Asmodeus to you wench! I have spoken and shall endorse Nachash's plan of desecration. Asmodeus departed straight to Satan's chambers, revealing Nachash's plan.

CHAPTER 8

RUIN OF THE HOUSE OF ADAM

In the late evening hours, a tiny newly formed imp demon named Ruin snuck to Cains alter, looked at it in awe, and began defecating and urinating on the food Cain so meticulously spread to appeal to Heaven and the spirit of Heaven came down and was repulsed by the evil emanating from Cains offering. Upon completion of his mission, the brief existence of Ruin came to an end as Satan dispelled it to Oblivion, providing Satan with plausible deniability in case a thorough examination was to take place no one could prove such and such demon is/was guilty of the heinous act because no such demon exists. Satan thought the plan an effective one. Time would prove him right.

Later that night, Adam asked, "Well, my sons, did you do as I commanded and offered the Lord a sacrifice?"

"We did as you commanded, Father, and the Lord favored my sacrifice," Abel said happily.

Adam looked at Cain, who had remained silent. "And what of you, my firstborn?" inquired Adam.

"You heard my brother, Father!" Cain responded heatedly, "It would appear your God doesn't love me."

"Nay, my son," began Adam, "remove such dark thoughts from your mind, as God loves us all."

Cain reluctantly responded, "If you say so, Father."

Adam looked at his despondent son, feeling great sorrow for him. "Please, my son," Adam began.

Cain stood up abruptly. "Forgive me, Father, but I don't have the luxury to tend sheep, thus doing nothing as they tend to themselves." Cain stormed out of his father's hut, feeling a building resentment.

"Father—," began Abel.

Adam lifted his hand for silence. "Abel, you must be patient and understand your brother's plight," Adam said to his youngest son.

"I will do as you say, Father, but Cain has always mocked me for tending sheep."

"I understand, my son. Will you do as I request of you?"

"Of course, Father," answered Abel. "Now, if you will but forgive me, I'm fatigued, and it has been an exciting day." Abel kissed his mother and father a good night and went to his hut.

That night Eve looked at Adam. "My mate, why is it the Lord has oppressed Cain? He spent all of five cycles of the sun making sure he picked choice food. Why then would our God give it only a glance while bestowing so much attention to Abel?" Eve asked.

"It is not for us to question the way of the Lord our God! Have you learned nothing from the garden?" Taken aback, Eve apologized. "Forgive me, Adam. I meant no disrespect."

"It is I who should ask for your forgiveness, beloved. The truth is, I am frightened by this turn of events. I thought the Lord would have equal favor with our sons, but this does not seem to be the case. So I am worried for them," Adam said, explaining his outburst.

"There is nothing to forgive. Come and lie with me. Let us rest and see how things look in the morning," Eve said, patting the mat of grass that was their bed.

Adam lay down beside Eve, wondering if this evening's event was going to be significant to Cain.

The following morning Cain arose as early as any who till soil does. He spotted his brother heading for his pasture. Cain was angered by the apparent joy filling Abel, who was nearly prancing on to his field.

Cain fumed the entire day, ruining a couple of harvest bushels as he pulled angrily at the plants.

As evening came, Abel almost stumbled over his brother lying in the field. "Cain?" Abel said, surprised at seeing his brother on the ground. "Are you hurt?" asked a concerned Abel.

"Why does God not love me, little brother?" Cain asked mockingly.

"Cain, you must not say such things," admonished Abel.

"Now you feel you have the authority to admonish me!" screamed Cain. "You stink of sheep dung, and if your God loves the fragrance of blood, perhaps he is as savage as the beasts of the field," asserted Cain.

"Brother, you blaspheme when you say this, and I will not accept such talk!" shouted Abel.

Cain's blood boiled and, without a thought, leaped to his feet, snatching up a stone. He delivered a fatal blow to Abel's skull. The fog of anger cleared from his mind, and Cain looked upon the dead body of his brother. Fearful of what his father would do, Cain ran into the wilderness.

While sleeping under a tree after an exhausting and hasty departure, Cain felt an overwhelming presence. In his mind, he heard a voice saying, "Cain, Cain, what have you done? Where is your brother Abel?"

"Am I my brother's keeper that I would know his coming and going?" Cain said, attempting subterfuge.

"Nay, I hear the blood of your brother call to me from the Earth. A most horrendous thing you have done, Cain, and for your arrogance and impertinence, you have branded yourself as a murderer of men, so sayeth the Lord your God."

"But, Lord, all men will hunt me, seeking favor with thee," complained Cain.

"Let it be that any man seeking vengeance against Cain shall be punished seven times over, with this mark shall all know that he is so protected. So proclaims the Lord God."

Cain rose from his rest, accepting his exile. He went deeper into the wild woods, hoping secretly to be killed by a wild animal. After several days Cain came upon some bandits who tried to rob him. Cain exploded in a ferocity that frightened the bandits and scared himself as well.

"Have mercy. Spare us, great Lord, and we shall pledge our lives to you," pleaded the bandits.

"Come then," said Cain. "We shall set forth and build a city, and we shall call that city Nod."

Cain's strong sense of leadership made him an excellent candidate for chieftain among the bandits. Cutting down a nearby forest, Cain built his fortifications. Slowly nomads began wandering to the city, seeking refuge from the hostile environment. Cain set guards for his town and was soon feared among the barbarians that raided caravans near his city. Soon it became known that the roads of Nod were protected by a son of Adam.

Many of the ancients revered Adam and extended the same respect. Cain earned a reputation for being a just ruler.

It was in this brief time of respite that Satan came to Cain. "Well, well, look at you," teased Satan. "Master of your domain, righteous ruler." He laughed. "They don't know you as I do, do they?"

"You don't know me, foul beast!" declared Cain.

"Stop with the compliments, Cain," Satan said mockingly. "But I do know you, kin slayer."

Cain was shocked into silence.

"Yes, my pet, I know about your innocent brother and that most foul thing that you've done to him," Satan teased. "I know of your defection from the Lord and your subsequent flight. You have but to worship me, and I shall aid you in building a mighty empire," Satan whispered to Cain.

"Leave from my side, foul one, for although I've harmed he that I loved and though the Lord cast me into the wilderness, I would never serve your foulness," declared Cain.

"Foolish mortal! Don't you know I could drag you kicking and screaming to Gehenna!" raged Satan.

"I don't believe that is the truth, evil one," Cain responded quietly.

"Oh? And why is that, foolish man?"

"Well," began Cain, "the way I see it, if you could have just dragged me, you would have. And seeing you didn't, I think it's safe to guess that you can't."

"I can do anything I want. Just ask your mother," teased Satan.

"No son of Adam will ever willingly join you, foul dog. You know the Lord protects me, and that's why you want me to join you!" exclaimed Cain, realizing Satan's purpose.

Cain began laughing. "Begone with you, dog, lest the Lord's ire visit thee seven times over. Get thee now unto your foul fiefdom and never show yourself to me again, pitiful beast." Satan glared at Cain. "You and the people you come to love will never know peace. I shall plague them with suffering, disease, and starvation. I shall put my foot on The Creators curse and shall add force to his punishment. The house of Cain will be short-lived".

He was gone with a roar, a puff of smoke, and a stench of brimstone.

The Visitation

Upon returning from his nocturnal ventures, Cain returned to Diego and listened while Diego related the threats issued by Satan as told to him by Ishar.

Cain questioned Diego: "How does this make you feel?"

Diego looked at Cain. "I do not fear the Dark Lord or his minions. Let them come," he said defiantly. "I will happily plant my foot with exceeding force upon his hindquarters."

Cain laughed with glee. "This is what I sensed in you, Diego," he remarked. "You showed little fear as a mortal, now as an immortal. Well…"

Diego smiled. "I assure you that when—" He paused. He and Cain grew eerily silent, waiting. With a roar and powerful stench of the underworld, a demon appeared.

"Slaves to Satan, kneel before me and be damned! Exclaimed the demon.

Diego laughed. "I don't think so, foul one."

Cain looked on silently.

"Fools!" shouted the demon. "Do you not know in whose presence you dare stand?" he challenged.

"Allow me," said Diego, bowing to Cain. Cain bowed in return. "As you please," Cain responded in a sophisticated manner. Diego continued, smiling. "A loudmouthed, foul-smelling pitiful excuse for a demon?" Diego asked teasingly.

Smoke and the smell of brimstone rose around the demon. "He is Haroth," said Ishar, who had awakened.

"You, imp! Come to me now, and your punishment will be exquisite," the demon roared.

"Okay, first of all, Ishar is not going anywhere he doesn't want to go," pronounced Diego. "Secondly, your manners leave much to be desired."

Cain couldn't contain his chuckle. The infuriated demon turned to Cain. "Perhaps you have some blessing protecting you, kin slayer, but your young and insolent apprentice has no such luck!" Haroth exclaimed. "Now surrender to me what is mine!"

Diego looked at Haroth and simply said, "No."

Furious, the demon launched himself at Ishar, who cringed at his approach. Just as he was going to reach him, Haroth felt a grip of steel fasten onto his ankle. "What?" Haroth asked, bewildered.

Diego held fast the demon. "I told you no, demon. What part of that did you not understand?" He asked sarcastically.

Screaming, Haroth spun around to break Diego's grip. Thrashing, with no sign of getting loose, the demon howled.

Now, now," said Diego contemptuously. "We'll have none of that."

The demon tried to spin on Diego, but Diego moved with him, confounding whatever attack the devil attempted. After a few moments of fruitless struggle, the demon stopped.

Diego looked at the demon. "Are we done?" Diego asked.

"Destroy me, but I am not the last," Haroth said.

"What is this thing about being destroyed with you guys"? Diego asked. "I mean do you derive some sort of sexual-like gratification"? Diego paused a moment while holding the demon at arm's length; after a moment, he loosened his grip. I shall not," Diego replied quietly. Releasing the demon. "You are free to go."

Haroth began whimpering. "What is wrong with you? I said that you might go. Why do you stand there and whimper?" Diego demanded, not comprehending the demon's behavior.

"Diego, you must destroy him, or Satan will punish him, thinking he failed." Explained Ishar.

Diego looked over at Ishar. "But won't he do that anyway, seeing that he did fail?" asked Diego.

"Yes, but not as severely if he fought to his destruction," Ishar said.

Diego looked at the demon. "Haroth, I have no wish to destroy you, but if it will spare you the fury of your master . . ."

Haroth looked at Diego with a look that, despite his nature of evil, looked like gratitude. Diego looked at Cain, who merely nodded. Diego held Haroth before him. "Prepare then, beast, to meet your lord and tell him I shall see him soon."

Haroth looked at Diego, trying to hide a small smile which was, despite the pain of demonic joy, Haroth embraced for the moment. "I shall, dark prince," Haroth responded, trying not to grin.

"Goodbye, Haroth." Diego ripped the head off of the demon, and the carcass burst into flames.

Ishar ran to Diego and dropped to his knees. "Master, thank you. I will serve you if you have me."

Diego looked over at Cain, who only shook his head goodheartedly. "Raising an army of demons, are we?" Cain asked sarcastically.

Diego looked at Ishar. "Little demon, you don't have to serve anyone."

Ishar began to whine and slowly rock back and forth. Diego looked at Cain, confounded.

"He is a demon, Diego. He must serve evil or perish," explained Cain.

"Yes, he'll go to hell."

"Go, Diego," Cain interjected. He will be exiled from hell, and with him being a demon, he may not go to Heaven," Cain clarified.

"Then where?" asked Diego.

"Oblivion," whispered Ishar.

Diego looked at Cain for advice. "Don't look at me!" Cain said. "You wanted to save him when I thought you should have destroyed him," protested Cain.

Diego looked at Ishar. "Little one, are you sure this is what you want?" asked Diego.

"You heard Haroth. He will not be the last demon to come for me. Master, say that I am yours, and I shall serve you loyally."

"How can I believe this when you are demon-kind?" asked a doubtful Diego.

"Master, you showed me kindness even knowing my nature. You could have destroyed me, but instead, you spared me, and when the demon Haroth came for me, you saved me. My loyalty is yours until you cast me aside or destroy me. Please, master," begged a frightened Ishar.

Diego looked to Cain for aid, but Cain had retired t the library. Diego sought him out.

"Cain," Diego called upon finding him immersed in his books. "Cain, why did you leave? I could use your advice."

Cain looked up from his books. "I don't think so, Diego. I'm beginning to think that the Lord God has a purpose for you, and I've already angered him once, and I'm not looking to repeat that scene," Cain expressed somewhat sadly.

"But, Cain, you are my maker and, I thought, friend."

Cain stood and put his hand on Diego's shoulder. "Diego, we are brothers, and whatever aid I can give, I will, even if we must battle with the father of lies but this thing with Ishar, I'm of a mind that a grand purpose is at hand and your decision may be vital, fear not as I will suffer the consequences beside you," Cain assured him.

Diego was relieved to hear that he had at least one ally.

"You know, of course, that Satan is going to send his minions one by one until one of them succeeds," warned Cain.

"You mean we get to empty hell?" Diego asked with almost childish glee.

"Diego, you do understand that we will be doing this ourselves, don't you?" Cain pointed out.

"What about your former disciples? Would they not assist us?" Diego queried.

"No, Diego, I believe some of my former disciples were consumed with the power they were given and are thoroughly evil". Cain said, sounding somewhat embarrassed. Some perished while others have simply gone their own way". Cain reported sadly.

"Why would you create evil Vampyres?" Diego asked.

"Diego, you must understand, when I was first turned, I had no guide, and all I knew was the hunger."

"So I am the only Vampyre that is not seduced by it?" asked Diego.

"Actually, no," began Cain. "There were two lads that might have been what you describe as good."

"Well, can we not enlist his aid?" Diego asked insistently.

Cain's expression turned thoughtful. "No, my son. On his second day, my firstborn felt the hunger upon him, so I took him into the night to feed. I, not having to worry about the sun, did not heed the approaching dawn, and my poor little firstborn burst into flames before we could reach the safety of shelter."

"But I thought you said . . ." Cain interjected.

"That I have others? I do, but they were made much later. I am older and my blood stronger, and I by that time had concluded none of my children could walk in the light as I can."

"So why can I?" asked Diego.

"I am not certain, but I think it might be that we are indeed part of The Creators' plans, which I, unfortunately, am not privy to," Cain concluded.

"But—," began Diego.

Cain raised his hand, quieting him. "Enough for now. I must feed. Will you join me?" he said invitingly.

"No. I will stay with Ishar. Go. We shall await your return," responded Diego.

CHAPTER 9
SATAN'S POINT

Cain exited the building of his latest snack when he began to feel what was becoming a familiar sensation. Not wanting to frighten what few people were about, Cain made his way quickly to the town's outskirts. "What do you want?" he questioned the seemingly empty air before him.

Satan materialized with the pompous grandiosity that one could only attribute to the Lord of Hell.

"Do you know nothing of being subtle?" sniped Cain.

"Do you know nothing of recognizing and paying homage to your superiors?" retorted Satan.

"Well, when the Lord God comes, I will."

"I am your superior, your master. You serve me, fool," trumpeted Satan.

"Satan, Satan, I think the Father keeps you around simply because you amuse Him," Cain said mockingly. "Yes, I think that as Lucifer, who I admit would have been my superior. However, he was so bright that he blinded himself. Yes, I think The Creator thought, 'O my me! How could I have created something so beautiful and so unbelievably stupid!'"

Satan's face remained calm, but Cain could tell by the increase of flames licking his legs he was becoming irate.

"Yes," continued Cain, "and for all that, the glory that was once Lucifer the morning star has instead become a withered, unloved, despised shadow of his former glory."

"Enough!" Satan shouted, stomping his foot and causing a minor earth tremor. "I did not come here to be insulted by you, dog!"

"Oh really?" interjected Cain. "Where do you go to get insulted? If it's a tavern, I'd like to know where it is."

Satan by now was furious. Then suddenly, he took a deep breath and said, "Cain, I did not come to fight with you."

Cain grew silent.

'Well, aren't you curious to say why I came?" asked Satan.

"It appears you are more interested in the saying than I am in the hearing," Cain responded.

Satan struggled to control his rage. "Your insolence will only lead to your destruction," he said heatedly.

"After all that posturing, that is what you came to say?" asked Cain condescendingly. He turned to leave.

"Cain!" Satan shouted. "I know it is unwise to harm you directly, but think, Cain, there are other ways."

Cain turned to face Satan. "You must be referring to the demon. He makes for a nice pet, and from you. Who would have thought?" Cain said, mocking Satan.

"The imp Ishar shall soon feel my wrath, but no, for another comes. One with power!" Satan exclaimed with judgmental glee.

"Oh, you must mean Haroth." Cain paused, allowing the implication to sink in. "Yes," he continued whimsically, "seemed a friendly enough demon. A bit of a braggart and a bit sloven if you ask me. You don't make as good a class of monsters as you did in the old days now, do you, old dog? Cain paused.

"Excuse me, it's been so long since I spoke to anyone near my age. As I was saying, this Haro."

"Haroth!" interjected Satan. "My demon. What of him?"

"Yes, Haroth, that was it." continued Cain, acting somewhat offended at the interruption. "As I was saying, this demon came into my gardens, huffing smoke and breathing fire and screaming that the dark god of the world demanded Diego and Ishar to accompany him to their judgment."

"And!" Satan demanded after Cain's pause.

"Well, Ishar put his head down and, of course, agreed.

"And!" Satan nearly shouted.

"And what?" countered Cain.

"Diego! What did Diego say!" asked an increasingly frustrated Satan.

"Oh, he declined to acquiesce to your invitation."

Satan stared at Cain. "It was not an invitation."

"That's what that demon said, and then my, my, he foolishly tried o force Diego."

"And?" asked Satan ominously.

"Well, perhaps you should go home. I think your demon needs reconstitution," Cain expressed with a tinge of pride in his voice. "But go to wherever it is you go to find body parts, as Diego ripped off this one's head," Cain concluded with a smile.

Satan looked at Cain with disbelief in his eyes and, in a sulfuric-laden cloud of smoke, was gone.

Cain smiled to himself. "I haven't had this much fun in millennia." He snickered.

Satan's Throne Room

In a flash of light and smoke, Satan appeared in his throne room. The imp, Nasr-din, stood close by, anticipating his master's needs, skittishly offering a cup to Satan. "A cup of innocent blood, master?"

Satan snatched the proffered cup, gulping it down without the usual savoring he enjoyed.

"Master, how may your servant serve you?" Nasr-din asked timidly.

Satan leered at Nasr. "Is not the imp Ishar of your clan?" inquired Satan.

"Yes, master," answered Nasr nervously.

"Would you vouch for his loyalty?" Satan asked slyly.

Feeling as if the father of lies was setting him up for something, Nasr began to pay very close attention to his following words. "My lord, how could anyone conceive of a manner to deceive you?" Nasr, sounding flabbergasted, said, "Easier to reverse the direction of the sun than deceive you, my dark Lord. You are the epitome of all that is deception. How could one possibly attempt such a thing?" Nasr finished, sounding awed at the thought.

Satan glared at Nasr. "Little jester, though all you say is true, I can't help but notice you didn't answer my question," Satan said pointedly.

"Forgive me, lord. I do not know if Ishar is loyal." Satan glared at Nasr. "Then why did you support Mastema's recommendation to allow the initiate to join your class of demons? Did I not say they would be your responsibility?" Satan asked.

"You did, my lord," conceded Nasr. "Then why is it that when I ask my chief jester if a member of his order is loyal or not, it replies with an I don't know?" Satan asked mockingly.

Nasr fell to his knees, begging. "Forgive me, Lord, if you would forgive. I was obeying my Lord Mastema."

"We," interjected Satan loudly, "are not in the forgiving business, in case you haven't noticed."

And with that, Satan raised his hand, and Nasr and his screams were teleported to the river of fire.

Arriving just in time to hear the fading screams, Mephistopheles appeared.

"You summoned me, Lord?"

"Yes. I am going to give Nargal a mission to complete. I wish it to be successful. Do you understand me?" Satan said quietly.

Despite the softness of the tone, Mephistopheles heard the veiled threat: fail and suffer. After receiving his instructions, Mephistopheles summoned Nargal, explaining to him his task as well as the displeasure of Satan should he fail. "Remember, you are not to be seen. Find out what you can then report to me," said Mephistopheles.

"Yes, master, as you wish," Nargal flared out, leaving Mephistopheles with a feeling he knew well—fear.

In his throne room, Satan looked over the torn body of Haroth. "How is it that you came to be this way, magician?" demanded Satan.

The suffering of a demon is that, though torn in two, they could not die and, depending on Satan's generosity—something the demons dreaded needing—it could take days, months, or years if Satan were so inclined. Fortunately, for Satan—not so for Haroth— his head was still intact. The talking head complained.

"Master, I went as commanded and ordered under your name that they join with me," wheezed out a torso-less Haroth. "The imp was ready to surrender; then I was savagely attacked by Diego and destroyed."

"You mean Diego and Cain destroyed you?" Satan corrected.

"No, Lord, only Diego. He is powerful, lord." Haroth clarified.

"He is a fledgling! Do not attempt to hide your incompetence with pitiful excuses!" howled Satan.

"No, my Lord. Listen, please. You must understand and listen to me."

"I shall," said Satan. "I shall listen to your screams as I send you to be picked at by the harpies."

"No, Lord! Noooo!" Haroth was cast unto the hill of suffering.

Satan turned to find Lillith standing behind him. "May I pleasure my lord?"

Satan grunted his accent, and they disappeared into his chambers. After satisfying his infernal lust, Satan rose from his bed of flames and strode over to his fountain that spewed liquid fire. Relaxed by the sight of it, Satan let out a sigh.

"What is it, my lord?" asked Lillith as she came up beside him, nestling her head on his shoulder.

"Do you think Ishar is traitorous?" Satan asked.

"The imp?" questioned Lillith. "My Lord, I think that entire class of demons somewhat questionable. I never bothered to know the imp myself. What are you thinking, Lord?" queried Lillith.

"I've sent the imp Ishar, Haroth the black wizard, and Nasrdin the jester/spy. All of these demons have suffered at the hands of Cain's new apprentice," growled Satan. "Now I shall dispatch the services of Nargal to deal with this upstart," claimed Satan.

"My lord," Lillith began carefully, "why not let me go first? I'm sure I would be able to entice him," suggested Lillith.

"No!" Satan demanded. "I want to know what's going on with these two arrogant creatures, and I want the apprentice Diego. He shall learn who his true master is. Besides, you think I don't know about your fixation on Cain?" snorted Satan.

"There is no fixation, lord," countered Lillith.

"Do you think you can lie to the father of lies, demoness?" You could not subdue his father, so you wish to slap the father by seducing the son!" Satan exclaimed. "I tell you what, demoness, if—and that's a big if—if Nargal fails, I will allow you to prove yourself. Am I not gracious?"

"Yes, Lord," Lillith said, bowing.

"Begone then. I have matters to attend," Satan commanded.

THE ESCAPE

Cain returned to find Diego gazing at a tablet in the library while Ishar squatted in a nearby corner.

"Welcome home," Diego greeted Cain. "You've been gone a while, and where have you been?" he asked. "Well," began Cain, "I went out to feed and ran into a friend of yours."

"A friend?" asked Diego. "Pointy ears, bad smell," Cain described. "Can you be more specific?" asked Diego.

"He means Satan," Ishar piped in. "Really? What did he want from you?" asked Diego. "Why, you, of course, Diego." Diego feigned surprise. "Me? Why me?"

"It would seem he is distraught over Haroth and I assume Ishar," stated Cain.

"Tell the worm he knows where to find me," Diego said pompously.

"No, Diego. I think it is time for us to leave here," commented Cain.

"But, Cain, his is your home, and we shouldn't let him drive us out."

"Diego, this building is just that. A building and I have no ties here."

Diego reluctantly agreed. "Fine! I just don't like running from a fight."

"I'm almost positive you will get your chance, Diego."

Diego turned to Ishar. "Well, little one, you may go free or join us, but I warn you, it will not be easy and will probably be very unpleasant," he warned.

"I am with you, Master. Where you lead, I will follow," said Ishar.

At that moment, Diego froze in place. Cain said, "I feel it too."

They turned to find Ishar gone. "Where did Ishar go?" asked Diego.

"I do not know," responded Cain. "But you can't tell me you're surprised. He is, after all, a demon."

Just then, Ishar appeared before them. "Masters," he gasped, "it is Nargal."

Diego looked at Ishar. "We thought you fled, and who is this Nargal?"

"Master, he is the demon that gathers information on prospects. Ishar said in a frightened tone."

"Prospects? Prospects for what!" demanded Diego.

"For hell, master," Ishar answered. "Satan sends him out when prospective souls try to escape his grasp," Ishar informed Diego. "Really?" asked Diego. "Yes, master. Really,". Repeated Ishar.

Cain looked at Diego. "Let us leave quickly," Cain warned.

Diego feigned, looking shocked. "Why Cain?" asked Diego with sarcastic concern. "What kind of hosts would we be if we left now, leaving poor old Nargal, who traveled all this way to see us if we left without first seeing to his needs?"

Cain was listening intently to what was occurring outside but answered Diego. "His needs are to drag you to hell! You wish to accommodate him?"

"Whatever gave you that foolish idea, Cain? We could always hear his offer with no capitulation."

"Master," piped in Ishar, "perhaps, Master Cain is right. These Nargal are vicious and effective."

"Nonsense," Diego said as he left to greet his uninvited guests.

"Master Cain, will you not stop Diego before he gets himself destroyed?" pleaded Ishar. "Come, little one, and you will see how powerful your Master Diego is."

Diego stepped into the garden, seeming casual in his stride. "Cain," Diego called, "could you tell me why it smells like the infected hindquarters of a diseased wild boar? It smells as if a leprosy-ridden corpse died and defecated on itself. You know what it reminds me of, Cain?" Diego sarcastically asked. "Satan's breath."

"What is he doing?" whispered Ishar. "He will only infuriate the demons."

Cain looked at Ishar and smiled. "You learn quickly, little one. Now watch."

Ishar looked again into the garden, where Diego was continuing his berating of the lord of evil.

"Yes, I understand that when God himself looked upon Satan, he had such pity for his ugliness that he mockingly named him morning star. He was the joke of heaven."

From the shadows, a demon flew at Diego, who caught him by the neck. "And where is it you think you are going, hell-spawned?" Diego mocked.

The demon struggled. "Fool! Give yourself to the Master, and perhaps he will have mercy on you," the devil warned. Ishar was looking around frantically. "What is it, Ishar"? Cain asked. still scanning the area, Ishar responded. "Master, that is not Nargal; he is one of his servants, a decoy." Meanwhile, the decoy made his threats.

Diego seemed to pause. "Let me think about that," he said, holding the demon still.

"You know what?" Diego asked after a moment. The demon looked at Diego questioningly. "You may be right," said Diego. The demon looked up, seeing Diego once again as prey. "Satan may forgive me," Diego continued, "but knowing who and what he is, I think I'll decline," he teased. The demon struggled helplessly in Diego's grip. The devil looked to the trees. "Ahh," said Diego. "Thank you. Tell your Master I'm sure I'll see him sooner than he wishes," he stated. And with that, he tore the struggling, screaming demon in two.

After the smoke cleared away, Diego looked into the woods. "Well, are you planning on cowering in the shadows all night?" he asked sarcastically.

With an explosion of smoke, Nargal stood before Diego, clutching his throat.

"We must help him," insisted Ishar. "That is Nargal-Din, a powerful demon. The Master doesn't have a hope!" whined Ishar.

"It is good to see your loyalty displayed, Ishar, but stand firm and watch," ordered Cain.

"Yes, master," responded a fidgety Ishar.

In the garden, Nargal held Diego by his throat, cursing in his face while Diego stared with what seemed a frightened expression. "Never in your darkest nightmares have you conceived the tortures my master has in store for you, fool!" Nargal screamed, squeezing Diego's throat harder. "You shall beg for mercy, but there will be none for you, Diego! Tonight you die!" roared Nargal.

Diego smiled at Nargal twisted his hand until Nargal released Diego's throat. Nargal's face transformed from fury to confusion to fear as he applied all his strength. "No!" Nargal roared.

"Yes," Diego replied calmly.

"You must die!" shouted Nargal.

Diego smiled. "You first, well take a second and think about how you threw away your sacrifice demon to gauge my strength, and wow, did you ever get that wrong." Diego then ferociously ripped the arms off Nargal, who howled in agony that was quickly silenced as Diego bare-handedly ripped off his head. "Say hello to shriveled face for me," mocked Diego to the dissipating smoke. Wiping his hands on his trousers, he turned to find Cain and an astonished Ishar and walked into the garden.

"Master, that was truly amazing," Ishar seemed to gush.

"Yes, yes, my boy. Excellent job. However, it is time we got going," declared Cain.

"Go? Go where?" asked a flushed and still somewhat excited Diego.

"We must leave here, my son, as Satan has all the patience of a sow, attempting to relieve herself of her unborn calf and about as much tact as swine that tries to consume its runts.

Diego looked at Ishar. "Ishar, you have appeared to grow pale somewhat," commented a smiling Diego.

"Yes, Master. Cain's description of what you would do to the demon Nargal made me a touch nauseous."

Diego looked at Ishar incredulously. "Ishar, you are a demon of hell! Why would such imagery disturb you?" asked Diego.

"Perhaps it is the influence of you and the good Master Cain."

Cain looked at Diego. "Gather what you wish, as we will soon depart."

"Where shall we go?" asked Diego.

"I have an old friend who I wish to see if he is still among us," said Cain.

"I'll just fetch my sword and—"

"Master, please allow me," Ishar volunteered. And with that, Ishar scampered off.

"You've got quite the pet there, Diego." Diego shook his head. "I prefer to think of him as my servant," corrected Diego. "You do know you do not require a sword any longer," observed Cain.

"Yes, I know," answered Diego. "But it is my family tradition that the men that go abroad have swords made for their particular fighting style." related Diego. "Ahh, yes, I understand!" exclaimed Cain.

With a loud clattering of armor, Ishar ran to Diego. "Here, master," said Ishar, handing Diego the battle accruements.

"Thank you, Ishar," said Diego while sheathing his sword. "I think I'll take only the breastplate and sword. You can leave the shield." He turned to Cain. "Shall we?"

Cain looked at Ishar. "I will follow closely, Master Cain." As a demon, Ishar had dimensional transportive powers that allowed him to go anywhere; however, his powers were beginning to wane as he drew away from evil and closer to good.

Cain considered that for a moment. "No, Ishar. I have something else for you to do." Cain then whispered instructions in Ishar's ears. Ishar's face went from frightened to curious to highly amused. Cackling, Ishar looked at Diego. Cain interjected before the imp could speak.

"Go now, Ishar," Cain ordered. "I will explain everything to Diego."

Hearing his name, Diego looked up from donning his gear. "What?" Diego asked.

"Are you ready? We should leave now," replied Cain.

"Lead the way," Diego said with a courtly bow.

"Oh my," quipped Cain as he floated into the air, with Diego hot on his heels.

"Fly beside me, brother," Cain called out.

Diego soared beside Cain. "To where do we journey?" asked Diego.

"To seek out one who might be amenable to our cause," Cain replied simply.

CHAPTER 10

INDIA-THE MAKERS RETURN

A star-lit sky provided a beautiful scene as Diego and Cain descended from their flight. "Where are we?" asked Diego.

Cain looked around suspiciously. "In the land of a dear old friend, something is amiss."

"What's wrong?" asked Diego. "I'm not sure, but wait for me here while I go look around."

"Around!" exclaimed Diego. "Around what? We landed in a forest and—"

Cain held up his hand to silence Diego. "I shall return shortly," Cain said before launching himself into the night.

"Damn it, Cain!" Diego complained to the now-empty air. "It's always something with you." Just then, Ishar appeared at Diego's side. "Master," said Ishar.

"Welcome back, Ishar. How did your journey go?" Diego inquired.

"Master, I was set upon by demons and—"

"What!" Diego interjected.

"A demon, master. I was attacked by a demon," Ishar sputtered.

"Well, tell me what happened and how did you escape"? Diego inquired.

Ishar looked around, perhaps looking for Cain. "I was in France, Master, when the demon Lilo commanded me to hell. Naturally, I refused, and he attacked me."

Diego was staring at Ishar. "And you defeated him?" he asked, astonished.

"No, Master. A dark lord, such as yourself, rescued me," Ishar revealed. Discovery dawned on the imp as he stared at Diego, realizing what the similarities were between the one who called himself Mulsine and his own Master!

Shocked, Diego replied, "What!" At the news, there might be another like him.

Out of the corner of his eye, Diego saw a blur streak at Ishar. Diego reached out, snatching what was surprisingly a beast, even more surprisingly, a full-grown Bengal tiger with unbelievable strength and speed.

Diego felt as if he were in for the fight of his life. The tiger kept breaking free of his grasp and, with preternatural agility, pressed his attack even though Diego kept catching and flinging him. The tiger paused, looking at Ishar and Diego, seeming to gauge whether he could get to one before the other struck. Diego spoke to the beast. "I don't know if you understand me, but we mean you no harm. If you attack my companion again, I will be forced to destroy you."

The tiger turned his head toward Diego and growled a low, threatening growl. It charged with incredible speed and adroitness. Diego viewed the awe-inspiring grace and beauty of the tiger as it swiftly bore down on him. He was so taken by the Tigers' grace it got uncomfortably close before Diego's awareness came screaming intensely to fight or die. Diego, oddly enough, chose neither; and as the beautiful, mighty, lethal tiger sprang at him, Diego seemed to disappear. The tiger, missing his mark, twirled and let out a bone-chilling roar, looked around, and saw Ishar, who was observing the battle. "Shit," said a frightened Ishar.

The tiger crouched as if to pounce, and Ishar vanished. It gave that ominous roar again but was cut off as a hand shot up from beneath the ground. Holding the tiger by the throat in a near crushing grip, Diego rose from the earth he had almost instantly bored into at the tiger's attack. Rising into the air, the tiger roared and struggled. But as powerful as it was, it had met its match with Diego.

Flying higher and higher, Diego tried speaking to the beast. "Stop! Stop struggling, or I'll release you." The tiger almost instantly stopped. "Ahh, so you do understand me. I thought you might.

Now I will set you down so you may be comfortable again, but you have seen my power. If you attack my companion or me again, I shall tear you apart with my bare hands. Growl if you agree". The tiger growled softly at Diego, who was in awe of the creature.

"Magnificent! You are indeed a wonder," Diego praised. The tiger, not hearing such words of kindness in a millennium, seemed to almost purring if such a thing were possible for this instrument of death.

Landing gently on the ground, Diego released the giant cat. The tiger walked a few feet away before sitting down and began cleaning himself. Diego could not contain himself. He exploded into laughter just as Cain was returning from his sojourn.

Landing gently, Cain smiled at the cat. The tiger, seeing him, roared and leaped at Cain. Diego, who was caught unaware due to his laughing fit, saw the tiger's tail flash by with Cain in the cat's path when, strangely enough, his arms opened as if to embrace the cat.

Before Diego could react, that cat slammed into Cain, bringing them both down. As Diego made to rip the animal off of Cain, he stopped when he heard Cain say, "How have you been, old friend?"

Diego was momentarily shocked that Cain was familiar with the great cat. He was then thunderstruck when he heard the cat purr, "I've missed you, Cain."

Taken aback, Diego uttered, "It speaks."

The tiger looked at Diego and growled. "It is a he."

Looking back at Cain, the tiger growled again, "Fast, powerful, but not very bright."

Diego heard what could only be a coughing-like laugh come from the tiger.

Cain stood, dusting himself off. Petting the great cat, Cain said by way of introduction,

"Diego, permit me to introduce you to the king of beasts, Shao-sin."

Diego looked at the tiger. "Shao-sin, a pleasure to make your acquaintance."

"My, what fine manners your youngling has, master," growled Shao.

"Master?" asked a befuddled Diego queried.

"Yes, Diego. After the cremation of my first apprentice, I flew here to India where Shao attacked me."

"Master, I was ravenous," Shao purred.

"Yes, Sin, I know," said Cain.

"Excuse me," interrupted Diego. "Sin?"

"Yes, Shao-sin, Sin."

"I see," said Diego.

"I drank from him but could not destroy such a wonderful beast, so I asked him if he would care to join me in immortality."

Diego looked at Cain. "You mean he could speak and understand before you . . . bit him."

"No, of course not. But much like when you were dying, I could communicate with you mentally, so it was with him," explained Cain.

Ishar stood not far away. Reappearing when things settled down, he stared intensely at Sin.

"Why do you stare, demon?" growled Sin.

Diego walked over to Ishar. "Sin, this is our companion, Ishar," Diego said, introducing the odd pair.

"I don't like demons!" growled Sin.

"Me either," replied Ishar.

Stunned, the great cat chuckled. "Really?" questioned an unbelieving Sin.

"Oh yes, our brave little demon even fought off the demon Lilo," said Diego.

"You what?" asked a surprised Cain.

"Well, actually, Master, I was aided by one of your brethren by the name of Mulsine. Shao's ears twitched upon hearing the name.

Cain sat back in silence. "So he has survived," Cain mumbled.

"Yes, master, and I was given to believe whatever aid you may require of him, he would gladly help."

Cain sat on a stump, contemplating this new information.

"Cain, what is it you wish to do?" asked Diego.

"I suppose we'll go to France and see what Mully is about."

"Master," purred Sin, "if I may?"

"Of course, Sin. What is it?" asked Cain.

"Master, one of your dark children has returned and wreaked havoc in my jungle.

If you would but assist me in bringing him to heel."

Cain looked furious. "Speak his name, noble king."

"It is Mmbyu, master," growled Sin.

Cain shook with anger. "What is it?" asked Diego. "Are you familiar with this man?"

"Yes," Cain answered. "After visiting India and augmenting Sin's abilities, I went into the city of Cylon, where I fed on an aristocrat.

Wishing for the companionship of men, I turned Mmbyu. I stayed with him and Sin for a century or so. I had learned with Sin more about my abilities."

The great cat purred, nuzzling Cain's hand. "And the limitations imposed on my descendants." Wishing them both well, I flew off to Greece, hearing of great men and new teachings." Cain snapped from his reverie.

"But the here and now is what matters. What do you wish us to know of Mmbyu, Sin?" "First, master, that he has raised a horde of picahs, a race of sickly vampire, and has elevated one as his disciple, who is called, Lord Yaksha, the disciple of the dark god." purred the great cat. "Yaksha's picahs terrorize the surrounding villages, drinking them nearly dry and offering his master Mmbyu virgins as a blood sacrifice."

Cain could barely control his rage. "Well then, I think it is time to pay this ungrateful swine a visit." The tiger seemed to chuckle. "Just so, Master. If you would but follow me," purred Sin.

"After you, your majesty," Cain said with a slight bow. The tiger roared and sprinted into the forest.

Cain looked at Diego. "He loves when I call him that."

Diego returned Cain's gaze. "I've never met a more powerful beast," Diego acknowledged.

"And he talks too," piped in Ishar.

"Yes, of course, there is that. Ishar, I want you to wait here for us."

"Come, Diego," said Cain as he flew off after Sin.

"Master," said Ishar. Diego glanced over at the imp. "Be wary, master," pleaded Ishar. "I believe that this one you now seek has converted to Satan's rule," observed Ishar. Diego smiled in satisfaction.

Transformation of a Killer

Born in the jungles of India, the Bengal Tiger was a stealthy hunter as his Mother and Father taught him to be, but they have been gone awhile now as poachers slew them. Luckily for the great cat, he was solitary by nature. He was a mighty cat with strict territorial markers, and woe be unto the animal that lingered in his domain. The cat ruled his jungle with a sense of equality. Unknown to all, this majestic cat protected the orphaned animals from greedy animals seeking easy prey and from human poachers like the ones that killed his parents. The younger felines began meowing "Shao." in his presence, meaning the "harmonious one." Never taking notice of such trivial matters, it wasn't until one day a man that flew as a bird came into his jungle. When a young tiger saw and growled his observations to the great cat. Curiosity drove the great Bengal. The Tiger ran to the last spot where the stranger that walked like a man but flew like a bird was last seen. He was quickly located as the man sat sobbing and rocking by a river-side. Seeing an opportunity, the great cat stalked over quietly. The man looked up; the cat was stunned to see blood issuing from the man's eyes. Shaking off the surprise, the cat lunged at the man. With no apparent effort, the small man threw the great cat as if it were a reed in the wind. Never had the cat been treated in such a fashion. The cat roared and charged the man who did not move. Hitting the man, the cat found it odd that the man didn't go down. The cat had hunted men before, and none acted as this one. All were terrified by the cats' presence, except for this man. frustrated, the cat bit the man, which seemed to shake him out of his stupor. "Ohh, you want to bite"? The man said aloud, although it sounded like gibberish to the cat. The great cat was shocked beyond belief when the man-thing bit him back. Then to the cats' surprise, the man began drinking his blood. The cat became weaker as his blood was being drained. The cat was confounded by the turn of events because nothing in his life prepared him for such a moment. Being more conscious than aware, the cat knew nothing of good and evil or souls and spirits nor God and the devil. The cat heard the man's thoughts in his head. *"You will. I offer you my blood; if you drink it, you shall become as I am. You will understand the words of men and become an immortal hunter"* the man projected. The cat purred his accent, the man cut his wrists, allowing the Tiger to lap at the blood. Soon the lapping became more frantic as the one who was called Shao began the dance macabre of the undead. Images raced through the cats' mind, images he couldn't possibly understand. Suddenly the cat heard the man's voice in his head, and much to his confusion, the cat, understood him. *"Who are you"?*The man asked, and the cat formulated a thought beyond his instincts which bewildered him as it was something he had never done before. *"The young call me Shao".* the great cat-related. *"You were dying Shao as I have drained most of your blood but your memories speak of a* cat *with a sense of pride and right and wrong so I offer you true power and ask only that you hunt faithfully beside me".* Cain proffered. Shao purred. *"My fangs and claws are yours".* The great cat growled. The state of mortality were stripped away leaving an immortal being. Shao sprang to his feet and roared experiencing more power then he's ever felt before. "I am Cain of Nod and I shall call you Shao sin". Cain exclaimed. Shao focused, growled. "How is this.." Cain waited a moment while Shao searched for the word. "Possible"? Shao asked. "That my friend is a long story we shall have plenty of time to ponder". Shao glared at him a moment. "well you appear to be feeling better". He observed. Cain looked at Shao. "Yes I am feeling somewhat better thank you". Shao responded gratefully. The great cats face took on an odd expression. "I find your words to be cumbersome as we in the animal world feel as we do without attempting to label everything". Shao observed. "Yes". Cain agreed. "That is true". Shao began to look very apprehensive. "What is troubling you my friend"? Cain inquired noticing the look. Shao growled. "I feel unbridled power coursing through me". Shao growled louder. "I recommend a good run followed by a hunt, now remember you will feel an urge to drink the blood, do not allow this to upset you". Cain suggested. Shao bolted from their spot, becoming a blur. Cain couldn't imagine the terror that spread throughout the region as Shao sped from end to end of the subcontinent roaring. Cain smiled. In a short time, Shao returned to the banks of the river of his transformation. "That was astounding! I'm not even short of breath," Shao said. "The undead does not need things such as breath or food; we only require to drink blood when the calling is upon us." Cain instructed. Shao showed his feline propensity for curiosity even though his rapid understanding of the human sense of civility and courtesy were developing and advised against it he prodded. "Cain, why did you come here? were you hunting me"? Cain looked at the city beyond Shao's jungle." No, my friend. In fact, as your skills sharpen, you will see in your memories what happened. The short story is that after the event that made me what I am, I was in a state of despair, but then I met a young innocent that almost convinced me that everything would turn out fine". Shao cocked his head asking. "and it didn't"? Cain shook his head. "By no means. My young friend was accosted by Satan who convinced him I was lying about my true nature,". Cain said in remembrance. "I made him as I made you my brother. Cain reflected. "As I was saying, my friend, confronted me as to why I wore a rag across my eyes when I was not blind." I wondered how he came by this information and how I presented myself among men." Cain clarified. "And"? Asked Shao. "I stupidly removed my blindfold and he was enraptured. "How is it that your eyes glow as lamps," He asked. "He then began to examine me more closely, noticing a lack of wrinkles and such. One night much to my dismay, he sliced his hand opens in front of me. You must understand I was still relatively young and had no real concept as to my power, my limits. seeing the greed in my eyes for the blood, he extended the wounded hand, asking. "Cain, why do you look at me in such a manner"? I fought the urge to pounce upon him and drink to my heart's content; instead, I explained my condition to him, promising him eternal youth and that we could walk in the light of day for a thousand years if he chose to walk with me. Shao was taken by the story. "So it was like adopting a kitten that isn't yours." Shao growled. Cain nodded. "Yes, in a manner of speaking." Cain said, agreeing with Shao's comparison.

CHAPTER 11

DISCIPLINING OF A DISCIPLE

On a hill overlooking a palace, Sin stood in a tree line, observing the surroundings.

Cain and Diego joined him. "What do you think?" asked Diego, assessing the situation.

It was a moonless night. Humid and windy. The wind carried a stench of blood to the preternatural senses of the trio on the hilltop. The Palace seemed to be bustling with activity. "What now, master"? Diego inquired.

"Me? I think I'm going to show my wayward disciple what real terror is, and then I'm going to rip Mmbyu to shreds," Cain coldly stated.

"Sounds like a plan. Sin and I will deal with the underlings," agreed Diego.

"Mmm, yes, demon food," purred the great tiger Sin. I will do an Ariel search for potential enemies and then signal you two to storm the gates. The loud screeching of the picahs could be heard.

"Careful, you two. Remember, Mmbyu has an apprentice or two," warned Cain.

"Ohh, goody," Sin purred. "Fresh meat." Cain motioned to them. "Wait for my signal. Cain launched himself into the night.

Diego laughed. "Come, mighty friend, let us show these creatures what real power is!" Diego exclaimed.

Breaching the walls was relatively easy. The picah guards fell before the mighty Tiger and his fearsome comrade. The Picahs was an offshoot of the vampiric family that never fully developed and were more or less mindless, blood-thirsty ravagers that obeyed only power. After the making of Yaksha, Mmbyu set him out to make him an army of undead, and although Mmbyu was a direct descendant of Cain, Yaksha was once removed and derived from a weak aristocrat. Yaksha could be seen whipping his picahs into a frenzy. The courtyard was filled with snarling, near-starved picahs.

"Who dares enter the domain of the dark god of Cylon?" the voice boomed from a dais high above the courtyard where Yaksha, The disciple of Mmbyu, stood.

Diego and Sin stopped looking up. "So, are you supposed to be this dark god?" Diego asked mockingly.

"Fool! I am the Yaksha disciple to the dark God Mmbyu, and you shall be his slaves!"

"Well," began Diego, "being that my companion is the king of beasts and I never took to the notion of slavery, I think I'll just decline the offer. Besides that, your twisted master who foolishly thinks himself a god shall today be destroyed," Diego ended with a smile.

"Blasphemous fool! The God Mmbyu cannot be destroyed. He is immortal!" screamed Yaksha.

"If by immortal you mean he could live forever, then no, you are incorrect as tonight he dies by my master's hand," mused Diego.

"Fools. You do not see the inevitable. Beg mercy and swear to serve the immortal Mmbyu". "I hate to interrupt your ranting, but you misunderstand," Diego interjected.

"You think your master Immortal? I mean to inform you that after my companion is done with him, the only immortality he will know is eternal suffering, and that may not be the sort of immortality you may be alluding to. Still, the one he will suffer nonetheless," Diego corrected.

Yaksha looked at the Tiger. "You think a mere beast, even with the blood of Cain, could slay my master?"

"You know of Cain?" asked Diego.

"I know of the coward that murdered his brother and with his curse made my master, who with his new power will destroy Cain and become the dark god Mmbyu."

"Does it hurt, Yaksha?" asked Diego.

"Does what hurt, impudent fool?" replied Yaksha.

"Well," began Diego, "a couple of things. How did you feel being a lapdog for a creature so low as to have to look up to see up a dung beetle's ass and two. Did you come by being so tremendously stupid genetically through your whorish diseased mother and your leprous father, or did that worm you call master pass it on to you when he fed? And just for your edification, Master Cain lives, your depraved master lied to you".

"Insolent fool!" screamed Yaksha. "I shall feed on the marrow of your bones."

Diego noticed that the picahs were milling about as if awaiting orders to attack.

"What are you waiting for, ugly?" teased Diego.

"He is rather ugly," growled Shao-sin.

"You shall meet your doom!" Yaksha threatened.

Making of Mmbyu

Shao-sin acted as a tour guide to Cain, showing off the beautiful countryside of India. Cain enjoyed roaming with Shao. The great cat wanted to introduce Cain to his animal family. "Well, they are not kin, but I've protected them from men and each other. Cain's face reflected concern when the suggestion was made. "Why do you wear a face of worry, master"? Shao inquired. Cain shook his head sadly. "My friend. Cain began. "Forgive me, I never thought of it, but it is not likely for your friends to accept your new condition." Shao looked at Cain as if he was crazy. "Why would you say such a thing? They are my family when no one else would protect them. I did". Shao said, upset at the notion Cain proposed. "Shao, you must understand, all animals fear the predator species, and you are well beyond that now. Now you are a supernatural predator, the instinctual fear you will stir will be well beyond their capacity to endure,". Cain shared sadly. "I realize your knowledge is extensive, master. Still, in this, you're mistaken." Shao declared. Realizing that only by going through the motions of trying to reconnect with those he thought of as his family would Shao see the truth Cain realized. This would be the most difficult portion Shao had with his transformation. When Shao attempted to return to his own territory, All those he protected before sensed the change in him and were terrified by it. There were some females that always purred whenever Shao was near, but now he was received with a raised back and hisses. When Shao tried to communicate in the language of animals, the only message they sent was that he was no longer welcome among them as he was no longer as they were. Shao angrily shouted at them. "Who saved you when other animals came to slaughter you? When men came and frightened the poachers who came for your pelts? It was me! Not one of you had the courage to face these intrusions upon your lives; it was me and me alone"! Shao shouted. As one body, the animals turned and fled from Shao in horror. He turned to Cain and bellowed a sound of loss that touched Cain deeply. Spending the monsoon season in different caves, Cain stood at the entrance of one that overlooked the city of Cylon. Shao strode up to Cain, asking. "What are you thinking, master. Cain stared at the city off in the distance. "I'm thinking about venturing to the city and finding us a warm, dry place to recline," Cain responded.

"We are fine here; we don't need the comforts of men." Shao spat. Cain looked at his feline friend. "Need, no. Desire, yes. Wait here, I shall return shortly". Cain directed and before Shao could raise an objection, Cain flew off toward Cylon. Scanning the area Cain found what he was looking for. A large house on the outskirts of town was lit with torches as the sound of merriment wafted up to Cain. Descending, Cain found a nobleman stumbling out of the main house, drunk and stretching while yawning. The man was short, round, with deepest dark brown eyes that seemed to look upon everything as if it were for sale. A sign of his prosperity that he hosted proudly was an annual festival the nobleman held, inviting dignitaries from other regions to visit and partake in trade making the nobleman liked, securing his position as a nobleman of Cylon. "Ahh, life is wonderful but predictable." The nobleman complained. "And what would you do if the unpredictable made itself known to you"? Cain asked, stepping out of the shadows. The nobleman was startled. "Who are you? How did you get past my guards"? He demanded. "I am the unpredictable you asked for." Cain responded. "Guards"! the nobleman shouted. "Now we shall see how clever you are." He threatened. Hearing the guards' boots running toward them, the nobleman turned his head to watch their approach while saying. "Now you will explain your presence here." Upon seeing the nobleman's distraction, Cain shot straight up where none could see. The guards approached the nobleman, the leader bowed. "My lord." The guard bowed by way of acknowledgment. "How may we be of service"? The nobleman pointed behind him where Cain had stood and ordered. "Take this peasant to the dungeons." He demanded. The squad leader looked dumbfounded. "My lord, of what man do you speak"? he asked. The noble spun only to find Cain gone. The guards, of course, thought the nobleman drunk. "He was here a moment ago"! The noble complained. The guard leader knowing his master ordered his men to search the compound for any uninvited guest. The nobleman was angered that the guards had allowed someone in who did not have an invitation, shouted. "Never mind, just tell my guests that the party is over and escort everyone off of my land." The noble shouted. Knowing his volatile temper, the guards went about their duties quickly. The noble retired to his bedroom stepped out unto his balcony, and saw a shadowed figure. he quickly drew his scimitar. So this is where you've been hiding". He said menacingly while pointing his sword. "I assure you the sword is both unnecessary and useless". Cain pointed out. "It protects me from you so it is very necessary". The noble claimed in correction. In a blur Cain snatched the sword from the mans hand and seated himself asking. "Won't you join me"? The nobles face took on a fearful expression. "Who or what are you"? he asked. "My name is not important, what is important is what I offer you". Cain said ambiguously. "And what would that be"? The nobleman asked suspiciously. "Eternal life". Cain answered simply. The noble tilted his head. "And how do you presume to offer me that which is not yours to give"? He asked doubtfully. "It is faster for me to show you rather than explain, may I"? Cain inquired. The noble grew anxious. "No doubt you are a warrior with extraordinary skills as your disarming me prove, will this display harm me in any- way"? The noble asked. "That would depend on your perspective as to what harm is". Cain responded sincerely. "I find your evasions unsettling stranger". As the noble finished his sentence Cain stood directly in front of him causing the noble to step back, Cain grabbed him saying, "Prepare yourself". The startled noble felt wind rush past him, chill envelope him. "Cain whispered. "Look down." The noble looked down and gasped. "What"? He attempted to question. Cain slowly descended so the noble could, in awe, view the countryside as they descended. Upon landing, the noble threw himself to the ground. "The power of life eternal is mine to give as I see fit, I desire the company of men, and I have chosen you." The noble bowed. I am Mmbyu, governor of this region. "Are you a god? Has Vishnu sent you"? He asked. Cain shook his head. "I come of my own accord seeking companionship, have you decided"? Cain inquired. Mmbyu scratched at his chin. "Will I be able to do as you"? He inquired. Cain shrugged. "My gift translates differently among my disciples. Mmbyu cocked his head. "In what way"? Cain smiled. "Have you ever spoken with a predator before" Cain probed. Mmbyu chuckled. "Of course not." Cain smiled. "Wait a moment." Cain thought about introducing Shao to Mmbyu as part of the intrigue that was part of what they offered. As Cain focused on the issue at hand, miles away, a startled five hundred pound machine of destruction jumped up from grooming himself. "What." He growled. He sniffed the air suspiciously. *Shao,* a mental whisper, his name in the wind. "Master"? He growled back. Silence. A strange silence, one that suggested a draft in a cave. Using his Vampiric awareness, Shao silenced his mind and thought of Cain. Cain's eyes blazed in awareness on the other end of this telepathic connection. *"Shao, come to me, my friend, unseen and unheard."* Cain mentally requested. Mmbyu sat staring at Cain, who smiled without revealing his fangs. "I bring more proof of my word." Cain informed him. "What sort of proof? I am no fool. I know of magicians that can hypnotize and have you believe the impossible. Cain nodded. "This is true but can any magician you know give thought and the power of speech to those we think of as beasts"? Cain challenged. Mmbyu's eyes narrowed in disbelief. "That would indeed be a trick of the gods." declared Mmbyu.

"No trick, simple fact," growled Shao. Mmbyu jumped at the sudden intrusion and nearly soiled himself being face to face, unarmed, against a jungle killer. It suddenly struck him that the voice came from the direction of the great beast. In great fear, he wondered how the beast got in. He looked past the animal when he heard, much to his surprise, The cat spoke directly to him. "No one is behind me. My master told me not to slay you, so for the moment, you are safe". The great cat growled. Mmbyu was at a loss for words; he slowly looked at Cain. "By what power do you do this"? He asked sensibly, which impressed Diego. "Excellent question with a long twisted answer, one that would require you to join my companion and me if you truly wish to know," Cain replied. "But I would no longer be human"? Mmbyu asked. "You will no longer succumb to illness, nor will you know death," Cain informed him. "And I would be able to fly"? He asked, almost breathless. "My gifts translate differently, so I do not know for sure. "Cain answered. "That kind of power and to live eternally? Yes, I'll join you". Mmbyu answered anxiously. "I have provisions, the first being no taking of innocent lives," Cain demanded. Mmbyu nodded. "Of course, do not our holy books say that the highest purpose of power is to serve the weak"? Cain tilted his head. "Is that so"? He asked. "With that also comes a test by one who would seek to corrupt you with promises of glory. You must resist him at all costs, do you swear to do so on pain of death"? Cain admonished. "I thought you claimed I would be eternal"? Mmbyu exclaimed, thinking he caught Cain in a contradiction. "All I have said is true, but the gift given can also be taken from you," Cain warned. Mmbyu paused for only a moment; the thought of immortality with just a fraction of the power Cain revealed was overwhelmingly tempting. Mmbyu agreed to Cain's stipulations. Cain took Mmbyu in his arms and whispered, "Remember your word to me." Cain buried his fangs in the new initiates neck and began the exchange of blood that would transform Mmbyu into an immortal. Mmbyu thrashed as if burning. Visions of him sitting on a throne as an empire chanted his name. A figure unknown to him appeared and whispered to him, *Do as you are compelled and a kingdom awaits you.*" Whispered a shadowy figure. Shao watched uncomfortably as he witnessed Mmbyu mutate into his immortal state. Opening his Vampyre eyes for the first time, he noticed Shao looking at him suspiciously. "Why do you stare at me in such a manner. Mmbyu asked. "I saw a dark shadow cross with your image,." Shao informed him. "I do not know what you're talking about,." Mmbyu insisted. For the next hundred years or so the trio explored the mysteries of the subcontinent until Cain felt an urge to depart. Calling his disciples to him Cain shared the news. "My friends something calls me back to the lands of my fathers, I must seek out the meaning of this compulsion. Shao-sin, Mmbyu, I expect you two to keep an eye on things while I'm gone. Do not permit evil to take root here and be mindful of the tempter for his mischief is always about. with his departure, Shao remained with Mmbyu for a season before he too departed, noticing that Mmbyu had been going against Cains dictates regarding the innocent as well as the beginnings of a blood cult. In his desire to rule, he made himself a disciple he named Yaksha and ordered him to create an army of undead that he could rule with the objective of creating a Nation of Vampires with Mmbyu sitting as its God.

CAIN CONFRONTS MMBYU

Cain soared high above the palace of his former disciple. He was buffeted by a steady warm wind and clear sky. Cain observed the lay of the land. His loyal disciples awaited his instructions at a tree-line that overlooked the palace, the sickening vermin that were the picahs groveled in the courtyard attended by what Cain assumed to be Mmbyu's disciple. Cain fixed his gaze upon the corrupt Mmbyu and dove, approaching the great hall unmolested, glided silently to the doors to the throne room.

Cain entered where Mmbyu sat upon an ornate throne. "Well, well, what have we here? A boy who never became a man and a Vampyre that thought himself a god" said Cain upon entering.

Mmbyu looked down upon Cain from his throne. "You shall not usurp me, slayer of men," exclaimed Mmbyu.

Cain floated up to eye level and hovered there. "I'm not here for your petty throne," he said.

"Then why did you come?" asked a nervous Mmbyu.

"Well," Cain began, "first, I thought I'd let my disciple tear your apprentice apart piece by piece before I destroyed you."

"Ha!" Mmbyu burst out. "You think your pup can destroy Yaksha and his legions? You are wrong again, Cain. You were wrong to kill your brother, you were wrong not to kill that silly tiger, who will become fodder for my picahs, and you are so wrong to think you can destroy me," finished an exasperated Mmbyu. Cain smiled. "I see you are under the assumption that it is just Shao and me, no my foolish child today you meet one that shall lay low all that you have raised, and in the end, I shall leave you powerless and those that you thought would aid you shall leave you to perish. Now, why don't you and I go outside and see how that turns out."

Cain invited, turned, going out to the balcony, where a hesitant Mmbyu joined him. Upon seeing Diego, Mmbyu looked at Cain. "Is this what you threaten me with? a youngling? And Shao sin"? Mmbyu shouted. Why are they still standing"? Mmbyu roared at Yaksha. "Did I not order you to destroy them!"

Yaksha looked chagrined. "Master, we've received no such orders," he said, fear infused in his voice. Mmbyu looked over at Cain, who only smiled, saying, "I didn't want you to miss the downfall of your apprentice."

Mmbyu spun around and screamed at Yaksha. "Kill them! Kill them now!"

The horde as one body turned to Diego and Shao-sin. "Well, it's about time," roared Shao and tore into the ranks with savagery never witnessed by Diego before. Picahs burst into flames left and right as Sin ripped through their ranks.

"Hey, leave some for me!" shouted Diego.

"Better hurry," snorted Shao as he spat out a picah head.

A loud horn could be heard over the din.

"Now you shall see why we are unopposed!" yelled Yaksha.

Amidst the slashing, screaming, and roaring, Diego heard what sounded like an army approaching. He looked up toward Cain. Cain, seeing what was unfolding, looked at Mmbyu, who wore the smile of the victorious. "All of these are creatures of your blood?" He asked. "Through Yaksha. Will you now yield?" asked Mmbyu.

"Why would I do that on earth?" asked Cain, feigning surprise.

Diego and Sin had by now destroyed most of the picahs that were in the courtyard.

"Cain," Diego called out. "We've got company. A lot of company."

Mmbyu addressed Cain: "Meet your doom, my former master."

"I think not," answered Cain.

As the swarm rushed toward Diego and Sin, Diego called out to Cain. "Really? This was the extent of your plan?" Diego asked sarcastically.

"You see, Cain, even your pup has no faith in you," Mmbyu gloated.

Cain called out, "Diego, do you believe in me?" Diego looked up with a look of exasperation, exclaiming loudly. "You want me to kill them all? Fine." Diego began moving forward to meet the charging mass. Beside him strode the great tiger Shao-sin.

"See the faith that boy has? Something you were always lacking, my apprentice," Cain said, criticizing Mmbyu.

The demons had entered the courtyard when Cain called out, "Diego, you and Sin step back." Diego heard the mental message. *"Take Sin into the air."*

Diego looked at Shao, who was busy ravaging anyone near him. Ripping the head off a demon he had by the throat, Diego called out. "Sin. To me." Diego floated into the air. The cat bunched his powerful muscles and sprang up to Diego, who hovered one hundred feet above the carnage.

Mmbyu turned to Cain. "What a pitiful trick, my former master." Cain only smiled. "Tell me what you think of this trick." He said to Mmbyu.

Cain walked to the balcony ledge and whispered, "Burn." The picahs screamed as they burst into flames so hot that Diego and Sin felt the blast of heat from where they hovered. "Amazing," purred Sin.

"No!" Yaksha screamed as his underlings were incinerated.

Diego and Sin floated gently to the ground.

"Destroy them!" yelled Mmbyu. Yaksha flew from his perch at a speed no average person could hope to follow, but he was not attacking an ordinary man. Diego snatched Yaksha by his outstretched hand and slammed him to the ground, stunning him.

Mmbyu looked on, shocked. "But how?" Mmbyu stammered. Cain smiled.

Yaksha gasped, "I will destroy you, dog."

Still holding the demon's hand, Diego broke three of his fingers in a quick snap. Yaksha roared in pain. "Now, that wasn't nice and a bit idiotic to threaten someone when they have you at their mercy," said Diego.

"My master shall destroy you all," Yaksha rasped menacingly.

Diego looked up at Cain. Cain turned to Mmbyu. "I gave you immortality, and this is how you show your gratitude?" snarled Cain. "You have beheld the destruction of your minions. Now watch as your apprentice precedes you to hell!" Upon the telepathic command of Cain, Diego ripped the head off of Yaksha.

"That was somewhat anticlimactic, wouldn't you agree?" purred Sin.

"Indeed," agreed Diego.

A loud wail of despair came from Mmbyu. In an attempt to flee, he flew down to the courtyard, thinking of killing Diego. As he landed in front of Diego, he was taken aback by Diego's apparent casualness.

"You die, dog!" screamed Mmbyu, who lunged at Diego, who surprisingly made no move to defend himself. Just as Mmbyu's fingers reached out for Diego's neck, Mmbyu was violently snatched back. Cain held him fast, lifting him over his head. Mmbyu struggled, cursing Cain. "Release me! I, too, have undiluted blood. I will return! Stronger, more powerful than you or your lackey once I join with Satan!"

Cain seemed to consider this for a moment. "You're correct, dog, so I'll. . ." With a quick motion, Cain flipped Mmbyu into a tight embrace, burying his fangs into his neck. "Wha . . . what are you doing?" asked a bewildered and nearly drained Mmbyu.

"Well, I got to thinking about what you said," projected Cain, *"and decided you might be right, so I've drained you of enough blood to make healing very difficult and painstakingly long."* And with that, Cain flipped the renegade vampire back into the air, caught him, and folded him until there was a loud crack of his spine snapping. He threw him to the ground, and Mmbyu landed like a broken doll.

"Now, Mmbyu," Cain said in judgment, "for the evil you spread and your betrayal of me, the one that made you, I have taken back most of the blood I once shared with you, leaving you unable to heal for weeks even with a fresh supply of blood, but I did leave just enough to be vulnerable to the sun again. So enjoy the rest of the night, for it is your last."

Mmbyu lay on the floor, gurgling incoherently. Cain turned to his disciples. "Diego, Shao-sin, shall we go?"

Cain and Diego flew off, with Sin keeping pace on the ground. "That is one fast cat," observed Diego.

Mmbyu writhed on the ground in excruciating pain as the tiny bit of vampiric blood attempted to heal his injuries. As the trio departed, a sinister figure appeared. "Ahh, look at you. What happened, dark god? Isn't that what you called yourself? hmm? If you had joined me when I first smelled your corrupt nature, you would not be in this predicament now". Satan taunted. For you arrogance I shall feast on you in hell dark God, enjoy the rest of your mortal suffering and prepare for your immortal one". Satan departed with a sinister laugh. Mmbyu cursed at Satan. A few hours into his torment, he could finally move enough to try sitting upright. Much to his chagrin, when he finally was able to, he sat up to a swiftly lightening sky as dawn rapidly approached. Screaming in agony, he dragged himself to a nearby grove of trees. Inches from it, he burst into flames as the sun rose over the horizon. So ended the tyranny of Mmbyu, the false God of Cylon.

CHAPTER 12

THE VILLA

Traveling through an ever brightening sky, the two Vampyre lords flew overhead while Shao-sin traversed the beautiful countryside of India and Turkey before approaching the borders of Syria. Looking down, Diego saw Shao dip in and out of valleys and make tremendous leaps over rivers, all the while keeping pace with that overhead.

Cain, Diego, and Shao finally arrived at Cain's residence in Tyre. They had covered vast stretches of land. Upon arriving at their destination, Diego looked over at Shao. "That was amazing! You're not even breathing hard," said an impressed Diego.

"Really?" Shao said, giving his version of a snicker, which amounted to a wheezing kind of cough.

"What is that supposed to mean, really?" asked Diego, picking up on the ridicule.

"I mean to say, Diego, that air is for the living, and since we are not technically alive . . .," Shao left the rest unsaid, hinting at Diego, waiting for him to make the connection for himself. "Oh, I see," Diego uttered, feeling stupid.

At that moment, Ishar appeared. "Welcome home, master." As Ishar approached, he pointed to the courtyard. "I thought you might be hungry when you got back, Shao, so I got you a nice fat ox."

"Little demon, I could stand to feed, but I like to hunt, so release the ox, so I may chase it down." purred Shao.

"Of course, Shao. I should have realized that. Is now a good time?" asked Ishar.

"Yes," growled Shao with anticipation of the chase. Ishar stepped off to release the ox when Shao addressed him. "Ishar, my thanks."

"Feed well, fearsome one," said Ishar.

Shao turned to Diego. "Fine little recruit you have there." And with that, he bounded off, hearing the ox braying as it ran for its short life.

Ishar turned to Diego. "Master, if I could speak with you and Lord Cain."

"What about?" asked Diego.

Ishar responded, "I think it best that I speak to you both."

Looking at the imp-demon quizzically, Diego capitulated to the request. "Fine. I'll meet you both in the library momentarily."

"Thank you, master. I shall arrive shortly," agreed Ishar.

Wondering at the mystery, Diego took to the air to see how Shao was doing on his hunt. Upon returning, Diego made for the library, where Ishar and Cain awaited him.

"Where did you go?" Cain asked Diego.

"I just wanted to see how Shao was doing on his hunt," answered Diego.

"And?" asked Cain.

"Doing what one expects cats to do, play with their food before eating it," answered Diego.

"I could never break him off that nasty habit. Well, Ishar, your request is fulfilled. Diego and I are here. What is so important?" asked Cain.

Ishar began his tale. "Remember when I went on that diversionary expedition, Master Cain? Well, I met an old disciple of yours." Ishar paused, waiting for a reaction. When none was forthcoming, he continued. "Well, I stopped off in France, and your suspicions are valid, as I was set upon by the ravager demon Lilo."

Cain's interest seemed to sharpen at that. "What are you saying, Ishar? That you fought a ravager?" Cain asked, shocked.

"No, master, although I told him what he could do with his offer."

Cain tried to keep from laughing. He looked at Diego, who was staring intensely at Ishar. "Continue," said Diego.

"Well," Ishar said, "he didn't care much for my denial, so he did what his type always does—roar and charge. At that moment, I became petrified and grateful for the existence you, master, and Lord Cain showed me I could have. Resigning myself to my fate, I heard a terrible scream followed by an eerie silence. I looked up to find a man of great stature before me; he said he was Mulsine, Pierre du Mulsine. And he asked why I was in his domain. I explained I was on an important mission for my lord, and he asked, 'Then why did you defy the ravager? Did I not serve the same master?'"

Diego and Cain looked at one another, wondering where this was leading.

"Mulsine said after I told him that I would return upon the completion of my mission and inform my master of his assistance he directed me to inform my master that he defends his realm against satanic forces and if you ever require his assistance, he would come to your call," finished Ishar.

"So, what do you think?" Diego asked Cain. "Can we trust him?"

Cain stood and walked to the windows.

"I met Mulsine during the First Crusade. He is old. He is powerful and hates Satan almost as much as I do," Cain mused.

"Trust him? Yes, I believe we can. Diego, I'd like you to take Ishar and speak with Mulsine, see if his word is true."

Just then, Shao hopped over the twenty-foot wall that surrounded the house.

"Well, old friend, did you enjoy yourself?" asked Cain.

Shao growled his response. "I had more fun slaying demon-kind." Shao looked over at Ishar. "No offense intended."

Ishar looked at Shao. "None was taken, great cat. Besides, you hate demon-kind. These days I'm only kind of a demon."

The four laughed at the attempt at wordplay. "Ishar, you may be developing a sense of humor," observed Diego.

"Let us be about our business then. Diego, you and Ishar find Mulsine," Cain ordered.

"What? Mulsine is about"? Shao asked eagerly. Cain nodded. "It would seem old friend." Cain acknowledged. "What of me, master may I go find Pierre?" growled the great cat Shao. Cain shook his head negatively. "Allow us first to see what side Pierre fights for before doing that, my feline friend." Cain insisted. "For now."

Go and hunt my friend, but be near in case I need of you," answered Cain. The great cat appeared not to be happy.

THE FRENCHMAN'S INITIATION

Pierre was a handsome boy who was spoiled by his Mother, Josephine. while not as rich as some of their relatives, Pierres' Father Jon-Luc was held in high regard as an advisor to the French Court. The favor was granted the Mulsine family because Jon-Luc was a brilliant tactician both politically and militarily, but the primary reason was Pierre's Mother, the lady Josephine, could trace her bloodline to Clovis, the first Merovingian king, Uniter of the tribes of Gaul, and founder of France. While Jon-Luc belonged to a minor noble family, he was enchanted by lady Josephine's beauty, and she was taken by his brilliance. Having met at a Ball at the Court of his Majesty Louis ix, they had a whirlwind romance, were soon married and Pierre was born to them a year later. Jon-Luc moved his family to Avignon so Josephine could be close to Marseille as she loved the sea. Pierre, when young, was often teased by those who considered themselves his peers. The fact of the matter was Pierre was peerless as he surpassed all those who dared rival him in everything from combat to academics. In large part because Jon-Luc did not want his son to lack for anything, and Jon-Luc knew A mighty sword joined with a keen mind would be welcome anywhere in the world. Josephine, on the other hand, believed her son needed to be brilliant, so she hired many tutors from many different disciplines so that Pierre was never lacking in intelligence. Born with what people referred to as a perfect memory, Pierre never forgot what he saw or heard. As the years passed, Pierre became infatuated with a pretty woman named Anna. Pierre would spend evenings writing poetry. There were days when Pierre would take Anna exploring the french countryside. On one such venture, Anna inquired, "Pierre, are you not concerned for your safety? I mean, there is so much banditry". She declared. Pierre only smiled. "No, my love, my father has provided for me well regarding my schooling." Not as naive as she pretended to be, Anna pointed out. "But I did not ask if you can add or tie your shoes, dear heart." She quipped. Pierre smiled, only saying. "Nor was I speaking of such my love. I refer to schooling as all that would encompass my education from adding, yes one plus one equals three, we all know that". Pierre teased. "Why would I ever consider tying my shoes"? Pierre gasped as if offended at the notion of manual labor. Anna stopped short and peered at Pierre, trying to discern whether he was teasing her or not. Seeing the playfulness in his eyes, she softly struck him. "This is why I am endeared to you, Pierre Mulsine; you are unlike others". Anna admitted shyly. Pierre looked at her askance. "And what would you know about the ways of others in your monastery, mistress Anna. With an innocent giggle, she asked. "wouldn't you like to know, Monsieur". Much to lady Josephine's dismay, Anna was an orphan with no family. Raised in an orphanage, she was schooled on the bible and was very religious, so when the one called Peter, the hermit, went through the French countryside preaching his gospel about freeing the holy land of Jerusalem from the grip of the infidels' Anna was enraptured and convinced Pierre to join her in listening to one of his sermons. Pierre's Father was against the idea while his Mother supported the idea but not the company. Doing as young men are prone to do, Pierre ignored his parents and attended the service with Anna. It was an overcast day, gloomy. Some would say a portent of things to come. The hermit spoke of the glory of God and how "we, as faithful Christian's were duty-bound to liberate the homeland of the savior." He proclaimed fervently. Anna turned to Pierre, gasping. "will you come with me"? Pierre's brows knitted together in concern. "You want to go to Jerusalem with this man to do something god himself could do if he wanted it done"? Pierre asked. Anna pouted. "You mock me and my beliefs Pierre", Pierre shook his head. "No. my sweet, I only doubt the knowledge and ability who has never seen battle to lead so many into hostile lands". He exclaimed seriously. Anna was unrelenting. "Do what you must, Pierre Mulsine, but I will be leaving with him". Anna declared before stomping off to her chapel. Pierre watched her leave, feeling despondent. Later that evening, over supper, Josephine noticed her son's mood and inquired about his seeming sadness. Relating everything that had occurred regarding the speech of the hermit and the disagreement with Anna, Josephine tried to advise her son. "Pierre, as a man, you will often find your skills and abilities will be sought after. I know you care deeply for this orphan but need I remind you that your line demands more of you". Pierre stood abruptly. "Forgive me Mother, but I know you don't like Anna, which may color your opinion; if you would allow, I will speak with father." Pierre stated matter of factly. "Do you presume your father to be more open than I"? Josephine asked. "No, mother It is only father knows what it is to love beyond ones' class and still get the result desired. Josephine could only smile as she knew her son referred to herself and Jon-Luc. "Do what you must, I believe your father is in the courtyard with his silly horse." His Mother said dismissively. Pierre bowed. "Thank you mother." Josephine waved her hand in dismissal. Exiting to their courtyard Pierre found his Father just where his Mother said he would be. "Father." Pierre called as he approached his Father who was grooming his favorite horse. "Ahh, my son. How are you this fine evening"? Seeing the look of consternation on his sons face, Jon-Luc stopped brushing his horse and asked, "what is wrong, Pierre"? Sitting under a cloudless night that held no moon but was ablaze in starlight, Pierre sat and told his Father of the days' events including the talk with his Mother. Jon-Luc listened carefully. "Son, you must forgive the pride of your Mother. Regarding this monk, he is spoken of even in the Court. My question is do you love this woman, Anna"? Jon-Luc inquired. Pierre took a moment before answering. "In truth, father, I don't think I've never been in love, so I don't know how to gauge if that is what I feel." Pierre admitted. Jon-Luc looked at his son. "My boy before I can advise you any further You must be able to answer that question." Pierre nodded his head. "I shall sleep on it father." Jon-Luc nodded his head. "Excellent idea my son, you are wise beyond your years Pierre." His Father complimented him. Pierre hugged his Father. "Good night father." Jon-Luc smiled. "Good night my son and don't forget to wish your mother the same." Jon-Luc reminded him. "I will not forget Father. Pierre strode back to the villa to wish his Mother a good night and prayed for inspiration in the form of an answer to his dilemma. The following morning Pierre left early to visit with Anna. Arriving at the boarding house where she resided, Pierre walked up to the house's Matron, asking for Anna. She looked at Pierre with a sad expression reporting that Anna had left very early in the morning with a group of people that were following the raving monk to Jerusalem. Pierre mounted his horse galloping all the way home to collect his gear as he intended to catch up with her. He arrived spraying mud as it was an overcast day with sprinkles earlier that morning. Pierre ran inside, scrambling for equipment to take with him when his Mother stepped into the room where Pierre was stuffing a bag. "Pierre, what are you doing"? Josephine asked. Pierre looked at his Mother. "I am leaving." Pierre said simply. "Leaving? Leaving for where". Josephine pressed. "I don't know exactly." Pierre admitted. Anna looked at her son's stricken face. "Are You going to chase that silly girl"? Josephine asked. Pierre did not answer but kept stuffing his bag. "Pierre, I asked you a question". Josephine demanded. Pierre looked up from what he was doing. "Yes, mother, that is what I am going to do." Anna looked at her son with deep concern. "Pierre, I beg that you stop and think about what you are doing, what you are throwing away." Anna pled. "You do not care to know how I feel Mother." Pierre insisted. Josephine took a deep breath. "Have you discussed this with your father"? She asked, knowing the regard Pierre held for his Father. Pierre shook his head. "You mean to tell me that this woman," Josephine began. Pierre looked up from his packing. "Anna, Mother, her name is Anna." Pierre snarled. Josephine looked at her son sadly. "Please, my son"? she pled. Pierre snatched up his bag. "I must go; please tell father the moment I get a chance, I will get word to him." Anna watched her son walk out and thought how much like his Father he was. "Be careful, my son." She whispered. Pierre rode fiercely until the poor horse died of exhaustion. Pierre kept going until he was relatively close to Bulgaria at the fringe of the Byzantine empire, where he ran across butchered bodies he recognized, from clothing and banners as coming from his region in France. Frantic Pierre searched through the bodies of the dead, praying Anna was not among them. After half an hour of searching, Pierre found scraps of clothing he recognized, and a few moments after that, he found the decapitated body of Anna. Releasing a blood curdling scream of heartbreak, Pierre sat beside the headless corpse of the woman he loved. There was no telling how long he was there, but a patrol of Seljuk Turks rode up and saw him there grieving. They dismounted their horses; Pierre was not stirred from his grief. One Turk laughed at Pierre, kicking him squarely in the head knocking him over. Pierre did not resist when they laid hands upon him, lifting him from the floor, slapping and punching him. Pierre only seemed to notice how the grayness of the weather reflected his mood and how the smell of blood and death seemed to call to him, and his only thought was I'm *coming, my love.* Pierre heard a scream and suddenly fell to the ground. Looking up, he saw a diminutive man holding one of the Turks in the air, and suddenly the Turk was headless as the small man bare-handed tore the Turks' head off. Then to his utter astonishment, he saw a huge creature he was unfamiliar with bound past the small man and slam into the remaining Turk and ravage him. The animal ripped the helpless Turk to pieces; that was the last thing Pierre saw before blacking out. Awakening, Pierre found himself atop a hill; there were no bodies, no awful stench of decay. Pierre sat up, trying to shake off his confusion, when he remembered the decapitated head of Anna. Tears sprang to his eyes as he looked around and noticed a small man standing by a mound. The overcast sky silhouetted the man in a stark manner giving him a surreal look. Slowly getting to his feet, Pierre now remembered the small man who remained still by the mound of dirt. Looking around and seeing only the countryside, Pierre slowly approached the stranger who spoke softly as Pierre walked up to him. "Have no concern, young knight. I have taken your beloved from those foul grounds and have laid her to rest here in these beautiful meadows unless, of course, you wish to return her to her family". The stranger said kindly. Pierre shook his head. "Their is no need, she was an orphan and except for the church she had no family. The stranger looked at Pierre. "She had you". He replied softly. Pierre, who was focused on the patch of earth where Anna rested smiled. "She did have me". Pierre responded. Looking at the small man Pierre expressed his gratitude. "To find such kindness in a foreign land is a welcome surprise". Pierre expressed gratefully. "If you do not mind my asking, what brought you to this dreadful place, foreign to you as you say"? The small man inquired. Pierre wiped dirt from his forehead while replying. "She did, I mean to say Anna did". The small man nodded. "A very pretty name". The stranger complimented. "Prettier was she". Pierre said lovingly. "Why than was she so far from you that she was caught up in such a violent incident"? The stranger queried. Pierre looked back at the resting place of his love. "As a child of the church she loved the word so when a monk spoke of reclaiming The holy city from the infidels she felt compelled to join the fight". "Fight? what Fight? these were not warriors,". The stranger criticized. "They called themselves the Peoples army' Pierre clarified. After a moment of silence, the small man asked." What shall you do now? return to your home, I presume"? Pierre shook his head. "No, I think not." Pierre fumed. "I will take up my beloved's battle and oust the unbelievers from our sacred grounds." Pierre said adamantly. The stranger asked. "Do you think that wise"? Pierre took a deep breath, looked at the small man, and swore. "What do you know of my loss"? Pierre paused a moment. "Forgive me, you have rendered me a service of worth, and I have yet to introduce myself, "I am Pierre du Mulsine de Avignon." Pierre introduced himself with a small formal bow. The small man bowed in return. "I am called Cain." The man said softly. Pierre fought back an urge. Cain smiled saying "Thank you." Surprised Pierre inquired. "Whatever for Monsieur? You have done me a service by carrying the body of my beloved here to this beautiful spot", Pierre waved his hand encompassing the area Cain had chosen. "And dug her a Christian resting place, it is I that thank you kind sir". Pierre expressed his gratitude. Cain smiled at the adroitness Pierre displayed when Cain attempted to act as if he was in Pierres debt for any reason. "What I mean to say Pierre is that like most people of our similar education my name cause's a certain unease. "Whatever do you mean"? Pierre said evasively. realizing for the first time, Cain seemed to be avoiding direct eye contact, and at that moment, Cain looked directly into the soul of Cain. "Let us not be coy Monsieur". Cain said lightly. Pierre was shaken as he stared into eyes so mysterious as to raise doubt as to one's sanity as the impossible seemed brought to life. "Is something troubling you, Monsieur"? Cain inquired. "Who, what are you"? Pierre asked, trying to calm a mounting terror. Cain looked at him calmly. "I am your means of exacting vengeance." Pierre looked at Cain suspiciously. "And what form would this take"? The sun began to set, which set the overcast day into a deep gray color. Diego grinned slightly. "First, I shall introduce you to the impossible, then probably frighten you witless, but as you think about it I shall introduce you to a miracle." Diego stated matter of factly. Pierre tilted his head. "I would be lying if I said I was not intrigued." Pierre admitted. "Show me the impossible you speak of." Pierre demanded. Cain nodded. "Very well, but remember when the impossible is made possible, terror is often the response." Cain warned. Pierre lifted his hand in protest. "I will garner my energies to maintain my composure." Pierre promised. From behind him, Pierre heard words mixed in with a low growl. "Is that so"? The gravelly voice asked. Pierre turned to the source of the words. "It will take more than a threatening voice issued from darkness to frighten me." Pierre declared. "Very well." The voice responded. Pierres' heart leaped into his mouth when from the shadows, a giant Tiger stepped toward him, stopping just inches from his face. Pierre panted heavily. "So you have managed to train a killer pet, that is very impressive. Pierre's knees turned into water when the giant cat whispered in his gravelly voice. "Pet? Did you call me a pet"! The cat demanded. Pierre felt as if he was losing this touch reality. Turning to Cain, he asked in desperation. "How"? Cain's eyes blazed brightly as he revealed his fangs. "By gods hand and the devils curse I am that which lives forever, my companion is the king of beasts, the mighty Shao-sin my disciple and I offer you Pierre du Mulsine the chance to get your full measure of revenge if you would but join me." Cain invited. Frightened Pierre looked at Shao-sin. Though his instinct told him to run he asked. "Is it true that I could avenge my beloved"? Cain nodded. "It is true. If you join me, I will show you more of existence than you ever deemed possible". Cain promised. Pierre nodded his accent, and Cain gave Pierre his immortal kiss. All of Pierre's mortal memories of his Father and his Mother playing on the beaches of Marseille. His Fathers smile, his Mothers embrace, and, finally, the gentle kisses of his beloved Anna. Upon awakening, Pierre stared into a fiery night sky, seeing the night as never before. Looking for the small man, Pierre saw The giant tiger standing, looking at him. "It wasn't a dream"? Pierre asked. Shao coughed a response. "No, not a dream. The master begs your pardon as you must now undergo a test of loyalty". Pierre scowled at Shao. "There was never mention of tests of loyalty." Pierre insisted. "Nor was there supposed to be one, but there is another, since my inception, that has taken to the masters' possible disciples." Shao informed. Pierre tilted his head in doubt.

"Who can withstand an immortal," He asked incredulously. "Shao whispered. "An Eternal". Pierre considered that for a moment. "But the only thing that is eternal is God." Pierre insisted. Shao grinned. "Is that so"? He asked facetiously. Pierre nodded then realized what Shao was referring to. "You mean".. Shao interjected. "Old rotten crotch." Shao said disrespectfully. "A hollow voice called out plaintively. "Now kitty-cat that was uncalled for. Suppose I summon a thousand flies to infest your stink hole"? Satan, who appeared in a cloud of sulfur and brimstone smoke, threatened. Shao snickered while Pierre stood terrified. "They would only confuse mine with your unclean one." Shao snapped back at the Lord of Evil. Satan turned to Pierre smiling. "I think you should listen to a proposal I have for you before you decide to join the buffoon, Cain." Satan Advised. Enveloping Pierre and himself in smoke and transported to another location that was serene. There was lush grass that kissed a small lake. The lake was fed by a waterfall. There was an aroma to the air supplied by lilacs and lavender; the air was abuzz with insects and colorful birds who sang melodiously. Pierre, after peering at his surroundings, slowly turned to engage his host. Satan had wisely remained quiet while the contradiction of Satans' reputation for evil and ugliness was belayed by this picturesque spot he brought them to. "I want you to know you are safe here with me, Pierre." Satan exclaimed to put Pierre in a state of ease. Pierre allowed a small smile while admitting. "I never expected," Pierre paused while he waved his hand, encompassing the scene. "This." He concluded, somewhat impressed. "This is in part what I offer you, access to a paradise with clearance to invite anyone you wish." Satan offered. Pierre looked around at the majestic scene. "At what price"? Pierre asked. "I don't want your soul if that's what you think." Satan claimed. Pierre looked surprised at this revelation. "I thought the devil always wanted a soul as payment for any of his gifts"? Mulsine queried. Satan snickered. "Oh no, my dear boy Cain gave me your soul when he made you a Vampyre. You see, your species is inherently evil as the source of all you are is born from a fire demon that derives from hell, ergo you belong to me". Satan concluded logically. Pierre took an unnecessary breath and considered what Satan explained. Pierre took in the scenery, which somehow looked slightly off; besides, he wasn't sure what it was but realized something was not right, but it gave him the emotional distance from the overwhelming news that he was damned, and it was his own need for vengeance that got him there. "Well, if not my soul, what price would I have to pay"? Pierre asked, seeking more information. Satan smiled, tasting victory. "Hardly an inconvenience to you at all; I ask only that you ignore the fool Cain who seeks to enlist ignorant bystanders in his age-long war against me". He exclaimed with frustration. Pierre smiled as his confidence returned. "Satan, I know you to be the Father of lies, a trickster that bends the truth to achieve his own selfish goals." Satan looked hurt. "Pierre, I was hoping you would be different and see through the fallacies." Satan complained. "I would tell you that while your story is compelling, I instinctively don't trust you, Satan, and the fact that you abducted me before I even had a chance to converse with the one that made me what I am raised suspicions. I would not take part in any fighting I don't know the facts about, and since you didn't let me gather any puts you on the wrong side of my confidence". Pierre revealed. The ambient temperature changed along with the scenery. Both the lake and the waterfall became fiery. The birds into flying demons and the buzzing bugs into nasty demonic gnat-like creatures. The aroma of lilacs and lavender turned into a vile, putrid smell of rot and decay. "And so the veil is lifted." Pierre muttered. Satan looked at Pierre furiously. "Begone to your foul master Pierre de Mulsine and know that you have made an enemy where you could have had an ally"! Satan threatened. Pierre found himself by Anna's grave. Waiting in the darkness stood Cain and Shao. The Vampyre Tiger roared upon seeing him. "Master, he has returned." Cain smiled. "Welcome back." Was his simple greeting. "Why didn't you tell me we are damned"? Pierre demanded straightforwardly. Cain shook his head. "Is that what he told you"? Cain chuckled. Pierre looked flustered. "Of course, that is what he told me; my question is, why didn't you warn me." Pierre again demanded. Cain looked at Pierre intently. "Pierre, stop and think. If we are truly evil, why would you expect any warning? Do you think demons consider the notion of fairness? and allow me to conclude with if you were truly damned, would Satan not just drag you to hell instead of trying to strike a bargain with you"? Pierre scratched his chin. "I had not considered that." He admitted. Satan is devious in his machinations, but he spoke the truth when he said that we, he and I, are enemies and that I would and will do everything in my power to foil his evil intentions. In this I welcome you but do not bond you to my cause it must be of your own free will". Pierre nodded in acknowledgment, asking. "And if I choose to stay awhile to learn then be off about my own business"? Cain grinned, "Then I would share what I know with a stipulation". Cain agreed. Pierre tilted his head in curiosity. "And what would that be"? He asked. Cain took on a serious countenance. "You may never drink the blood of the innocent or fight against good for the sake of evil on pain of death" Cain warned. Pierre was slightly taken aback at the dictates. "Remember Pierre, we are not evil despite the rumors of the ignorant." Pierre nodded his acceptance. "It shall be as you say." Pierre swore.

CHAPTER 13

TWO DISCIPLES

Enjoying the feeling of the air passing through his hair Diego flew through a half-moon, cloudy night.

Diego gently touched down, with Ishar materializing beside him. "This is where I met the dark lord Mulsine, master," claimed Ishar.

Diego scanned the area with what was rapidly becoming an acute psychic ability. Feeling a push-like force off to the west, Diego noticed a small village. "Ishar, this way." Diego flew to where he felt the energy emanating from when suddenly it seemed to disappear. Stopping in mid-flight, Diego floated to the ground, fully alert for any Satanic trickery.

Upon landing, Ishar appeared beside him. "What is it, master?" he asked.

Diego, looking around, answered, "I'm not sure, but stay alert."

From a tree line off in the distance appeared a figure. Seeing this, Diego attempted to scan him when he heard telepathically, *"Hold, brother, ask your demon friend of me."*

Diego looked at Ishar, who appeared to be listening. He quickly focused on Diego.

"Master, there is the dark lord I spoke of."

In the blink of an eye, Diego stood beside Mulsine. "Well, finally. I am pleased to meet you," said Mulsine.

Diego looked at him, assessing him. Tall, long black hair tied in a tail. Green eyes, small-mouthed and fancy if somewhat dated attire. "I'm afraid you have me at a disadvantage, sir, as I am not acquainted with you," Diego announced in the fashion of the court.

Mulsine bowed. "Forgive me. I am Count Pierre du Mulsine, former French knight and disciple of the immortal Cain."

Diego, recognizing the manner of the French court, reciprocated the gesture. "I am Diego Torrolisimo de Cadiz, Spanish knight and also a disciple to the immortal."

Mulsine smiled. "It is a pleasure to finally meet you, my brother. Perhaps we could retire to my villa?"

Perhaps we could retire to my villa?"

Ishar stood beside Diego. Mulsine smiled at the imp-demon. "Never have I seen one so cursed fight his nature with such determination. You are also welcome, Ishar," Mulsine graciously invited.

Ishar appeared taken aback. "Great Lord, never have I felt as welcomed as with Lord Cain, Master Diego, and yourself. I most humbly accept," expressed Ishar.

"My, but he does go on," observed Mulsine.

"Yes," agreed Diego. "But he is swiftly becoming a trusted friend."

Mulsine looked at Ishar. "By all that's holy, Ishar, you appear to be blushing," teased Mulsine.

"How can that be, master? I am not." Ishar trailed off, seeing the smile on Mulsine's face. "I see," said Ishar, "you are mocking me."

Mulsine said, "You misunderstand, little one. I only tease as friends do."

"Oh, I see. Your remarks are meant to tease without Mal-intentions?" asked Ishar.

"Of course, little one. Now let us begone."

Ishar vanished in a puff of smoke.

"He is a sensitive creature, wouldn't you agree, Diego?"

Diego, who had been peering at the village, said, "You don't know what you've signed up for, do you? Ishar seems to be unique among his kind, and he has gone past his fear," said Diego.

"Now that I can attest to, as I've seen that scrawny, tiny imp insult a powerful demon with no regard to his safety," agreed Mulsine. They flew low as they got closer to the village; the two stopped as they heard a blood-curdling scream come from the direction of the village. "Quickly!" said Mulsine. "We must see what evil is afoot." The two vampire lords blurred into town to find Ishar atop a demon's head, attempting to claw its eyes out. "Crazy imp," murmured Mulsine. The demon finally got a hold of Ishar and flung him through a barn wall. Diego, seeing this, flashed by the demon, unsheathing his sword. Slicing. The demon rocked back and forth for a second before his head separated from his body, which burst in flames.

A brave village boy who was trying to fight off the demon turned to Diego in fear, thinking to skew him when he was snatched by Mulsine. "Now that's a bad boy," he chided before sinking his fangs into the lad's soft young flesh.

"Noo!" screamed Diego, charging at Mulsine. Pierre stopped feeding to face Diego. Blood dripping from his fangs, he turned to face Diego, only to find himself dropping the boy to catch an unconscious Diego.

Hearing a sudden ferocious scream, Pierre found himself trying to fend off a maniacally savage Ishar. Mulsine reached for the imp, only to have him vanish before his eyes. Reappearing beside the fallen Diego, Ishar grabbed him, hissed at Mulsine, and vanished with Diego.

Confused, Mulsine focused all his vampiric senses on Ishar's trail.

Unfortunately, Ishar, being only an imp, and one that was losing the support of hell, was not powerful enough to transport Diego all the way home, materializing a few miles away. Ishar focused on Cain. "Master, we need you. Lord Diego is hurt". A response echoed in Ishar's mind. "I come."

Ishar looked over Diego with concern. "Do not worry, my Lord. Master Cain will be here shortly."

Mulsine blurred into the clearing Ishar took refuge in. Ishar saw Mulsine, and his back bristled, prepared to sacrifice his existence for the only being that ever showed him compassion. "You shall not take my master, traitor. I will rip you to pieces before I allow you near him."

Mulsine hesitated. Not out of fear, of course, he could easily destroy the imp but was impressed by his loyalty to Diego and display of bravado. "Be at peace, little one. I have no desire to harm my brother," explained Mulsine.

"Why then were you trying to kill him?" asked a suspicious Ishar.

"Ishar, I assure you, no such thing occurred. We saw you thrown through the wall, and Diego moved with incredible speed, decapitating the demon that threw you. A young boy must have thought Diego a demon and went to stab him. My thought was, well, if he's trying to kill us, he was fair game, and to be frank, I was hungry. I then began to feed on the boy when I heard Diego scream and charge at me, so I dropped the boy and turned to face him, and he collapsed," Mulsine finished.

Ishar still looked at him suspiciously. "I have called for Master Cain. Let him judge the issue," Ishar countered.

"As you wish, little one," responded Mulsine.

Cain arrived while Diego was still unconscious. "What happened?" Cain demanded.

"Master, the only thing I know is that I was ambushed and began to battle a demon when I was hurled away." Ishar began, "only to return to hear Master Diego screaming at Mulsine, and when the master approached him, he collapsed, and Lord Mulsine was holding him, so I attacked him, grabbed master Diego, and tried to travel home. But I didn't have the strength, and I was forced to wait in hiding. Then Mulsine arrived, and I told him to await your arrival. I did not trust him, Master Cain, and swore I would do what I could to protect Master Diego," finished Ishar, who was scowling at Pierre.

Cain looked over at Mulsine. "Pierre, do you care to explain yourself?" asked Cain.

Mulsine dropped to his knees. "My lord, never would I betray your trust."

"That remains to be seen. We cannot stay out here. Let us return home," decided Cain.

"But, master," said Ishar, giving Mulsine a sideways glance, "Is that wise?"

"Your concern is touching, Ishar, but Mulsine is one of my children, and if he's betrayed me, well, he'd know the consequences."

"Master, Mmbyu and Yaksha were of your brood, yet they still betrayed you," Ishar. Pointed out candidly.

"While that may be true, Mmbyu was something Mulsine is not," said Cain.

"It would be assuring to know what that is, master, if I may ask?" Ishar added, still uncomfortable with the notion of speaking freely.

"Stupid. Mmbyu was stupid and greedy and loved mischief. In my vampiric infancy, I gave no thought to the maturation process of our kind and how mischievousness can be corrupted into evil". Cain admitted. "Mulsine is none of those things. He was first and foremost a gentleman who found solace in his books. It was the love of a woman that pushed him into The mire of the first crusade. The Mulsine family was a minor noble family. Pierres' war was personal and short-lived as it was focused on those that murdered his beloved. It was in this decrepit state I found him. I promised him vengeance and long life. The vengeance was enough for him, so he joined me. Now let us return to our dwelling."

"Thank you for confiding in me, master." The Ishar projected feeling more unity than ever for what he was now beginning to think of as his coven. Cain took to the air, Ishar teleported himself to the manor.

Mulsine followed closely behind Cain, explaining the event. *"Master, I would never betray you. You must know that!"* Mulsine projected.

Cain glanced at Mulsine. *"I do believe you, Pierre, but I need to hear what* happened *from Diego himself and in case you have not noticed, Ishar had taken to Diego, unlike anything I've seen before,"* Cain observed.

"Yes, he is quite a fierce little creature, and I never thought demons could love, but it appears that he loves Diego," Mulsine projected.

Cain agreed. *"Yes, it is a bit unusual. Even the demon that infects me only abides in me because he hates Satan for usurping his power, and we've come to an understanding that as long as Satan is my enemy, he would aid me".*

CHAPTER 14

HOMECOMING

Diego awoke to find himself in front of the fireplace, with Ishar curled by his feet. He looked around and saw Mulsine reading an ancient tablet. "Sumerian?" Diego asked.

Mulsine looked up from his reading.

"Sumerian, yes. How are you, Diego?" asked Mulsine. But before Diego could answer, Ishar leaped into his arms.

"Master Diego! Are you well, master?" Diego gently set Ishar aside. "Yes, little one, I am well. But what happened?"

"Master Cain will explain upon his return," answered Mulsine.

"And we're supposed to just wait for him?" asked Diego.

"If you'd like some answers, then yes," countered Mulsine.

Diego looked frustrated. "I do remember charging at you; I thought you were doing something . . . evil."

"Considering we are Vampyre and drink the blood of humans to survive, one might say we are the epitome of evil," answered Mulsine.

Diego mulled over that for a moment. "I suppose that would be a fair categorization," admitted Diego.

"But, master," chimed in Ishar, "you are not evil. I lived in hell; I know evil."

Diego looked confounded. "Neither good nor evil? What am I then?"

"We are the gray walkers," answered Cain as he entered the room.

"And what, pray-tell, is a gray walker?" prodded Diego.

"We walk in the light and the darkness. We guard heavens' gate," answered Cain.

"That is a ridiculous thing I've ever heard," said Diego.

"Why, Diego? Why is it ridiculous?" asked Cain.

"As Pierre pointed out, we are killers of men, slayers of the innocent," Diego explained.

"Mulsine, yes. Myself, most definitely. But not you, Diego. No, my son. Not you at all," finished Cain.

Curious, Diego asked, "How's that now?"

"I have been going over your, shall we say, incidents, and I see one commonality."

"And that would be?" Diego prodded.

"Innocence," answered Cain. "Innocence? But I'm not innocent! I'm so far from being innocent that I would need a map to find it," responded Diego.

"Diego, consider the bull and the child. What did they have in common?" asked Cain.

"How should I know?" responded Diego.

"Think, Diego, when you slay the demons, nothing happened to you. But when you tried to feed on the innocent animal and saw the blood of the child on Pierre's lips, you passed out," finished Cain.

"Are you saying I am doomed to starve? That I'm a feinting vampire?" asked a highly concerned Diego.

"No, my son. I believe you may only draw the blood of the wicked," answered Cain.

"Master, I have never heard of such a thing!" Pierre piped in adamantly.

"I see," said Cain. "And because you never heard of a thing, it isn't possible?" asked Cain.

"No, master. You are the oldest and knew the Lord God, so it makes sense you would have a better understanding of his ways," answered Mulsine demurely.

"And the reason you're not always this respectful, Pierre, would be what?" asked Cain.

"I feel this to be an important event, and I yield to my maker. Besides, someone has to give you a hard time, so you don't get bored," Pierre answered with a touch of sarcasm. "How considerate of you, Pierre," said Cain, returning the sarcasm.

"That can't be right," countered Diego. "I killed before I was Vampyre. I lay in wait on hell when I was dying; I heard the approach of Satan! What has changed to allow me the grace to stand before my Lord?" voiced a befuddled Diego.

"I don't know with certainty, but you did reject him." Cain pointed out. Diego shook his head." No, I didn't reject him. Because my choice, as I understood it was eternal servitude to Satan or walking in the light drinking blood, I like to drink. Wine, blood, I did not think there would be much difference,". Diego admitted. Cain looked at Diego sadly. "I wish I had the answers you seek Diego, but considering that the vile son of perdition has taken such a strong personal dislike of you, and the fact that you spoke with the logos, which, may I add, has never happened before I think you are blessed in ways we don't understand yet."

Pierre stared at Diego. "You've met the Christos?" he asked, flabbergasted.

"Yes. Don't make too much of it," responded Diego.

Pierre looked hard at Diego. "Don't make much of it? Seriously? How am I not supposed to make much of that piece of information? Seriously?" Pierre asked in exacerbation.

Diego looked at his companions. "I need to be alone for a while."

Ishar, who had curled by the fireplace, leaped to his feet. "Master?"

Diego looked at Ishar. "No, little one. You stay here while I go collect my thoughts."

Ishar sat with a scowl.

"Where are you going, my son?" asked Cain.

"I shall return shortly, Cain." Diego walked out and took to the sky. Ishar looked at Cain, then Mulsine, and as if reading the imp's mind, Cain said, "Go, but stay hidden. Remember, Diego is powerful, and he may detect your presence. Let us know if Diego requires our assistance for anything."

With a squeak of delight and some smoke, Ishar disappeared to trail Diego.

"Is it something I said?" asked Mulsine. "And does it always smell so bad when Ishar appears and disappears like that?" Pierre complained. Cain chuckled. "You think that's bad? Before Diego turned him away from darkness, he carried the stench of hell on him. It has been diminishing since."

Mulsine appeared puzzled. "I've never seen or heard of a demon turning from Satan," he said. "That, his heavenly visitation and the bewildering affliction of blood sickness he suffers." Cain clarified.

Evils Throne Room

The room glowed from the fire that decorated the edge of the room—emptying as sycophants exited the room as the Lord of Evils Chamberlain ushered Satans' entourage out as Satan demanded privacy to deal with yet another disappointment.

Flames licked at the heels of the son of perdition as he sat on his throne, staring down at his chief succubus, who kneeled at his feet, affecting a contrite disposition. Tell me why I shouldn't cast you into the lake of agony, Lillith"! demanded Satan. "My lord, I sought only to do your will." Lillith pleaded, fear filling her words. "You think to lie to the father of lies"? Satan grunted with irritation in his voice.

"My lord," Lillith begged. No! Be still. I know you went out of vindictiveness to Adam, seeking to corrupt Cain. Satan exclaimed, knowing the animosity Lillith held for the puny human that dared reject and renounce her.

But, my Lord, would not the corruption of Cain cause Adam an agony that would be satisfying to you? As when Cain was first turned by Adramelech?

Satan stared angrily at Lillith. Never mention that traitor's name in these halls again! Satan ordered. The room was silent for a moment, reeling from Satans' fury; a moment passed before Satan reluctantly admitted. Yes, that was satisfying, but you forget, demon, that Cain didn't turn. He was possessed, and he and the fire demon have joined their essences in a common cause, their hatred of me! So the satisfaction you refer to was fleeting at best.

Lillith ignored the demotion to her by calling her a mere demon. Yes, my Lord, that was an unforeseen event, agreed Lillith sardonically.

Satan, hearing the sarcasm, pierced Lillith with an evil glare. Perhaps you need to spend some time alone, my little demoness, Satan said menacingly.

Lillith began to tremble as she understood his reference. My Lord, I assure you the well of oblivion is not necessary, she gasped.

Oh, but I think it is. It will give you time. Satan paused to allow the implication to set in. Time To consider your transgressions.

No, Lord, I beg you! Lillith screeched. With a glare and a wave of his hand, Lillith was cast into the Lake of Oblivion, where awareness in total silence and darkness that could never be described existed. Even the screams of the imprisoned could not hear themselves scream as the darkness swallowed all sound and light, where existence is recognized but doubted at every turn of thought which were unceasing.

Satan sat thinking of the impudence and repeated failures of his minions. *Perhaps I should go visit this creature myself. No*, thought Satan, *I will bide my time, sending one minion after another until I find this damnable renegade's weakness and exploit it to his detriment.*

Beelzebub and Molech entered the throne room. The demons bowed before the Lord of darkness. My Lord, they said in unison. Satan motioned them forward. There is one above, a disciple of Cain. The demons glanced at each other, somewhat surprised. My Lord? They asked. My Lord, the bane of mankind has been silent for centuries. What makes you think he is about mischief? I am the Lord of mischief, fool, and I detect the order of such coming strongly from him. From Cain, my Lord? He has left us alone, and we have done likewise,". said Molech. Beelzebub cringed at the awaited retort. Molech, why do I tolerate your shortsightedness and inability to pay attention to details? Satan asked menacingly. My Lord? Molech asked. "If you would have but listened, you would have heard me say Cains disciple! Satan growled. Pardon, my Lord. The demon lord begged. Satan glared at Molech. This is hell, demon. What pardon would you expect? Why should I consider such a notion? Molech knew to choose his next words very carefully if he wanted to continue existence outside of perpetual punishment. "That is is for my Lord to determine, mine is to do what is required of me? Well said, observed a somewhat mollified Satan. However, this is no usual command, Molech. This disciple is surprisingly powerful, though new to immortality. This is where I think your advantage lies. First, trace his descendants, then let him know that every day that he refuses to pay homage to me, one of them will die" dreadfully, horribly with a terror not born of the earth but an unleashed demon. That should subdue that rebellious nature of his, claimed Satan. My Lord interjected Molech, why not give me leave to go and take him, by force if necessary. Have you seen what he has done to Lillith? Or heard that he is converting Ishar the imp? Who has done anything remotely like that? Of course, there was the convincing of the demon Legion to enter the herd of swine and kill themselves by the Son of Heaven. Satan looked down on the demon lords continuing his rant. â€œHave you met our new guests, the greedy Mmbyu former disciple of Cain, who was destroyed for betraying the laws of his master and was sent to us to suffer his pitiful and self-righteous screams of agony? How about his pathetic, sycophantic apprentice Yaksha? Or his idiotic picah slaves? How about the devious Nargal of my secret forces? These are some of the casualties inflicted upon us by the Disciple of Cain. Have you not taken notice? Knowing that nothing pleasing was going to come from this exchange, Molech hung his head in a semblance of humility. No, my Lord, I have not noticed. Beelzebub flinched at the response. Well, permit me to share that this, this disciple of Cain has sent them all back torn asunder. A look of surprise reflected on Molech's face. Yes, demon, as I said before, he is very powerful. You may request what support you need, but the less you ask, the more I will hold you in my favor. Do we understand the command issued forth? Asked Satan. Of course, my Lord. Your will shall be done. Molech bowed in obedience. Satan waved his hand in dismissal, sending the two demons off to be about their Masters' demands. Well, it seems as if you are gonna have your hands full, Molech. Beelzebub observed.

HELLISH DISCOURSE

After bowing out from the dark one's presence, They found themselves in Beelzebub's lair of pestilence. Disease-carrying insects carpeted the floor, and flies buzzed about. Beelzebub, with a look of feigned concern, asked Molech. "So how are you going to approach this"?

Molech looked at his fellow demon, trying to ignore the swarm of flies buzzing around his head. "The only way I know how," he answered.

Beelzebub let out a low growl. "What?" Molech asked. "Do you have a better suggestion?" Beelzebub shook his head, wishing to discretely get himself as far away as possible without it becoming obvious as to his intention. "No, no, no. You have been here more than long enough to know. If our lord finds I've had even a passive hand in assisting you". Beelzebub hinted. "But you heard him say I could request assistance!" Molech huffed angrily.

"Molech, we both know that anyone that aids you will not only share whatever reward the master may offer on successful completion, but they also share your punishment if you fail. Hearing your plan to overwhelm this particular subject gives me little to no hope of you succeeding. By the way, what reward were you offered?" asked Beelzebub.

Sidestepping the question, Molech responded with, "You have such little respect for my powers, Bee-al?"

"Not at all, my perfidious comrade. I just take note of how cautious Satan acts around this one. He's banished Lillith to the Lake of Oblivion."

Molech, who was pacing back and forth, stopped in his tracks. "I did not know this." He said, startled at the fact that this new nemesis has the Lord of evil so upset that he would banish one of his oldest and favorite demonesses to the lake of oblivion made Moloch more apprehensive about the mission set for him by Satan.

"Yes," Beelzebub continued. "I have a very disturbing feeling that this Diego character is going to bring mischief to our gates by the time he's done."

"Hmm," grunted Molech. "I shall take everything you said under advisement. Curses upon you, Lord of flies."

Beelzebub looked at his ancient comrade. "Upon you as well, evil one."

Exiting, Molech went in search of Nargal, of Satan's secret police chief.

CHAPTER 15
DIEGO

Diego sat on a rock in the mountains of his home in Cadiz, Spain. Diego sat, mind swirling with the imagery he was having trouble comprehending. How could so many have perished, he wondered. Unknown to Diego, he had been gone almost a century and had arrived at the end of what was called "the black death." Unable to shed tears, Diego let out a wail that was heard not only in his province. Satan rubbed his hands together in glee to hear the now-immortal Diego scream in such mortal pain.

Summoning Nargal, Satan asked, "And what of a relative? My plan will only succeed if we have a hostage."

"As commanded, Lord, I've captured a descendant of his." the newly reconstituted demon reported.

"Very good. Now we'll see who he praises! The first killer of man that allowed such a thing to happen or me." Satan cackled.

Diego saw his old family estates in ruins. "How could this be? How could such a thing come to pass?" Diego looked at the bloated corpses, feeling an overwhelming desire to destroy something. An overcast sky reflected Diego's mood.

Just then, Ishar appeared. "Master." Diego looked at him with a look of sadness that sent the imp reeling back. "Oh, master, to see you in this state, it is affecting me in a way I do not understand." The devoted imp whined.

Diego felt wonder while in the midst of tragedy. Could this demon empathize? he wondered. "What you may be feeling, little one, is my sadness and sense of loss.

Ishar was stunned. "But, master, that is impossible! My kind does not know empathy, sympathy, or compassion. The dark one says that it will affect our abilities to serve him."

"This may be so, Ishar, so you have to ask yourself, who do you serve?" said Diego.

"I serve the Dark Master Diego, the disciple of the Dark Lord Cain." With that proclamation, Ishar's face seemed to light up. "Is this what it feels like to be good, master?" asked Ishar.

"Just a taste, little one, and if it is my power and you so wish it, you will know more," answered Diego smiling despite his grief. *Was he counseled by a demon? Ahh, what other surprises does life have in store"*? Diego wondered.

"Can we go back home, master?"

Diego liked that Ishar was referring to Cain's villa as home. "In a bit, Ishar, first I must seek answers." Was Diego's morose answer.

DIEGO'S PERUSAL

Diego walked through the ruined and almost barren streets of his ancestral home.

Seeing a peasant gathering scraps of crops from barren ground, Diego approached a peasant slowly so as not to startle him. Clearing his throat to get his attention, Diego said, "Excuse me, señor."

The peasant was startled despite Diego's effort to avoid that. "I mean you no harm, amigo," Diego said quickly. The man crossed himself with the sign of the Savior while he backed away. Understanding the man's fear, Diego copied the man's actions by crossing himself. "I do not serve evil as you see," said Diego. The peasant stopped retreating and stared at Diego. "I just want to know what happened here and if you have any information about the Torrolisimo family," Diego said.

The peasant looked at Diego. "You look like Don Rodrigo and his son Don Carlos."

Diego was momentarily shocked into silence hearing the name of his long-deceased grandfather and father. "You must tell me, amigo, what happened?" he demanded.

The peasant, frightened by Diego's vehemence, started telling the story. "Well, it started with the sickness."

"Sickness? What sickness?" asked Diego.

"Here we called it El Muerto negro," said the peasant. "They say that El Diablo put a curse on all of Europa."

Diego was stunned at the extent of Satan's malice. "And my family!" demanded Diego. "What happened to my family?"

"Your family, señor?" Then it hit the peasant. "You are a descendant of the highlanders?" the peasant asked incredulously.

"Tell me," Diego insisted.

"Well, mi don, it is a sad story, but after the illness ravaged the town, strange evil things started walking the night."

"What do you mean, evil?" asked Diego.

"Senor, I mean that you would hear howling in the night, screams as people were taken away." shaken at the news, Diego countered. "That could just be foreign enemies."

The peasant shook his head. "I wish this was true, señor, but it is not. It became so terrifying that the highlanders came down from their mountain to do battle with the hell-spawned creatures, but, alas, the highlanders fell, and so did the old patriarch, courageous Don Rodrigo, and his son, the noble Don Carlos."

The peasant, finishing his tale, looked up at Diego and was shocked to see blood falling from his eyes like tears. "Dios Mio," the peasant said, stepping back and repeatedly crossing himself.

Diego stood statue-like, eyes glowing, blood tears streaming down his face. Ishar stayed hidden, seeing the grief in Diego's eyes.

"I will avenge you, Father!" Diego huffed in a quiet voice.

The peasant looked at Diego, unbelieving. "You, you are Diego, son of Don Carlos?"

"Si. I am," answered Diego.

"But you died many years ago!" The old man shook his head. "No matter. Senor, you must get back to your family estates. You have a cousin; Manuel still toils there." Diego looked at the peasant. "A cousin? Manuel? He still lives"? Diego repeated. The peasant nodded. "Si, last I heard." The peasant confirmed. Diego took a gold coin from his pocket handed it to the peasant, who took it gratefully. Diego, mindful of his surroundings, not wishing to terrify the villagers, took a walk up to his family's great hall.

The Torrolisimo Ancestral Home

To the peasant, it seemed as if Diego suddenly disappeared. A moment later, Diego stood outside the gates of his family home. Casting out with his vampiric senses, he took note of a small group of people still within its walls. As he continued to scan, he sensed an evil recently departed.

Entering the grounds stealthily, he scanned for a familiar presence. Diego detected a peasant exiting the stalls. He was shocked to see what appeared to be his old manservant Pablo. The realization struck that Diego may have been looking at the former servant's grandson struck him with an odd nostalgic force. Whether he was as trustworthy was yet to be seen. Diego telepathically disturbed the bushes close by him. The servant, hearing it spun brandishing a knife.

"Who's there?" he called out.

From behind him, Diego, disarmed, grabbed him, covering his mouth to prevent his screaming, and flew off to a nearby hill.

"This is probably not the best way to make an introduction, but we are flying to those hills there where I will place you down, and we shall speak. You see that I have power. Do not scream or try to run, or I will slay you. Do we understand one another?" asked Diego.

The terrified servant nodded his head vigorously in the affirmative. "Good," said Diego as they floated to a clearing.

Upon release, the servant dropped to the ground, kissing it. "Señor, what are you doing?" Diego asked.

The servant tried to fight back his fear. "We f-f-flew. Like a bird, we flew."

Diego smiled, having briefly forgotten the feeling of rapture on his maiden flight.

Unfortunately, Diego's smile had an adverse effect, like dried blood, tears, fangs, and glowing eyes were indicators of something evil in this servant's mind. Frozen in fear, the servant asked, "What do you want from me?"

Seeing his discomfort, Diego asked, "What is your name?"

"Why do you wish to know my name?" the frightened peasant asked. "I will not aid you in casting a spell on me."

Diego felt a small degree of courage this servant was displaying. "I do not wish to cast any spell, amigo. If you will allow me, I am Diego Torrolisimo de Cadiz," Diego said by way of introduction.

The servant looked, first of course with disbelief, followed by curiosity, and ending in recognition. "But this is impossible. My grandfather used to speak of a gallant and rebellious knight who became a mercenary for the English."

"Yes," agreed Diego.

"And that this knight, against his father's wishes, went to retake the Holy City," continued the servant.

Again Diego agreed. "Yes."

"But it is said that the knight fell!" the servant exclaimed.

"Yes," echoed Diego.

"I remember the portrait of you that hung in the great halls astride a magnificent stallion." The peasant noted. "Yes." Agreed Diego. "My horse Viento."

"But that was more than a hundred years ago!" The peasant observed incredulously. Diego tried appearing meek. No mean feat for such a powerful predator as Diego was becoming, although, upon reflection, the glowing eyes, fangs, and bloody tears probably were not helpful.

"Now, will you tell me what your name is?" Diego asked quietly. The servant was looking at Diego as if to assess his credibility. Diego stood, permitting the scrutiny. "Well?" he asked. "Are you satisfied?

"Don Diego, is it truly you?" asked the dumbfounded peasant.

"It is truly," answered Diego.

"But how? How is such a thing possible?" asked a frightened and confused peasant.

"That is of no matter. You will tell me what happened here, now!"

The peasant bowed. "Forgive me, mi don. I am Jose Pina, a former apprentice and aspiring squire. When I returned from my visit to my family in Barcelona, my grandfather told me of the events with the dark beings and how both Dons were slain.

He then charged me with the last living relative, a son of Señora Anna de Torrolisimo. Grand niece to the Lady Inez Torrolisimo. His name is Manuel." Jose cast his eyes down, pausing in his tale as if to summon strength.

"Stopping a tale in such a fashion leaves one apprehensive, Jose. Now finish."

Jose looked up with tears in his eyes. "I failed, my lord."

"What?" Diego bit back the wail building inside of him.

"Forgive me, master, but I had never seen such creatures, and while I killed a few of them, the battle was a ruse to capture your family member."

Diego looked at Jose, seeing genuine remorse. He touched him gently. Diego's hands were so cold that Jose jumped back in shock.

Diego went on as if not noticing the reaction. "Do not concern yourself, Jose. I'm sure you fought bravely, and perhaps one day I can repay your family's loyalty to us," said Diego.

"A chance to get at those evil creatures would be a suitable payment, my lord," Jose responded.

"Be careful what you wish for, my friend. I may draft you into my service," Diego answered.

"Anything, my Lord! Anything you need."

Diego looked at Jose and smiled. "Do not be so quick to throw away your life, young one. There is much more to both the light and the dark you may wish to never know," warned Diego.

Jose looked Diego in the eye, bravely saying, "You have but to command, my lord."

"Really?" asked Diego somewhat skeptically. "We shall see. Remember what I told you about the dangers of awareness. Await me or my companion's return."

Jose looked around him. "Companion? My Lord, what companion?"

"It is, as I said, not all is as it seems. Ishar, come out of hiding. We will return home," Diego said to seemingly empty space. Then to Jose's surprise, a small demon appeared beside Diego.

"Master, how did you know I—" Diego held up his hand to quiet Ishar. Turning, he faced Jose, who stood in surprise and fear at the sudden appearance of the demon. "Remember, things are not always as they seem, Young Jose," Diego said mildly, waving goodbye and ascending into the air as Ishar disappeared in a cloud of smoke while Jose stood there with his mouth agape in awe, wondering what the return of Diego meant for the people of Cadiz.

CHAPTER 16
CAIN'S VILLA

After what seemed an eternity, but which was a little more than a small part of the dawn, Diego arrived at the villa, Ishar appearing beside him as he lightly touched down.

Cain was in the courtyard with Shao-sin. Upon landing, Diego said to Ishar, "Stay here. And I do mean for you to stay here this time. Do not follow me, or I will be upset with you," Diego demanded in a tone Ishar seldom heard from his master.

Diego turned to Cain. "Where is Pierre?" he asked.

"It is dawn, my son. Pierre does not have the good fortune of walking comfortably in the light," answered Cain.

"Very well," Diego responded. "I will take a brief leave of you, master. I shall return."

Cain motioned to Ishar to escort Diego. The poor little imp wrung his hands and whined quietly. Somewhat befuddled, Cain asked, "Ishar, what has gotten into you?"

Diego looked at the imp, who he was, strangely enough, beginning to have an honest liking of. "It is not his fault, master, as I forbade him from following me," explained Diego.

"Diego, are you mad!" exclaimed Cain. "You do realize the dark son of perdition has fixed his gaze upon you and means to bring about your destruction!"

Diego looked at Cain squarely in the eyes. "One could hope, master." And with that, Diego bounded into the air, taking flight.

Cain stared at his rapidly departing disciple. "What is he thinking, Ishar?" Cain asked the imp offhandedly. "Diego is without a doubt the most powerful being I've ever produced, but even his strength and speed is no match for Satan *and his* hordes."

Ishar began telling Cain of the events of the trip and Diego's meeting with his former servant, who still pledged loyalty to his house despite the destruction of most of his family by dark horde raids. He also told Cain how Diego's grandfather, as well as his father, were slain and how a surviving relative was enslaved by Satan's minions.

Cain sat down, taking in this last bit of news. "This reeks of Satan's meddling. Diego would be walking into a trap if he sought his relative," Cain mused.

"What now, master?" asked the huge cat Who silently entered the room.

"How fast can you run, Shao?" asked Cain.

"Like the wind, from one end of the world to the other," growled Shao, getting a sense of his meaning.

"Yes!" exclaimed Ishar. "That is brilliant, master. Diego said nothing about Shao following."

Cain smiled at Ishar. "Yes, little one. A bit devious, however." Cain looked at Shao, who gave what appeared to be a toothy grin before running off with such velocity that one could hear the splitting of wind.

"Master, do you think Master Diego will be safe?" asked Ishar.

"All I do know, Ishar, is that who or whatever gets in the way of those two will regret it deeply. Now come and let us darken the villa so that we may awaken Pierre."

"Master, I thought vampires had to sleep in the day?" Ishar queried.

"No, Ishar, most are weakened and cannot come into direct contact with the sun, so they sleep."

"But, master, you and the master Diego walk in the sun and retain your strength."

"I am possessed by a fallen angel, and to be frank, I do not fully understand why Diego has taken on the attributes that he has."Cain

Confrontation

Splitting the air, Diego flew at a fantastic speed. Approaching the coastline, he saw an orange smudge that turned into a glow.

Using his preternatural vision, he zoomed in and focused on the glow. He was horrified to see the ruins of his family estates bathed in flames. He pushed himself to blistering speeds, landing with massive impact, sending a plume of earth and rock into the air. Rising from the vast dust he sent scattering, Diego saw Satan holding a man, clawed fingers wrapped around his neck.

Satan glared at Diego. "Ah, a fortuitous opportunity has risen. Well, met Diego Torrolisimo de Cadiz. Had I known it was your family giving me so much trouble when my minions were implementing the plague in this part of the world, and you were gallivanting about in your little Crusades, I would have wiped out all traces of your mortal family immediately".

Diego saw at Satan's feet lay Jose. Catching his look, Satan said, "Do not concern yourself with this deluded peasant. He is merely unconscious. Diego, answer me this, how is it that your family survived as long as they did with such ridiculous bravado? Hmm? I mean, this silly little man tried to attack me. Me! I thought it was both funny and tragically pitiful. I know you are thinking, how can I rescue them? Well, you can't! I offered you the opportunity to join me—several, in fact—and you repay my courtesy by destroying my servants," fumed Satan." Diego considered the possibilities. He could save Jose or the peasant Satan held, not both. "I would have gladly gift-wrapped them for you, but the smell of them prevented me from doing that. Let me ask you, is it that you don't bathe in hell, or do you bathe in the manure of damned beasts? Because to say you and your kind are malodorous is a level of an understatement I have yet to achieve," Diego responded mockingly.

"Always with the jokes, Diego? Well, will you laugh when you are the very last of your people? Utterly alone as I slay anyone even remotely related to you? Hmm? What, no jokes? Nothing clever you wish to amuse me with"? Satan quipped mockingly. "Only that I am going to shove my hand so far up your ass that you are going to be my hand puppet," threatened Diego.

"Very colorful imagery, Diego, and my scathingly witty response to that is." Satan hauled Manuel up. "Say goodbye to your cousin." As Diego sprinted to him, Satan cut off the head of innocent Manuel blood sprayed from the decapitated body, spraying on Diego, who collapsed to the ground.

Upon awakening, Diego found himself bound by what appeared to be a thin length of chain. He attempted to break the paper-thin chain, only to find that he couldn't. He struggled mightily against the unyielding chain, to no avail. Pausing to assess the situation, he noticed Satan exiting one of the last buildings, standing with a beautiful woman draped on his arm. Satan approached Diego, who was kneeling on the dirt.

"Well, well, dear Diego. Who would have known that killing such a weak simpleton would bring you to your knees." Satan laughed mockingly.

"Release me, pig, and we shall see who would be on their knees," Diego challenged.

"Now, why would I do that?" Satan chided.

"So that I may relieve you of the misery of your life," Diego retorted.

"You are a bold one, little Vampyre. How about you swear allegiance to me, and then I will not only release you but reward you with this beautiful woman?" Satan stepped aside, giving Diego a clearer view of the woman that stood beside him. "This is Lenore," said Satan by way of introduction. "Is she not spectacular?" Lenore slowly spun in front of Diego, her low-cut robe opened in all the right places.

Diego admitted to himself that she indeed was, spectacular and had he known such a woman as a mortal, and he probably would have never left home. Diego caught himself recognizing the spell of mesmerization and shook it off.

Satan continued, "You have only to worship me as your god."

"Satan, the odor of the world's sin is upon you," Diego said.

"Yes, a lovely aroma, wouldn't you say?" Satan acknowledged, ignoring Diego's comment. "More like someone bathing in pig's manure while a diseased cow urinated in it." Diego spat. Glaring at Lenore, he spoke softly. "I know this creature for who and what she is." Diego looked at Lenore. "You may have fooled our first mother and father, and you may have convinced Cain to slay his brother, but I know better, harlot. As for you, Satan, you are no god. You are, but a poor imitation of the grand spirit consigned to the flames of hell for thinking yourself above your station."

"Well, suppose I change your mind?" Satan queried.

"Nothing you can say or do to me will ever do that, you diseased dog," responded Diego.

"Really?" Satan taunted. "Let us test that assumption, shall we?" He motioned, and a badly beaten Jose was dragged and thrown before Satan's feet.

Diego roared and struggled against the chain. "Don't bother, Diego; that is Anglicore, the unbreakable. A small gift of Michael when he snuck up, bound me, and cast me out of heaven. So you see, there is no escape for you." Satan turned his attention to Jose, the servant, and said, "Beg now for your life. Convince the stubborn creature to join me, and I will not only let you live but will give you long life and vast wealth," proffered Satan.

Jose looked at Diego, then at Satan. "Thank you, no. If my master will not succumb to your bribes, neither shall I."

"Foolish mortal! This is not the living heir to this fallen house. He is not even a man! He is immortal, and while you rot in the grave and I drag your pathetic soul to hell for exquisite torture, he will still be alive. Why suffer for that when I can extend your days and make you prosperous?" Satan asked.

Jose looked at Diego. "What do you think, Don Diego?" Jose asked. Diego looked at the man that was willing to stay behind and guard his descendant.

"I would not think any less of you, Jose. You stayed when you could have run. Do what you feel to be right," Diego said sadly.

"How very touching. Now, if you're done?" Satan taunted.

"It would appear that I am," said Jose. "Master, forgive me for leaving you."

"Finally," Satan said. "All these displays of chivalry are giving me a headache. Now denounce your master, accept me as your one true god, and all the things I said you would have shall be bestowed upon you."

Jose slowly rose to his feet, raising his hand to pledge. "So I swear from this day forward, with every breath, with all my strength, I shall revile you, Satan. You are a fool who knows nothing of our line to think you can slay one of our own and we would join you? Ha. No wonder the Lord cast you from his gates. You are no god, Satan. Just a malcontent with father issues."

Satan stared at Jose. "You are a fool mortal, and your death will be agonizingly slow, and when you die, I will roast you in my flames while hell-born maggots eat at your soul," Satan admonished. Motioning to one of the demons in his vanguard, Satan ordered, "Kill him, but do it slowly and let the helpless master listen to his servant's screams. And make it last."

"As you will, my lord," responded the demon.

"Look now upon the misery you bring upon those who love you, Diego. Are you sure you won't join me? I'll even extend the courtesy of allowing your manservant to live if you but acknowledge me as your god," Satan said.

"No, master, don't."

Satan backhanded Jose, knocking him unconscious. "Silence. Diego, do you have something to say"? Asked an amused Satan.

"I do. Foul one, you've destroyed my house that has stood for hundreds of years, you murdered my last living blood relative before my eyes, and now you seek to torture my servant because of his loyalty to me?"

"Okay, I see where this is going, but you cannot harm me. It is written that the final days shall see the final battle, and oh yeah, I'm a participant, so please don't bore me with threats against me," Satan interjected.

"You, as always, misunderstand me, dog. It is not you but every agent you send to do harm or sow mischief upon mankind that I will strike down. My family's blood shall hunt and torment you and your kind through eternity if need be. Great woe for the day you made an enemy of my house," Diego said menacingly.

"House. What house? You mean these burned-out shells. Your arrogance is amusing, Diego, but I will send some interested parties that will cut you into little pieces and bring those pieces to me in hell, where I will direct the denizens of my domain to befoul your remains with urine and excrement. Then I will spread what remains for my minions and imps to eat so you may become demon shit. And just to make it fun, I will alleviate the suffering of a damned soul for a moment if he sings a ballad of Diego the arrogant and how his arrogance now has him as demonic dung for his Lord and master Satan to fertilize his fields of rot". What do you say to that!"

Diego looked up. "Are you still here?" Diego said, feigning surprise. "You must forgive me, Satan, for I do not speak the language of beasts. Is that even accepted as a language among sentient beings? Or do you have to be mentally deficient to grasp such barbarity?" Diego mocked.

Satan glared at Diego with hate-filled eyes. "You think yourself clever, little suckling, but it will be my mercy you will hunger for soon enough."

Diego looked up at Satan. Still bound, he sat cross-legged, appearing comfortable.

"You know, you just might be right about that, as I would now ask you to show me the mercy of killing me or do whatever it is you say you're going to do unless, of course, your plan all along was to bore me to death with inane drivel that oozes forth from your lips, disguised as intelligence but its odor betraying the defecation it is."

Satan, growling, stuck his face inch's from Diego's, who winced at the smell emanating from Satan. "Soon." Satan threatened. He turned to a demon. "I want him slowly skinned to the bone, then burn his flesh and bones." Satan paused, then smiled. He looked at Diego and smiled. "First, chop off his head so he can watch.

Diego met Satan's gaze "Nice touch," commented Diego offhandedly.

Satan almost smiled. "You like that?" With a sinister laugh and the smell of brimstone, he was gone.

A demon stood over Diego. "Well, well, this is the upstart giving the master trouble? He does not look like much to me."

Diego shifted his glance to the demon. "That is because I'm not in my evening wear," Diego mocked.

The demon roared, "Dog! Soon you will pay homage to the Dark Lord Satan."

Diego laughed. "Demon, I'll pay you right now if you but bathe. Whew! You have the type of odor one can taste," Diego said, enraging the demon.

"Fool, do you know to whom you speak?" the demon said furiously.

"In point of fact, no. However, I'm sure that will be rectified momentarily, as your kind suffer identity complex and wish to boost your name any chance you get," Diego mocked.

The demon roared and hit Diego with tremendous force. The report of the strike was loud. Diego looked at the demon, not appearing disturbed by the blow. "I apologize, as I did not hear what you said. A mosquito landed on my face, and they are a bit distracting."

The demon's chest heaved as its anger continued to build. "Fool! You will beg for mercy, and I will deny it to you, as I, with great pleasure, shall beat the insolence from you before casting pieces of you throughout creation!" the demon threatened.

"Well," began Diego, "I've always wanted to see the rest of creation." The demon raised his hand as if to strike him again. Diego looked it in the eye. "Demon, if you strike me again, I'll be forced to take it personally, and that will be very, very bad for you."

The demon slowly lowered his hand. "You think yourself something special, don't you? Let us ask your servant." The demon motioned for Jose, and two of his subordinates threw the servant at the demon's feet.

"Now, what have you to say, Vampyre?"

Diego looked at Jose on the ground. "Forgive me, loyal friend."

"Beg mighty Satan for succor, and perhaps I'll let your little friend live," said the demon coyly.

"The only thing I would beg you or that piss ant of a master is to take a bath. Please, you stink horribly," Diego said defiantly.

The demon snatched Jose by the hair and hauled him into the air. Screaming, Jose shouted, "Be damned with you, cursed one! May you and your kind rot in pig shit for eternity."

Diego admired the courage of his diminutive friend but knew Jose had crossed a boundary with the demon.

"Another insect who thinks himself clever." Finishing his provocation, the demon sliced open Jose's stomach, dropping him to the ground and laughing.

Seeing what the demon was going to do, Diego shut his eyes to prevent his ailment from striking at this inopportune moment.

Diego roared, "There will be no mercy for you, swine fornicator."

The demon laughed. "You are in no position to make threats." Raising his hand to strike Diego again, he was interrupted by a tremendous roar. The demon collapsed to the ground, unable to stand. Diego peeked and noticed that the demon's entire back portion of the leg had been torn away.

Screaming in pain, the demon writhed on the ground then burst into flames. As the other demons attempted to approach the scene, a blur of motion ran past at such tremendous speed that it took Diego's heightened preternatural sight to follow it. Diego smiled, saying softly, "Here, kitty kitty."

Another demon went down, gurgling on his fluids as Shao-sin ripped its throat out. Pausing, he looked at the last of the demons still standing. In a deep baritone, Shao growled, "Leave now or perish." The demon looked at his brethren that numbered twenty and, with no further hesitation, vanished in a puff of smoke reeking of sulfur.

"Shao," Diego called to the great cat. Not sensing any further threat, Shao walked over to Diego and pawed at the chain restraining Diego freeing him. Glad to be free of the chain, Diego dashed to where Jose lay bleeding.

"Forgive me, mi don. I've failed you." Jose coughed.

"No, my friend, you have not. You are brave and loyal, and your memory will survive the ages in me."

Jose coughed again, weaker this time. "I'd rather walk with you," he said, staring intently.

Diego, with closed eyes, looked down. "My friend, you know not what you ask."

"I do," Jose responded. "I know what I ask." Jose coughed again.

"Diego, he will not make it through the night," Shao informed him.

"I will not take an innocent into this damnation!" Diego was torn as he knew his last mortal family friend was slowly dying. Diego focused. "Master, I need you now!" His silent scream was heard. Moments later, it was followed by a crash of thunder. Cain and Mulsine came flying in. Observing the situation, Cain quickly deduced the reason for Diego summoning him. "Diego, are you sure"? Cain asked, seeking confirmation.

Diego nodded in the affirmative. Cain's fangs pierced Jose's neck. He drank his blood and then gave Jose some of his blood as the transformation once again delivered its dark gift.

CHAPTER 17
JOSE'S TALE

Born to a house of serfs and farmers, Jose and his family were fortunate enough to be born under the banner of the House de Torre. While he was of the peasant class, Jose aspired to be more than his birthright of being a serf. The House of Torre was renowned for raising any family or servant that showed an aptitude that would be beneficial to the house. El Patron, Don Rodrigo, Duke of Torrolisimo and knight of the Order of Tower and Swords, was the first to implement such a controversial decision, that which allowed for the elevation of social status. Many traditional families rebelled against the notion; however, as the house, Torre began gaining in academic, militaristic as well as agricultural pursuits due to new and unconventional ideas brought by unconfirmed minds, other houses began utilizing the practice. The policy started by the Patron was followed and continued by his heir, Don Carlos. Although frowned upon by other Noble houses, it was the notion of Don Carlos, like his father before him, that great houses could be greater by not allowing bias, prejudice, or status to dictate the future of the talented. Because of this policy, the House of Rodrigo was held in great esteem by the peasants of España, and many clamored to join the great house.

Jose grew up hearing the tales from his grandfather of a young son of the house Torrolisimo named Diego, who had joined the Crusades when he was a very young man. Sadly for the house, Diego had disappeared, and the house had gone into great mourning, as Diego was well-loved by his family. Approximately thirty-odd years after this great disaster, another befell their region as inexplicable tragedies began to occur. A young Jose saved a caravan that was ambushed by a pack of rabid wolves. The caravan filled with grain in preparation for a forthcoming winter was a vital food source. The attack was unexpected as the wolves usually kept to their hunting grounds. It was fortunate for the caravan that the Duke had sent out a patrol to assure safe passage for the caravan. The patrol rode up as the caravan riders attempted to beat the wolves back with poles—the leader of the patrol charged in with Jose at his heels. The wolves broke off the attack of the caravan but unlike any previous attack made by wolves, instead of fleeing attacked and dragged down the patrol leader, who was killed instantly when the wolf pack leader tore out his throat. His victory howl was short-lived as Jose decapitated the beast. Leaderless the other wolves paused a second and, as a body turned their attention on Jose. The young squire dug his heels into his horses' flanks charging the rest of the pack. At that moment, the rest of the patrol caught up with and joined Jose in the charge. The wolves turned to run but not before three more of their number were slain. After a brief chase to clear the area, the patrol returned and escorted the caravan to Cadiz, where the caravan leader gave a full report on the event, the odd behavior of the wolves, and the bravery shown by the patrol, particularly the valor of Jose. The old Duke Threw a celebration to salute and accept young Jose as his squire; he then charged him with the safekeeping of his youngest heir, Manuel. "This is a great responsibility I give you." The old Duke pointed out. Jose bowed deeply. "Sire, I am honored beyond words, and I would lie dead before any harm came to an heir to our great house," Jose swore.

Then the Duke, silver-maned, brandishing his family sword, "el Fuego de Cielo," went forth with his son, Don Carlos, to face the ever-increasing attacks against his people.

The Duke never expected a hoard of hell-spawned demons to come forth to do battle. With the heart of a lion and the stubbornness of a bull, the Duke set forth against the demons. On an ominous cloudy day, the Duke and his son Don Carlos engaged the enemy.

Great cries went forth as the noble Duke, his heir, and their knights set forth. With a horrendous clashing of steel against scales, the old Duke laid devastation upon the advancing demonic horde. A platoon of hell-spawned creatures attacked Carlos while he was trying to evacuate one of the villages. The battle was brutal as men and demons fell on both sides. Carlos rode through a pack of demons; his warhorse, with flaring nostrils and wide eyes, stomped demons head, crushing it while Carlos was cutting off heads on both his left and his right side. Jose, the squire of the Duke, fought as one possessed. Alongside his Lord Rodrigo, he saw why this powerful man rose to the position he has for, although aged, seemed as if years were shed off of Rodrigo as he fought with youthful vigor. "We have them on the run, father," Carlos shouted to the old Duke, who smiled. "So it would seem," Rodrigo responded. He then ordered his men to cease fighting as the hellish rabble scrambled to retreat. "We should run them down and destroy every last one of them." Carlos demanded. The old Duke shook his head. "No, my son, we should tend to our wounded. If all is as it seems our enemy has an inexhaustible supply of demons and we have limited men and resources. I will petition the king for aid". Rodrigo told his son. Gathering the wounded, the men gave a shout of victory.

While riding back, Azel, commander of a squad of assassins, let loose his killer elites, who, awaiting the end of the battle, lay in ambush for the battle-weary knights.

As the Duke and his son rode over a rise, the demons attacked with bows and arrows.

Carlos was killed immediately as an arrow pierced his throat. The Duke was severely wounded as a poisoned arrow pierced his chest plate. Immediately surrounded by the rest of his troops, they bravely fought off the attack. Rodrigo was taken home, where he charged his squire.

"Jose, You did well today," said the old Duke, "I hereby charge you with the safekeeping of my last heir. The brave Carlos has fallen, and Manuelito is the last of my line."

Jose looked at the old man with tears in his eyes. "Si, mi don. With my life, will I protect your family."

The Duke winced in pain as the poison ravaged him. Great wailing went forth that night as the strong and brave Duke succumbed to his wounds and died.

Jose awoke from his visions, screaming. Cain put his hand on his shoulder, holding him down. "Easy, Jose," said Cain.

Startled, Jose gasped, "Who, who are you?"

Mulsine stepped forward. "He is your savior, your maker, and your new lord."

"My, what?" Jose asked. "I have but one master. That is Don Diego."

Diego walked up. "Jose, mi amigo, are you all right?"

Jose looked up and saw Diego. "Master, you are well."

"Yes, my friend. And I don't believe Cain will be upset if you call me master, but, Jose, Cain is your maker, not I."

"Maker? Maker of what? I am made already," Jose said, pointing out the obvious.

"I apologize, my friend, but it was by Cain's blood that you live, not mine," said Diego.

Cain let Jose get to his feet. "Your blood?" Jose asked Cain.

"Yes," replied Cain.

"But what does that mean?" Jose asked. "And what was that painful vision I just witnessed of a time now many years passed."

Diego said, "Come, Jose, I'll explain everything to you."

Jose froze in his tracks as he spotted Shao-sin. The tiger approached Diego with a purr that sounded like a mild roar.

"Master, look out!" warned Jose.

Diego petted the huge tiger. "Jose, this is Shao-sin, the finest and most ferocious of tigers and a member of our little family. You need not fear him."

"Our p-p-pet?" Jose stammered. The purr turned into a growl as Shao looked at Jose.

Jose backed up a step. "It is as if it understands me!" said Jose, shocked.

"He does," Diego informed him.

"But how is this possible!" asked a startled Jose.

Diego looked to Cain. "Tell him everything," said Cain.

"Everything?" asked Diego.

"Yes," replied Cain. "He is, after all, one of us now, unless you wish me to destroy him. Jose looked at the smaller man as if he was joking, but when he looked into his eyes, there was only death in them.

"Master," said a frightened Jose, "I have always been loyal to you and your family."

"Yes, my friend. That is why I didn't do it myself. I could not bring myself to damning you." "Damning me how?" asked Jose.

"Come, I will explain everything to you."

Diego and Jose walked into the woods, where Diego informed Jose of Cain as well as of Shao, Mulsine, and himself.

Jose almost staggered. "So you are saying you are Vampyre and immortal?" asked a shocked Jose.

"As you are now," agreed Diego.

Jose slowly backed away. "Then why did Cain offer to destroy me?" Jose asked suspiciously.

"We are in a war against Satan, Jose, and if you would turn to him with the power of Cains immortality, then our maker would destroy you." responded Diego.

"But, master, you know I serve your house. I even tried to protect Manuel from demons! How could you not trust me?" Jose asked.

"I do trust you. The fault is mine. When I saw you lying there bleeding to death, I had to offer you this chance to continue living. After all, you were willing to give your life in service to my family, so I felt obliged to give you your life back."

"Do I have powers?" Jose asked.

"Unimaginable power, my young friend. However, Master Cain has rules we, his children, must obey. We do not attack the innocent, only evil. Will you do well by this?" Diego asked.

Jose stared at Diego as if for the first time. "Master, your eyes are as bright as jewels reflecting light."

"As are yours, my friend," Diego countered.

"So it is true then? I am Vampyre?"

"It is true," answered Diego.

Jose let out a loud whoop and went running along the fields at an incredible speed,

Shao comically shook his head. "Children." He said, mocking Jose's behavior. "I know, right." Agreed Diego. Cain looked at the three disciples replying. "If I remember correctly, not one of you responded any less childlike as your powers awoke. Shao, you ran as if you just discovered running, and Diego wanted to see how far he could fly and how fast". Cain looked to Mulsine, who argued defensively. "Master, I didn't say anything"! Cain nodded in agreement. "You didn't say anything but you sure went on a killing spree when you were first turned. Diego looked at Mulsine curiously. "And what may I ask would have that been about"? Mulsine shrugged his shoulders. "Someone brought harm to someone I loved." Mulsine responded quietly. Taking the hint Diego responded simply. "I would wager it was something they deeply regretted" Mulsine only nodded. Returning to were Cain, Diego, Shao, and Mulsine awaited him. Jose strolled up to them. "This is unbelievable," Jose said. "I'm not even tired from my sprint."

"And you never will be again," said Diego.

Jose looked at Cain. "I swear my undying loyalty to my maker Cain and master Diego," Jose swore.

"It's about bloody time," growled Shao.

Jose jumped back, which carried him much farther than he intended. He slammed into a tree twenty or so yards behind him. The elders knew it was Jose's unfamiliarity with his current state and the power that came with it that caused the reaction; nevertheless, Shao could not stop laughing at the fledglings reaction. Jose Sprinted back to them, where he looked at Shao. "It speaks?" asked a surprised Jose.

Mulsine burst into laughter. "Yes, he does. And if you want to continue doing the same, I recommend most strongly never to refer to Shao as 'it' again."

Jose looked at Shao. "My apologies, Shao. This is all new to me, and I've never seen an animal that could speak. I promise if you give me a second chance, we will become the best of friends," Jose said in an apologetic tone.

"Not likely, but I accept your apology," Shao growled. "Diego, Mulsine, come. Ishar awaits us." Cain reminded them.

"Shao, would you escort Jose to the villa?" asked Diego.

Shao growled his compliant but acquiesced.

Rite of Passage

Jose looked in awe as Cain, Diego, and Mulsine flew off into the night. Turning to Shao, he asked, "Can you fly?"

"Perhaps. I've never attempted such foolishness." Shao scoffed.

"How could you say that?" asked Jose in mild surprise.

Shao looked at Jose. "Why is it that man always seeks to be outside of his Nature? I am a tiger. Not a bird. I like birds, especially as a snack. This is my Nature. Big tiger, run fast, eat food, my Nature." Jose considered this for a moment. Shao said, "We should get moving."

"Where are we going?" Jose inquired.

"To Lord Mulsine's villa," answered Shao.

With that, Shao became a blur as he descended the Cadizean mountain that was the ancestral home of Diego and streaked toward the Andalusian plains.

Jose caught up with Shao, both running faster than the eye could follow, mere smudges for any sharp-eyed individual that was in direct line of sight.

Around the city of Saragossa, Shao noticed Jose slowing down. "What is wrong?"

Jose came to a stop. "Starting to feel weaker."

It was then Shao noticed the growing light that was the telltale sign of approaching dawn. "Come with me," Shao growled. Casting out with his natural predatory instincts combined with his preternatural vampiric senses, Shao saw an empty shed and raced to it. Once inside, Shao began digging furiously into the earth.

"What are you doing?" asked Jose, staggering in behind him.

"Have you fed yet?" growled Shao.

"Fed? Do you mean eaten? No."

Shao nudged Jose into the hole. "Get in," he growled again.

Jose looked somewhat shocked. "You want me to do what   ?"

Shao bumped Jose into the hole before he could finish his sentence.

"What are you doing!" Jose exclaimed.

Shao pawed at Jose's hand, reaching for the edge of the hole.

"If you want to live, you will listen"! Shao warned. The blood of Master Cain has made us. Diego and I are immune to the sun, but you are still newborn and have not been fed. Because you are feeling weak, I think it best that we take this precaution and keep you out of the light until the master says otherwise," explained Shao.

Jose looked at the small enclosure. "And what am I supposed to do while I'm here?" Jose asked.

"Rest. I will look for nourishment. Bury yourself, have no fear, and for the love of everything you hold dear, await my return."

And with that, Shao went to explore and find food for the two of them.

As the day wore on and evening approached, Jose came out of his near-coma sleep feeling a presence nearby. Thinking it to be Shao, Jose burst from his grave-like bed, only to find a beautiful woman in the shed.

"Who are you?" Jose demanded.

Reacting as if she was surprised by his appearance, the woman screamed and then stammered. "Some call me Lolita," she replied demurely. "And you, sir, who might you be?"

"I am Jose de Torre," he answered.

"Of the House Torrolisimo?" she asked.

"The same. You have heard of us?"

"Who has not?" she asked. "There are many stories of how evil befell the house and how the old Duke Rodrigo and his son Carlos went forth and did battle with demons."

Jose smiled. "Yes, that is my Duke, the bravest of the brave, and his valorous son Carlos."

"Yes, but I heard they were felled and the house destroyed," she said.

"True, but vengeance shall be ours!" Jose said before pausing. *I burst forth from the ground, and this woman speaks to me as if she is not frightened".* Jose mused.

"What is it, my dark prince?" she asked, capturing him with a stunningly beautiful gaze.

"Why would you call me that? I am no prince." Jose protested.

"Oh, but you are my lovely prince." Lolita began walking slowly toward him.

Jose felt himself being swallowed by her stare. "W-w-wait," Jose stammered. "How is it you are not frightened?" he asked.

"Why should I be frightened? Because you are undead?"

"How did you know that?" Jose asked weakly.

"I know much about you, my dark prince." Lolita was mumbling under her breath when Jose realized she was atop, straddling him.

"How did she come to be on top of me?" Jose wondered.

"Do not concern yourself with such trivial things, my love," she whispered with a silken voice as if reading his mind. Her eyes had become his world.

"I shall not worry," Jose slurred. "I have never felt such a feeling," he said, immersed in her eyes.

"And you shall never feel anything again, Jose de la Torre," she whispered. Jose heard the threat but seemed unable to respond.

"What have you done to me?" Jose gasped.

"Nothing, my love. Only preparing you for the dark Lord's arrival."

Jose tried to struggle but found himself unable to do so. "You are now mine, Joselito. Do not despair. I'm sure the master has plans for you."

"Bruja!" The door to the shed was flung open.

Lolita spun around, hearing her ancient name. "Shao-sin. The kitten that would walk with the immortals," mocked Lolita. "You may tell your master that he need not worry about his newest convert, as he is now mine," Lolita gloated.

"Witch most foul, you and your order have unbalanced Nature. You are a plaque on the world, and I will kill you and any of your remaining sisters," growled Shao.

"I do not think so. And how is it that you somehow feel justified accusing us of unbalancing the natural order of things when you are the personification of Nature unbalanced, A talking cat indeed"! Lolita mocked. Now, come to me, little kitten, and I will show you true peace," promised Lolita.

She was shocked to hear the grumbling laugh from Shao. "Witch, your mesmerizing tricks do not work on me, or those descended from the blood of Cain.

"Fool!" Lolita shouted. "Is this fledgling not of Cains blood"? Lolita demanded. Here I rule. Do I not have this sorry excuse for a Vampyre under my control?" she asked, pointing behind her at Jose.

Shao looked with what could have been interpreted as a sneer. "I think not, witch."

Suddenly Lolita felt a powerful hand grip her throat. "What!" she choked out. Lolita struggled against Jose, matching his strength.

"Bite her!" Shao shouted. Confused but compliant, Jose sank his fangs into her neck. With the warm gush of blood pouring down his throat, Jose felt incredible power surge through his body. He drank greedily as Lolita weakened and slumped into Jose's arms. He continued feeding ravenously.

"Enough," roared Shao.

Drunk with pleasure, Jose continued draining the ancient witch. Shao swatted a powerful paw at Jose, knocking him aside.

"What are you doing?" Jose screamed.

Quietly Shao explained, "Never drink their last drop, for death resides in it, and we must never make her one of us."

"But she is beautiful and . . ." Jose shook the cobwebs out of his head, and realization dawned on him.

"Thank you, Shao. You saved me."

Shao looked at Jose. "I didn't do it for you, but your death may have distressed Master Diego, and I would not have that. Especially at the hands of these witches," Shao said, deflecting the compliment. "If you want to thank me . . ." He turned, looking at Lolita. Jose, understanding the unspoken request, walked over to Lolita, who lay on the ground, bloody and weak.

"My prince, please spare me. I did as I was commanded," Lolita begged.

"Since you like to follow orders, Lolita, Bruja, or whatever your name is, I have one last order for you."

"Anything, my prince. You have but to command."

"Very well," Jose agreed. "Here is your last command. Die!" With that, Jose reached down, snatching Lolita, and snapped her neck. Looking down at the broken corpse, Jose felt an odd sadness; trying to shake it off, he looked at Shao.

"How much farther?" Jose asked.

Shao growled and sprinted away. He was running with liquid grace, Jose. feeling as if he was just reprimanded, he took off after Shao, who looked at Jose when he caught up to him and replied. "Not far. See those mountains over there?"

In the distance, a mountain range cut into the horizon. "What about them?" Jose asked.

"They, my young friend, are the Pyrenees."

"Shao!" Jose called out. "Are we on a sightseeing tour?"

Shao glanced a Jose. "Young and dumb," he growled.

"Hey, you don't have to get personal." Jose protested.

Shao made a sound that Jose assumed was the giant cat's way of snickering. "My apologies, Jose. I didn't know you were so sensitive."

Jose looked at Shao. "Was that a laugh, or are you choking up a hairball?"

"Humor? Who would have guessed you possessed the intelligence for observational hilarity," Shao nearly purred.

They came closer and closer to the mountains. The wheat in the field whipped their legs as they ran by.

"That was uncalled for, Shao," Jose complained.

"Was it now?" Shao mocked, enjoying the banter.

"So you think you're so smart, kitty?" asked Jose.

"No thinking required," Shao responded.

"Okay, smart . . . cat, tell me this, what happens when an object traveling along in a north-to-south axis and an object traveling slightly slower in an east to west axis traverse one another?"

Shao shook his head. "Boy, are you stupid.,"?

Before Shao could finish his statement, Jose had stuck out his foot, tripping the great cat and sending him sprawling. After a half dozen bounces and decent slides, Shao came to a stop. Spitting out grass, he looked back to see Jose laughing and, between gasps, pointed at Shao.

"Aww, kitty, go boom?"

Shao growled, "Dead meat!"

Jose saw the look in Shao's eyes and took off as fast as he could. Shao quickly caught up to him and clipped his foot with his paw, sending Jose sprawling much as Shao did.

Jose stood up quickly, brushing the dirt off.

Shao coughed out his laughter. "You were right, Jose. That was funny."

"You die, Cato!" Jose shouted.

Shao hissed. "Catch me if you can, meat sack."

With a whoop, Jose sprinted at Shao, whose preternatural abilities coupled with feline reflexes gave him a quickness advantage. As Jose arrived, Shao had already taken off, looking back and teasing Jose. Under a half moon and clear skies, two disciples of the immortal Cain played a game of cat and mouse that also served as a training session. "Oh my, but you are a slow one," Shao mocked over his shoulder to a chasing Jose.

"Come to me, kitty, I'll show you slowly," Jose raged playfully.

"I'd imagine you have perfected the art of moving slowly. Is this what one would describe as the turtle technique?" Shao laughed.

Jose grunted. Digging deep, he managed more speed, whispering, "Here, kitty, kitty."

Jose slowly began to catch up to Shao. "I've got you now, furball."

Shao looked back and smiled. "I think not." With that, he increased his speed. "What's wrong, Jose? Cat got your tongue?" Shao laughed at his witticism.

Jose took a breath and lunged at Shao. The great cat sensing this nimbly, stepped aside. "Missed me," Shao laughed. Jose and Shao crisscrossed the Andalusian plain in this fashion. Running over green plains pocked with sunflower and purple Spanish sweet peas with a midnight blue sky as a backdrop sent the new vampiric senses of Jose into a state of ecstasy.

Leaps and great bursts of speed later, with Jose still trying to catch Shao, they found themselves approaching the foot of the Pyrenees. With one last great effort, Jose followed Shao's intricate and irregular pattern of running and leaping. Finally, Jose caught Shao midair by the tail. Shao yelped as he and Jose hit the ground, rolling and laughing. "That was fun," observed Jose.

Suddenly Shao leaped to his feet and started swiping at Jose. Connecting with a powerful paw to the head, Jose reeled. "Hey, Maricon! What do you think you are doing?"

Shao slowly advanced, swiping fast, vicious swings at Jose. After getting hit a couple of times, Jose became frustrated.

"Fine, you want to fight, let's g—" Jose never got to finish the sentence, as Shao popped him in the mouth.

"Hijo de Puta," Jose spat out. "You want to fight? Let's go."

Shao, silent and intent, combined attacks with feints, tagging Jose repeatedly. After getting slapped a dozen times or so, Jose managed to duck a blow intended for his head. Shao came harder and faster. Jose's eyes widened as he saw the ferocity of the attack. Moving with speed, he was not aware he possessed, Jose began to time Shao's movements, avoiding getting hit. As suddenly as he began, Shao stopped and began bounding up the face of the mountains that were their destination.

Jose looked at the retreating cat. "What the hell, Shao!" Jose shouted. "Stupid pendeho cat. One minute we're playing, the next he tries to kill me. You know, I will tell the masters. Perhaps you are so old you are beginning to lose your tiny little mind."

Shao crested the edge of the mountain and began pounding earth furiously. Jose looked up to see Shao smiling at him, but what was more attention-grabbing was the mini avalanche tumbling toward him. "Dios Mio," said Jose as he had to leap, dodge, and duck around the rocks. Finally, it was over, and Shao stood on the precipice, looking down at Jose. He smiled and began his descent on the other side.

Jose cursed the cat as he finished the climb and began his descent. Upon reaching the bottom, Jose looked for the now-missing cat. He looked into the trees sind saw nothing when suddenly he caught a whiff of the cat's odor. He fixed his vision on where he believed the smell emanated from. His vision sharpened tenfold as he concentrated on seeing Shao.

Then an inexplicable feeling directed him to look to the right of the tree he was looking at, and sure enough, there crouched the great cat in near-perfect camouflage, difficult to discern. Laughing, Jose sprinted to the cat, who had begun to clean himself.

"It's about time," Shao said between licks.

"That is disgusting! Are you licking your balls?" Jose asked, pretending to be shocked.

Shao purred. "I'm sorry. That was rude of me. Did you want some?" he asked sarcastically.

"Enough of this nonsense. Are we far from Master Musline's villa?" Jose asked.

"Just over the rise on the horizon. We should be there shortly," answered Shao.

"Excellent! Let us be off then," Jose suggested.

CHAPTER 18

CAIN'S MANOR

Ishar paced back and forth, unable to shake an impending sense of doom. He longed to search for a way to convince the only living, or more precisely the un-living, thing that mattered to him. With a sense of frustration, Ishar recalled the promise he had made Diego regarding staying put until he returned.

"You don't realize the depths of my former master's devious nature, Master Diego," Ishar mused aloud.

"Why would you think that?" said the voice of Diego in his head. Thinking he had an inner dialogue with himself using the voice of the one he missed, he continued with his chain of thought. *"Satan is beyond evil, Master! His corruption spreads through the world like a virus."* Mused the imp. Ishar hoped Diego was safe and returning soon.

"Well, well, well, little Ishar, a pet?"

Ishar spun around, seeing Nargal, One of Satan's demon spies, the gatherer of ruinous information, speculations, rumors, or outright lies. This demon whispered hateful lies in the ears of Emperors and peasants alike.

"Hello, Nargal. Has your Master let you off your leash?" asked Ishar.

Nargal hopped down from where he perched in a tree. "So, old comrade, what new tricks have you learned among the unwilling?" asked Nargal.

Ishar stared at his former comrade. "Why have you come, Nargal? Satan finally has the sense to kick you out?"

Nargal approached Ishar. "Brother, what is happening to you?"

"First, Nargal, we were never brothers, and we were barely comrades, and what under the creator's name are you speaking about?" Ishar asked vehemently.

Nargal winced. "How is it that you can utter his title and not feel the suffering of oblivion," he asked curiously.

"What," began Ishar, then he understood what Nargal was referring to, "I do not know. Perhaps because it wasn't a conscious effort," he speculated.

Nargal looked at him enviously. "But this is impossible! None may utter, you know, that name again since the Master forbade it with the threat of oblivion for any demon that dares mention *his name* again."

Ishar smiled. "What name is that Nargal, do you mean—"

"Stop, Ishar! The Master will be very displeased with you," warned Nargal.

"My master is the Vampyre Diego; our earthly father is Cain and—"

"Noooo!" shouted Nargal, holding his ears. Looking at Ishar unbelievingly, he vanished in a cloud of smoke.

"I seek the forgiveness of my Lord God the heavenly Father." A feeling unlike any other suffused Ishar. Never in his entire existence had he felt the love and mercy that is God the Father. Sinking to his knees with tears of happiness, Ishar looked to heaven. "Father, forgive my nature. Your servant Diego has opened my eyes, and you, most blessed Father, have opened my heart. I will do everything as you instruct. Lord, I thank you and pay homage to your divinity. I beg that the masters are safe from the fury of the fallen ones."

Descending from the clouds, Cain, Diego, and Mulsine saw Ishar on his knees, his words drifting up for them to hear.

"Well, thank you, Ishar. I've become fond of you myself. but Ishar, did you just pray to the Almighty"?" Diego asked, amazed.

Hearing Diego's voice, Ishar turned his tear-filled eyes to Diego, who was gently landing. Ishar threw himself at Diego's feet. "Oh, master, thank you, thank you."

Diego, slightly embarrassed by the display of affection, turned to Mulsine and Cain, who stood looking equally perplexed. Seeing Nargal, Diego called out."Nargie! So glad to see you so quickly reconstituted," exclaimed Diego.

Nargal had hoped to fool Ishar into thinking that he had come and gone. He realized that his spell of invisibility could not work against one as powerful as these dark lords, uncloaked.

"I've only come to warn my infernal cousin of the impending doom of this pathetic coven of yours, but I see now it is too late for you, so I shall leave your doomed house," the demon threatened.

"Ah, Nargie, that's no way to be. Stay. We're having a ripping good time!" Diego teased.

Cain smothered a laugh and explained the inside joke to Mulsine, who smiled in response, asking. "Master, you are saying Diego is acquainted with this demon?" asked Mulsine.

"You will come to see that our young brother here is full of surprises," responded Cain.

Mulsine's attention went back to Diego. "Do tell." Mulsine retorted. Meanwhile, Diego was continuing to assault Nargal with inane disingenuous inquiries. "So how's old Haroth? I hope he isn't too torn up over our last meeting".

The ambient temperature rose along with Nargal's temper. Observing this, Diego asked Nargal, "If you're going to do that, would you mind stepping away from the Date trees? They're Master Cain's favorite, and we wouldn't want to upset him now, would we?" By this time, Cain was rolling on the ground, howling, a chilling sound that slowly turned into a tenor-sounding laugh.

Nargal vanished in a plume of smoke while Diego taunted his retreating essence. "Don't forget to give my regards to the rest of your demonic brothers and remind them that the celebration of our Lord's crucifixion is coming, and I will be visiting soon to assure they give proper respect!"

Cain, Mulsine, and Ishar stepped up to Diego, although a more accurate description of Ishar's approach was leaping and hooting. Diego turned to face the approaching trio. "Well, that was fun!" he exhaled.

"That was incredible!" Ishar exclaimed. "I've seen Nargal take on popes and bishops without blinking, but you, you, Master…,

Diego interjected. "All right now, little one, it was a moment of fun, that is all."

"Fun? Do you call that fun? As if everything is a big joke or simply here to amuse you. What if it had been a trap? What then, my young knight?" Cain admonished his prize apprentice then braced himself for what he knew was going to be an explosive reaction from Diego.

But beyond Cain's understanding and expectation, Diego relented. "Forgive me, Master. I just so enjoy getting on the last nerve of the horned one and joyfully dance," he explained.

Cain stood, somewhat shocked, a feeling he enjoyed every century or so.

"Yes. Well, be that as it may". Cain muttered, seeking to continue in his castigation. "One would do well considering the judgment of others before committing to action. Especially when there is the welfare of others to consider," Mulsine interjected.

Diego looked at his pensive-looking elder and smiled. "Elder Mulsine, do I gather correctly in saying your tone smacks of concern?" Diego taunted.

"Gather what you will, youngling. You need only know only that sitting can be a painful activity to partake in when one has a foot firmly embedded in one's posterior."

Diego smiled. "Noted." He acknowledged.

Cain let out a slow breath. "Are you hens done clucking? Diego, remember we must meet Shao and Jose."

Diego nudged Mulsine. "Look, Pierre, Father, has his happy face on." Mulsine coughed out a laugh, and even Ishar giggled.

Cain took on a serious visage. "You dare!"

Diego and Mulsine shot into the air while Ishar vanished in smoke.

Cain let his Vampyres go for a moment before smiling to himself and began chasing what may be the strangest coven in the history of covens.

In mid-flight, Diego instructed his imp. *Ishar*, Diego thought.

The imp responded, *"I am here, master."*

Ishar, go to France and find Mulsine's villa. There is a new fledgling that goes by the name of Jose. Find Shao before appearing to Jose. He does not know you yet and may try to destroy you.

Ishar responded, *"As you command."* With that, his presence vanished.

Mulsine felt the sudden departure. *"Why did you send Ishar ahead?"* asked Mulsine.

"I am concerned for Jose, Pierre, being new to the war. Satan may think him our weak link."

"And is he?" Mulsine projected the question.

"He has the blood of Cain as you and I, but he is very enthusiastic and might get himself in a bind." Diego projected his fear.

Pierre thought for a moment. *"But did you not hint that Shao is with him?"*

"Yes," Diego agreed. *"However, although there are few who can protect as Shao does, no one can be saved from their own foolishness."* Diego quipped.

Cain, flying just behind them, sped up. *"You are correct, my son. We must make haste."*

The trio flew across the black Mediterranean Sea, approaching Greece.

Diego thought to Cain, *"Anyone here you remember?"*

Cain smiled. *"Yes, but I'm sure they have moved elsewhere by now. It's been a while,"* he answered somewhat sarcastically.

Mulsine joined in on the telepathic communication. *"Tell us, master, who did you know?"*

Cain reflected on those times. *"Are you familiar with Alexander of Macedonia?"* asked Cain, shocking both Diego and Mulsine.

"Did you know Alexander the Great, master?" Mulsine inquired mentally.

"No, I didn't," responded Cain.

"But you said . . .," Diego chimed in.

"I didn't say anything. I do, however, remember him."

Diego said aloud, "And this matters because. . ."

"Because, my dear disciples, I knew his General Seleucus," Cain informed.

Mulsine shook his head. *"You mean the founder of the Seleucid Empire?"* Mulsine projected his question.

"The very same," responded Cain. *"At the end of his reign, Seleucus and Ptolemy were arguing over a region where I resided. Anyway, they began a battle, killing many people. I could not listen to the constant wailing of the orphans and widows, so as a demonstration of my power, I single-handedly wiped out one of his legions then openly presented myself*

to them."The wind whipped through the hair of the trio as they flew over the beautiful islands of Naxos and the Silver islands of Greece.

Diego and Mulsine hung on Cain's every word. "What happened, master?" asked Diego.

"Well," Cain continued, *"they both decided they would punish my impudence. So they chained me and set archers to fire upon me."*

"Master, what did you do?" asked Mulsine, catching a stray bug and noisily spitting it out. Cain glanced over at Mulsine and signed with a finger over his lips for Mulsine to keep his mouth shut before continuing.

"Wall after wall of arrows descended and pierced my body. I sank to a knee." Cain paused for dramatic effect.

Diego looked at Mulsine. *"Don't you hate when he does this?"* He projected.

"Most assuredly," Mulsine projected his agreement.

"Do what?" asked Cain, feigning innocence.

"Stop toying with us and finish the story," Diego flared.

"You need to work on that patience, young one, and, Pierre, you should know better," Cain admonished.

Mulsine was mildly shocked. "What did I do?" he pleaded aloud, catching a few more bugs for his effort.

"What did I say about bugs, Pierre?" Cain teased. *"As I was saying before being so rudely interrupted"*—Cain looked first at Diego, then Pierre.*"Are we done with the interruptions"*? Cain inquired. He was taking their silence as compliance Cain continued. *"Good. Now Seleucus was a pompous man, and his pride was great, which would cost him in the end. Anyway, he walked into the middle of the square, making a grand speech about how all enemies of Alexander would meet a similar fate."*

Cain paused just long enough to drive his disciples to a fever pitch awaiting the conclusion to the story. Seeing that they were practicing the patience he spoke of earlier, Cain continued. *"So I waited for his self-congratulatory speech to end. I then began laughing. Softly at first, then louder as I got to my feet. Seleucus had his back to me as he addressed his legions. The warriors, though, saw me stand, and my laughter spun that fool of a general around. I snapped the chains, and before Seleucus could give the order to fire, I was among them. I killed hundreds of men and stopped in front of Seleucus, who was just beginning to draw his sword. I said to him, 'Go ahead.'"*

"What did you do, master?" asked Mulsine.

"Nothing," answered Cain.

*"Well, what did Seleucus do?"*Diego projected.

"Oh, he plunged his sword into my chest. I then sank to my knees, looked up at him, and said, 'You think you know evil, General, don't you?' I stood up, grabbing the hilt of the sword, saying, 'That was not deep enough. Let me help you". So I pushed the sword deeper.

"The general began to back away, asking what kind of demon I was. I grabbed him by the chest plate, raised him over my head, and said to him, 'I am the demon of death. Shall I now take you?' With my most horrid Vampyre visage did I threaten him. "Know that for every tear the widows and orphans spill shall be visited upon you a hundredfold. Never do I want to hear your name connected with such butchery again. Do we understand each other"? He pleaded that he did then had the audacity to beg me to make him one of us," Cain finished.

"Well, obviously that didn't happen," chimed in Mulsine.

"Acute observation. Pierre, did you formulate this obvious conclusion yourself?" Diego projected sarcastically.

Pierre looked at Diego. *"No one likes a wise-ass, Diego."*

Diego hoped Mulsine would take the bait.*"Well, then you must be loved by all, my brother."*

The trio flew up the heel and through the Italia boot, quickly approaching Rome. Mulsine gazed at Cain. *"Bring back memories"?* Mulsine projected lasciviously.

Cain smiled and projected telepathically. *"Mulsine, at times you concern me as to how wretched you think."*To both disciples, Cain projected. *"Many."*Diego and Mulsine remained quiet for a moment, thinking about another of the Master's tests. After a few moments and much distance, the two disciples looked at one another. "Really!" exclaimed Diego verbally, forgetting Cain's earlier warning against flying and attempting a conversation at the same time. Spitting bugs out of his mouth, Cain sent telepathic laughter. Diego silently shouted, *"Oh, so funny!"*

Mulsine grabbed his head, wobbling in mid-flight. *"Merde! Diego, mon ami. Your scream. Please don't do that again."*

Cain looked at a slightly abashed Diego. "Mi Hermano perdoname," he said, somewhat confused. Diego looked over at Cain, thinking, *"Master, I . . ."* Diego projected his confusion. Cain steered the communication in a different direction.

*"Have you ever heard of one called Gaius Germanicus?"*Cain interjected telepathically. *"Or perhaps you're more familiar with ...*

CHAPTER 19

BEFRIENDING A DEMON

It was a chilly evening with a bright moon that appeared as an eyebrow as if a great eye was kept upon the mortal world, perhaps one of the reasons early man worshipped the moon. Now she had her eye on two vampiric descendants of he that was said to have brought murder into the world.

Jose and Shao awaited their masters, passing the time with Shao explaining to Jose how he came to be. He finished his tale with, "And I have been friends with and companion to Master Cain for almost a thousand years, as measured by man." Jose stared at the giant cat. "You are amazing, Shao-sin."

Shao purred, "When you're right, who am I to argue"? Jose laughed, enthralled by the great cat. "And how do you . . .," Jose trailed off. "What?" Shao purred. "You know," Jose said tentatively. Shao did know but enjoyed playing with the younglings. "It appears to me, Jose, that you are having difficulties communicating. Have you been drinking from the tavern dwellers? All that alcohol might be doing something to you". Shao suggested smugly. Jose cut his eyes at Shao. "Listen, Cato, don't act like you don't know what I'm talking about. You know, the act. You know."

Shao contained his laughter. "How am I supposed to know when you can't even say . . . oh, you mean mating?"

Jose looked relieved. "Yes! Thank you". He exclaimed, somewhat exasperated.

Shao began grooming himself, knowing he was frustrating the young Vampyre. "Well, like most animals. I mount and ride them till they purr." Jose looked at Shao and thought he saw a small smile. "Forgive me for saying, but you are one dirty kitty." Jose laughed.

Shao stood to his full six feet. "First of all, farm boy, I am a majestic Bengal tiger with vampiric prowess and longevity."

"Dear sweet lord, are you going on again about how majestic you are, Shao?" came a voice from above.

Shao looked up. Silhouetted by the quarter moon floated down Cain, flanked by Diego and Mulsine. "Father!" Shao roared. "Well, met old man."

Shao charged at the trio, leaping into Cain's arms while simultaneously slapping both Diego and Mulsine with his paws. "It is good to see you, master. I have done as instructed.

Cain petted Shao. "I never doubted you, my son."

Shao reminded Jose of a house cat the way he purred and rubbed against Cain's leg.

"Shao, take Diego and teach him the way of sightless hunting," Cain instructed.

"Is that fair, master? I wanted to," Shao stopped, knowing even the slightest changes in Cain's moods. "As you command, master. Come, Diego. Let us patrol the area."

Diego looked between Shao and Cain, feeling as if he had just missed something.

Mulsine looked around. "Where is Ishar?" he asked.

Jose looked over at Mulsine. "Who?"

Cain focused then pointed to a spot by his fig tree. "He is there."

Jose looked around. "Okay, is this get-the-new-kid type of joke because I'm not laughing."

Cain heard the frustration in his newest convert's voice. He projected a mental command to Ishar, who was, in fact, invisible in the yard. *"Ishar,"* Cain projected.

"Yes, master," came back the reply.

"Ishar, I want you to stay invisible and occasionally disturb something Jose can hear."

"As you wish," projected Ishar.

Cain looked at Mulsine, smiling. "Pierre, tell Ishar that he is needed." Being one of Cain's oldest disciples, he knew what his master was doing.

"Ishar! What are you doing? The master has need of you!" demanded Mulsine.

Jose looked around, thinking this was a joke. "Ha ha ha! Very not funny. Why are you." Jose spun around, hearing a rustle behind him. Cain smiled. Jose jumped as if something poked him. "Madre de Dios! What the hell is going on here?" demanded Jose.

"The first thing you need to learn, youngling—"

"Excuse me," Jose interjected, "but can we stop with the youngling thing? It's starting to irritate me."

Pierre looked at Jose. "They do grow them bold in Torrolisimo, don't they?"

Jose looked at Pierre. "Si," he answered curtly.

"Of course, forgive me," Cain said, bowing to Jose. "The first thing, *youngling*, Cain continued, blatantly ignoring Jose's complaint. "Is, be aware. Know that nothing is as it seems. See what isn't there. Hear what is silent. Smell that which has no odor."

Jose looked at Cain. "Let me see if I understand you correctly. You want me to detect the undetectable?"

Mulsine gazed at Cain. "He's not as stupid as he looks."

Jose shot Mulsine a withering look. Turning back to Cain, he asked, "How do I do this, master?"

Cain smiled. "Open yourself, my son. Feel everything around you as if you are a part of it."

Jose jumped again as Ishar poked him again. Furious, Jose attempted as his master instructed.

"No, Jose. Anger clouds; calmness brings clarity. Try again."

Ishar poked Jose a third time, trying to keep him off balance. Jose breathed through his wave of anger, and slowly his perception heightened. At that moment, Ishar came in for a fourth attempt, only to find his hand caught by a powerful grip. "Got you!" Jose shook Ishar, who turned visible under the onslaught. "A demon!" Jose exclaimed.

"No, Jose. Did not Master Cain say to you that not all is as it appears?" Mulsine protested as Jose shook the imp violently.

Jose held on to Ishar, pointing at him. "Yes, but a demon? Have we not taken an oath to fight their kind?" he asked adamantly.

Cain said softly, "Jose, do not harm Ishar, or Master Diego will be very upset with you," he warned.

"But, master, I do not understand." Jose pled.

"Yes, Jose, you do not understand. Do not allow ignorance to be the root of your convictions". Cain warned his young apprentice.

The confusion was apparent on the young apprentice's face, so Cain explained further.

"Diego saved his life, and Ishar was willing to sacrifice himself and face Satan's wrath to help Diego. Now you will release him and reflect on how you found him. Understood?"

Jose nodded. "Yes, master, I understand."

Ishar, who had remained frozen, wiggled in Jose's grasp.

"If you don't mind," Ishar complained, pointing at Jose's hand, who, staring at Ishar, whispered. "Only because my Master demands it do I release you demon. Your kind is treacherous and not to be trusted, but the Master trusts you, so shall I". Jose, upon releasing the imp, quietly backed away, rubbing his wrist.

Cain approached and touched Jose's cheek. "Worry not, my son, for you did well today. You now only need to understand the lesson. I'm sure that you will," Cain concluded.

Jose looked up. "Thank you, master. I'll retire to the study then."

"Go feed first, my son, for, on the morrow, while you rest, contemplate what you've learned today," Cain advised.

Jose bowed himself out.

"I miss those old courtesies," Mulsine said. Cain grunted in agreement.

"Well, what do you think?" asked Mulsine.

"I think he'll make a fine addition to our little family," Cain answered somewhat cautiously.

Mulsine, being his disciple since the First Crusade, knew when his maker was being disingenuous. "Master, is there something you're not telling me?"

Cain paused. "I do have a concern, Pierre. It's Ishar."

Mulsine, not used to seeing Cain befuddled, became alert. "What is it, master?"

Cain shook his head. "I'm not sure yet, Pierre. Cain answered in a seldomly heard confused tone.

A PATH FOUND

They were outside of the beautiful port city that was Marseille, France. an ancient port developed by the Phoenicians in 600 b.c. North was the Etoile chain. A string of mountains that looked down on the bustling village.

Diego was put off by the seeming redundant training that Master Cain was putting him through. "Shao-sin, this is ridiculous! I am a master killer. I do not require lessons," stated Diego sounding a bit petulant. Shao Shao bit back a scathing rebuke and instead responded by growling. "Oh really?" He retorted. "And where did I find this master killer last I saw him?" Shao teased. Diego mumbled something unintelligible.

"I'm sorry, what?" Shao teased again. "I'm getting old, and these ears are not as sharp as they once were."

"On my knees in front of Satan," Diego admitted grudgingly. A cool wind blew in from the south, scattering the clouds and unveiling a half-moon as if peeking in on the immortal activity.

"Yes, on your knees in front of the one you would call your enemy," Shao stated sarcastically. Diego shot him an evil glare. "I'm sure you never want to find yourself there again and may even want a little revenge,"? Shao asked in a gravelly voice.

Diego stared at the cat. "You know I do. Why all the sarcasm? Did you have to chew the crap out of your fur again?"

Shao looked at Diego. "Really? That's what you're going with? Have I unknowingly denied you a treat? You really should cut back on those you know, bad for the digestion. Are we done now? Did you get the complaining out of your system yet?" Shao asked. "I tell you what, kitty. You certainly got a pair of balls on you." Diego observed. Shao tilted his head to the side. "Diego, do you want to get bit? Now stop looking at my balls, and let's train."

Diego capitulated, knowing how stubborn the great cat could be. "Fine," he exhaled. "They are gross looking anyway," Diego muttered.

Under the moonlight, Shao-sin taught Diego the art of the hunt. "Sight is only a part of it. One must learn to use all their senses when hunting, especially with your unique situation," Shao said in reference to Diego's burden.

"What do you mean unique?" Diego asked with a hint of sarcasm.

Shao growled. "Unique in the way that you are the only Vampyre I've ever heard of that faints at the sight of blood. Would you prefer the word cowardly response instead?" Shao teased.

Diego checked his anger. "Shao, you do not know me if you think me a coward," he said with death in his voice. "Besides, what do you know of it?" he responded dismissively.

"Master Cain has shared with me. I know your problem. What I intend to do is show you how to be effective even though innocent blood is shed before you," growled Shao.

"So please stop being so sensitive," Shao complained. "Ignoring Shao's remark, Diego argued. "But the Son has cursed me," complained Diego.

"No, my brother. He has sublimely gifted you". Shao argued, "He saw you fight in his name, he saw you try to resist evil, perhaps he has judged you not fully evil. If so, this may be your chance for redemption," Shao pointed out.

"I do not believe myself that blessed, but if there is a chance, so be it," Diego said.

"Excellent. Let us begin." Shao proceeded to teach Diego the art of stealth, hunting by smell, sound, and the innate gift of proximal sensitivity, an inner radar that pinpointed prey's location through the feint electrical charges the brain emits. Diego took to the lessons almost immediately. "Very good, brother." Shao purred.

"Shao, tell me something. When we were in India facing Mmbyu and his slaves, Master Cain gave a scream that made me feel as if I would explode. Could you speak on this?" Diego asked.

"I believe you speak of what I call the wail of despair," Shao growled.

Diegos' lifted an eyebrow upon hearing the dramatic name.

"What is this wail?" Diego asked, curiosity rising.

"Do not quote me, as I am guessing, but I think it is tied in with the fallen spirit within our master that wails his anger at his sense of betrayal. Anyone with the blood of Adremalach would be instantly consumed by his avenging fire," Shao purred almost reverently.

Diego reflected for a moment before saying, "Wait, both you and I were there, and while I was most certainly discomforted, I felt no danger," Diego retorted." Did you"?

Shao seemed to mull over that information before saying wonderingly, "He must have mastered the wail! That is astonishing!" gasped Shao.

"In what way?" asked Diego.

"Don't you see? It must mean that Master Cain has established some type of agreement with the fallen spirit within him," Shao said excitedly.

Diego looked at him as if he had lost his senses.

"Well, that not only makes perfect sense but to me seems painfully obvious," Diego declared. Shao snickered, "Not as clear as one would think, Diego. When the master was first possessed, he went insane with his grief over his loss of everything and went on a feeding rampage that many tale weavers of the day we're giving the credit, or blame, depending on your perspective, to evil. It's one of the reasons Satan thought it would be easy to plunge the master into final damnation."

"How would he go about doing that?" Diego asked.

"By denouncing God and accepting Satan as his lord," responded Shao.

Enchanted by the story, Diego asked, "And is this the time you came to be?" Shao purred. "Yes. After going through his rampage and telling Satan where he could stick his pitchfork, he came to India. I think he sought peace among the mystics. What he found was a very large and very hungry tiger trying to stalk him. Obviously, things did not go as I planned, and I believe Cain was hungry for companionship, so we traveled together, and he attempted his first coven. It was where he lost his first convert and was saddened, thinking he would never be able to speak to another man again. That is when he met Mmbyu, an Indian nobleman who was obsessed with the masters' physical beauty. The master was so grateful for the company and hospitality that he naively offered Mmbyu immortality. In part, I think, as I said, the reason being gratitude, the other part being selfish and wanting companionship". Shao then walked up to Diego with razor-sharp claws tore a long strip of cloth from his shirt, the cloth dangling from his claw. Diego looked at the ripped shirt displaying dismay. "What the hell did you do that for"? Shao's head dropped for a moment growling. "For the love of the master, stop whining and put this over your eyes." Shao directed.

Diego took the rag. "Tell me again why you are tearing into my clothes"? Diego inquired. Shao growled, "Your impatience is your greatest weakness and frankly very annoying." Shao complained.

"Fine. Great and mighty cat! What do I use it for?" Diego asked. Shao began to purr. Diego, thinking this highly suspicious, looked at Shao. "Why are you purring, mighty hunter of mice?"

Shao acted offended. "First, you know nothing of hunting mice, and they are difficult to catch. second, meat sack, if you don't want to follow Master Cain's instructions," Shao let the sentence hang unsaid. "No, no, no. I'll do it." Diego looked confused for a moment. "What is it you want me to do?" he asked, slightly embarrassed. Shao purred, "Glad you asked. You are now going to learn vision beyond sight."

"What beyond what?" asked Diego.

Shao walked slowly to a nearby precipice. "You can launch yourself from this cliff and soar with the eagles."

"Yes and?" Diego asked, walking up beside Shao.

"We have varying talents amongst our kind, Diego. You, for whatever reason, have shown growth far out of proportion compared to those of your brothers. Master Cain knew upon seeing you that you're a latent potential."

"Thank you," replied an uncertain Diego, curious as to where Shao was going with this information.

"Diego, I want you to tie the rag across your eyes."

Diego unhesitatingly tied the torn shirt, now a rag across his eyes. "Vision beyond sight?" he asked.

Shao purred, "Just so. Now, tell me what you see."

"I see darkness!" exclaimed Diego. "What am I supposed to see?" he demanded.

"Tell me how your imagination describes our surroundings," Shao purred.

Diego described the entire location down to the last detail. "We are standing on a cliff. I see the villa a few leagues to our west. It is surrounded by a high gray wall with towers. I see the formation of boulders off to—"

Shao interjected, "Okay, stop. What is it that you think you are doing?"

"I'm doing as you instructed!" he said, somewhat perturbed. "And rather well, I thought."

"Do you now?" Shao asked in a growl that carried a mischievous tone that Diego heard. "Are you prepared to face all obstacles for your training? Because if not, tell me now so I won't waste time better spent licking myself."

Diego bristled at the subtle challenge. "Let's see what you got, kitty," he said mockingly.

"Interesting choice of words, Diego. You will follow me without taking the rag from your eyes." Sounds easy enough," Diego said confidently.

"Does it now? Well, allow me to sweeten the pot with an incentive," Shao growled.

"What—" Diego was cut off mid-sentence as a powerful blow that sent him sprawling connected to his head.

Looking up, Shao growled, "Catch me if you can." He sprinted the way they had come. Diego sprang to his feet, hot on Shao's tail.

"Here, kitty, kitty," he said, sounding menacing. "Come to me, you foul dropping of a diseased pig."

Diego charged at Shao, who had gathered his enormously powerful legs under him and burst into blinding speed, his paws churning up rock and earth as he charged down the small mountain. At the base of the mountain, Shao looked back and saw Diego bearing down on him.

"Come to me, kitty," Diego hissed.

Shao bolted away from the villa. Diego was amazed at the giant cat's speed, which was detectable by the sound of splitting wind. After about a mile or so, Shao snatched up a piece of wood and ran even faster. Hearing the cat's pace quicken, by way of increased thumping of Shao's paws on packed earth, Diego opened up like one of the wild Andalusians he loved riding so much when he was mortal. The cat suddenly stopped, and Diego charged to the spot where Shao sat waiting. As Diego drew rapidly closer, Shao hurled the piece of wood he had picked up earlier to about thirty feet away from where he sat. Diego suddenly changed course, hearing the wood hit the ground. He was streaking to the wood. Stopping, he stood there. Shao leaped at him, striking him forcefully and knocking him down. Diego stood up, spitting grass.

"What the hell, Shao!" he exclaimed.

"What the hell indeed. You were using your memory earlier," reprimanded Shao, "when I distinctly remember telling you to use your vision!"

Diego turned to the sound of Shao's voice. "How did you know I was not?" Diego asked.

"Spaniard, please, I've been a hunter for thousands of years. I can spot a weakness when revealed." "But how did you know?" Diego asked.

"My first clue was your description of the cliffs. You described what we had passed, not what was in front of us. I also noticed that you were listening to me. Finally, you were chasing the log." "Clever," grunted Diego.

"Now," said Shao, "I am going to beat you about the head and body until you get this, okay?" Before Diego could respond, Shao landed a resounding paw on his head. He jumped back snuck one in his stomach before jumping behind Diego, biting at his calf. This went on through most of the night, with Shao tirelessly pawing, scratching, and biting Diego from a myriad of positions.

Calming himself, Diego felt a strange sense of detachment—a feeling of being separate from his body, as if he was watching Shao pick at the helpless person before him. It took a moment, but Diego discovered it was him from a different perspective. Envisioning Shao's paw reaching up to smack him again, Diego quickly snatched the paw and flung Shao a few dozen feet from him.

Growling, Shao attacked again, with Diego avoiding the strike and bite attempts. Shao leaped in frustration. Diego caught him and threw him. Landing on his paws, he shook his head. Walking back slowly, Shao complained, "You felt a need to throw me, brother."? Shao complained.

"Absolutely." Diego smiled, taking off the blindfold. "Well?" he asked Shao.

Shao looked him up and down and halfheartedly grunted, "Not bad. Let us return to the villa."

Diego bowed. "After you, master Shao." The great Bengal looked at Diego, grunted, then bolted for Mulsine's villa.

CHAPTER 20

LESSONS

"The first thing you need to learn, youngling." Cain began

"Excuse me," Jose interjected, "but can we stop with the youngling thing? It's starting to irritate me."

Pierre looked at Jose. "They do grow them bold in Torrolisimo, don't they?"

Jose looked at Pierre. "Si," he answered curtly.

"I apologize; I meant no offense." Cain responded facetiously. The first thing, *youngling*, Cain continued blatantly ignoring Jose's complaint. "Is, be aware. Know that nothing is as it seems. See what isn't there. Hear what is silent. Smell that which has no odor."

Jose looked at Cain. "Let me see if I understand you correctly. You want me to detect the undetectable?" He asked in disbelief.

Mulsine gazed at Cain. "He's not as stupid as he looks."

Jose shot Mulsine a withering look. Turning back to Cain, he asked, "How do I do this, master?"

Cain smiled. "Open yourself, my son. Feel everything around you as if you are a part of it."

Jose jumped again as Ishar poked him once again. Furious, Jose attempted as his Master instructed.

"No, Jose. Anger clouds; calmness brings clarity. Try again."

Ishar poked Jose a third time, trying to keep him off balance. Jose breathed through his wave of anger, and slowly his perception heightened. At that moment, Ishar came in for a fourth attempt, only to find his hand caught by a powerful grip. "Got you!" Jose shook Ishar, who turned visible under the onslaught. "A demon!" Jose exclaimed.

"No, Jose. Did not Master Cain say to you that not all is as it appears?" Mulsine protested as Jose shook the imp violently.

Jose held on to Ishar, pointing at him. "Yes, but a demon? Have we not taken an oath to fight their kind?" he asked adamantly.

Cain spoke softly, "Jose, do not harm Ishar, or Master Diego will be very upset with you," he warned.

"But, master, I do not understand." Jose pled.

"Yes, Jose, you do not understand. Do not allow ignorance to be the root of your convictions". Cain warned his young apprentice.

The confusion was apparent on Jose's face, so Cain explained further.

"Diego saved his life, and Ishar was willing to sacrifice himself and face Satan's wrath to help Diego. Now you will release him and reflect on how you found him. Understood?" Jose nodded. "Yes, master, I understand."

Ishar, who had remained frozen, began to wiggle in Jose's grasp.

"If you don't mind." He said, pointing at Jose's hand, who, staring at Ishar, whispered. "Only because my Master demands it do I release you demon. Your kind is treacherous and not to be trusted, but the Master trusts you, so shall I". Jose, upon his hand, released the imp, who quietly backed away, rubbing his wrist.

Cain approached and touched Jose's cheek. "Worry not, my son, for you did well today. You now only need to understand the lesson. I'm sure that you will," Cain concluded.

Jose looked up. "Thank you, Master. I'll retire to the study then."

"Sleep, my son, for the sun rises, on the morrow, you will have to feed."

Jose bowed himself out. The sky grew paler as the sun touched the horizon.

Jose retreated to the farthest corner where he set up temporary bedding; upon laying to rest, he saw images of Satan on a mountain top speaking to him. Beside him stood a beautiful woman calling him, "My lord Serrate." Many images followed. Jose/Serrate flying?! Many people bow, thrones, crowns, and armies. The seductive images continued through Jose's rest cycle.

Pierre watched as his younger sibling retreated to rest.

"Well, what do you think?" asked Mulsine.

"I think he'll make a fine addition to our little family," Cain answered somewhat cautiously.

Mulsine, being his disciple since the First Crusade, knew when his maker was being disingenuous. "Master, is there something you're not telling me?"

Cain paused. "I do have a concern, Pierre. It's Ishar."

Mulsine, not used to seeing Cain befuddled, became alert. "What is it, master?"

Cain shook his head. "I'm not sure yet."

Out in the French countryside, Shao and Diego patrolled the area. "Why do you think the Master has us looking for"? Shao inquired. The sun broke the horizon, and the stars faded from sight. "I'm not sure, but I'd imagine he senses some evil afoot, and since it was so close to dawn, he sent us." Diego assumed. They spent most of the day searching the area around the villa. after an uneventful patrol, Diego and Shao returned to the villa where Diego took to reading while Shao stretched out in the garden Shao sniffed at the air, and Diego looked up from his perusing of an ancient Sumerian tablet written in cuneiform.

Mulsine entered the courtyard where Shao and Diego were enjoying a moment of repose.

Diego looked at Mulsine. "How did you come by these wonderful tablets?" he asked in wonder.

"Master Cain gave them to me as a gift when I kept asking if the tales of Gilgamesh were true," replied Mulsine.

"And are they?" asked Diego.

"I'll tell you the same thing the master told me," said Mulsine.

"And that would be what?" asked a slightly annoyed Diego at Mulsine's evasions. "He said, Pierre, whatever gave you the idea I can read Sumerian?"

Diego smiled. "That must have been infuriating; what did you say then"? Diego inquired. "Again, I will defer to the master's style of sharing," he said; Mulsine paused, enjoying the fact that he was annoying Diego. "What?" Diego asked heatedly.

Mulsine smiled. "Learn as I have. You have time," he replied sarcastically.

Shao sprang to his feet as the door to the back rooms opened. He sped to welcome Jose home but stopped short of him, still sniffing the air.

"This is how you greet me, Shao?" Jose asked.

"You carry a smell I know and dislike, Jose," growled Shao.

"Well, perhaps I need to bathe, but there is no reason to be rude about it," declared Jose, in the hope to lighten the sense of tension he felt emanating from the great cat.

"No amount of bathing can wash away the smell you are carrying, Jose."

Mulsine and Diego entered the foyer.

Jose asked, "Is Master Cain about?"

Mulsine walked over to Jose. "Would you mind first telling us where you've been?"

Jose looked at Mulsine. "Where I've been is no concern of yours. Are you my wet nurse? Am I a child that needs to explain his comings and goings?" Jose asked defiantly.

Diego watched quietly as Shao ambled over to him and sat, still growling.

"Why am I being treated in this fashion!" Jose looked to Diego. "Master!" he pleaded. Diego raised his hand for silence. "The sun rises, and you as of yet have the strength to resist it. You risk much by testing that ability, but you seem fatigued; go rest. I assume that you fed already?" Diego asked.

"Of course, master, I am content, but I will go rest as you say." Jose beat a hasty retreat to his darkened chambers under the penetrating gaze of his three vampiric brothers. "Well?" asked Mulsine.

Shao's growl echoed Mulsine's question, which was directed at Diego.

"Well, what?" Diego asked facetiously.

"Diego, stop playing games. You know of which I speak," Mulsine said insistently.

Shao growled, "Little brother, I know he and his family served you and yours, but it would seem . . ." Shao's accusation hung in the air.

Diego sat heavily in a chair. Exhaling sadly, he responded, "Yes, brothers, I smell the dark one on him as well."

Cain entered the room. The three stood at his entrance. "You are correct, my sons. Satan seeks to corrupt him, seeing that he is the weakest among us," Cain observed.

"What shall we do, master?" purred Shao.

Cain looked directly at Diego. "We will do nothing," Cain said, raising his hand to silence Diego's objections. "You must listen to me," he implored. "As each of you was tempted by him, so must Jose so we can gauge his commitment."

Diego stood up. "Jose and his family have always been loyal to my family. I will not discard him!" Diego argued vehemently.

"The person you knew as Jose de Torrolisimo died that night in your village. We are speaking of the vampire Jose who may have a taste for power. If this is so, then his lust for power shall corrupt him, not us. Diego, this is something you must try to understand," Cain said in a sad voice.

Diego stomped into the yard where the sun, having broken the horizon, kissed the garden and washed over Diego, bringing with it a cool breeze from the Mediterranean sea.

"Diego." Diego looked at Mulsine, who was squinting in the light. "Diego, I admire your sense of loyalty to those you care for, but we must not ignore the truth."

Diego spun on his heel silently and went to his chambers.

Cain came up behind Mulsine. "Pierre, we must give him time to accept the truth. Jose was his last link to his family, so let us not judge too harshly."

Mulsine nodded in acquiescence. "As you say, master." He entered the house, for though he could withstand the light of the sun, it still caused him discomfort.

SATANIC RENDEZVOUS

Jose waited for late night. Not hearing movement in the villa, he quickly left to the mountains to make his rendezvous.

In the chilly night air, Jose made his way to the meeting place. Satan was waiting dressed oddly enough in a monk's habit.

"Do you hold nothing sacred?" Jose commented sarcastically.

Satan smiled at his approach. "On the contrary, my dear Don Jose, I utterly respect the priesthood. After all, some of my most devout followers are from that lovely sect."

"You lie!" Jose shouted.

"My dear don Jose, with time, you will learn that I don't lie. What I'll admit to doing is fostering lies man tells himself to ease the burden of his ignorance."

Jose chuckled softly. "Really? And how is this accomplished?" Jose asked sarcastically.

"That is the easy part. Do you recall what I said about the fundamental pillars?"

"Yes," answered Jose uncomfortably.

"Of course you do. Well, not to belabor a point, it is easier for man to believe in absolutes; hence I am not the Lord's tool of punishment, but rather his equal polar opposite. Even though they say he is all-powerful, they fear me more than they love him."

"That is blaspheme!" Jose argued.

"Really? Does not man pay more tribute to my altars of war, lust, and greed far more than assisting the poor?"

Jose scratched his beard, seeing the logic in Satan's argument. But he was unable to think of a way to refute what to him was a simple truth.

"Look at the Crusades," Satan continued. Who were all those men dying for? Jesus would not lift a hand in his defense, yet let be slain hundreds, nay, thousands of people, innocent or not. The church that claims to be his voice on earth says that the prince of peace would let people, good or bad, be condemned to hell just because they wouldn't follow him or support his church. Christ, for lack of a better word, was a socialist, while the world since the inception of trade is more imperialist and capitalist. What most fail to understand is that by saying that if I could go to war against God, then I must pose a threat to his rule. How can a weaker force threaten a stronger one? It must mean then that I am equal to that force called God."

Jose looked at Satan. "While I admit you make a valid point or two, I do not concede to the conclusion of your argument. God is all-powerful and has no equal," Jose stated stubbornly. "Wait," Jose exclaimed suddenly as a realization dawned upon him. "Are you trying to tell me that the angels tipped the balance, and that made you as powerful?" asked a shocked Jose.

"Yes!" agreed Satan. "That has been my point for millennia. My lieutenants insist that the darkness rules, hence the coup attempt.

I tried to get Cain to assist me in restoring balance, but some incompetent demons, including my former lover Lillith, made that impossible by instilling everlasting hate for me in Cain." Jose looked surprised. "How did they manage that?" asked an enthralled Jose.

Seeing his eagerness to hear more, Satan continued. "Well, you know that Lillith seduced Adam, condemning Man-kind to mortality. Mastema, a demon lord of sorcery, taught the witches a spell of binding that trapped poor Adramelech, a fire demon, in the infernal state he is in. Source of the immortal Cains power. Even he believes that I betrayed him. To be wrongfully accused of a thing for thousands of years tends to be disturbing. What I need is to find powerful disciples who I would infuse with the power of negativity and with their aid restore balance, thereby pleasing our Father, who I angered in my youth," Satan finished, sounding both hopeful and despondent.

Seeing the confusion on Jose's face, he said, "Don Jose, it was good of you to listen, if not believe, what I had to say." Satan continued. As pitiful as it sounds, I have no one to relate to, and there is no hell like that of silence. That being said, I will take my leave of you to ponder what I've said. I hope to see you soon. Be well." Satan softly diffused in glowing lights as opposed to the usual smoke and stink of brimstone, all thanks to a spell of sedition Lillith shared with him. Then Satan was gone.

Jose stood there for a moment before hearing the rustling of leaves behind him. Turning, he saw Agrat coming up the slope. Jose was struck anew by her beauty. Upon approaching him, she fixed him with a dazzling smile that was augmented by a blue-black night canvass that was the night sky, lit by a rising moon, with stars appearing to adorn her outlines. "Angelic," whispered Jose to himself. "Good evening, dark prince," Agrat greeted him.

"Beautiful princess, good evening, an evening improved upon greatly with your presence," Jose responded, enchanted by the sight of her. "And what would my prince apply his will toward this evening?" she asked.

Jose paused as he thought he heard anxiety in her voice. But why would she? Jose then realized her greeting, and her manner bore a slight trepidation. Dark Prince. Jose remembered her way of greeting him. *Is it possible she knows?* he wondered. "My will would best be served if I understood the reason for your apparent fear," claimed Jose.

Agrat took a fearful step back. "It is Satan. He told me what you are and how you came to be," she replied, unsuccessfully attempting to hide her fear.

Anger swelled in Jose's chest when he felt a warm hand in his. He looked over at Agrat, who had clutched his hand. "My Lord, be not angry with Satan. He saw how I was taken with you, and he said he felt a certain obligation to warn me since he had rescued me from foul demons. He didn't want me to be ignorant of certain facts," Agrat explained.

"So you know of me?" Jose asked, shocked.

"I know what Satan told me, and though others have maligned his name, I found him charming and sincere. He spoke very highly of you, saying that though Cain was older, Diego powerful, and Mulsine wise—I'm assuming these are members of, what did he call it? Coven? He says that though you are the youngest and the weakest among them, you are undoubtedly the wisest."

Jose looked at the sky and the rising moon, occasionally covered by wispy clouds. "None of this frightens you?" Jose asked. Agrat smiled. "No, lord. I was born into a house of warriors. I fear little."

Jose looked at her with fierce eyes. "I am not little!" he pointed out.

"Nay, lord. I did not mean to imply that you are, only that—"

"That what?" asked Jose feeling and thinking things he would have never thought, such as giving Satan the benefit of the doubt and the strange feelings he had for this beautiful, seeming helpless woman.

Agrat hesitated for a moment. "I feel oddly drawn to you, my lord."

Jose's heart leaped with excitement, which reversed itself with a realization. "But I am immortal, which means I would have to watch you grow old and die. I'm not sure…." "My lord," Agrat interjected, "I am not without gifts."

The comment confused Jose. "What do you mean by that?" he asked.

Agrat explained, "My bloodline, my Lord. I am a descendant of the witches of Endor of a past long gone. Satan said that he would awaken the power within that has gone dormant."

Jose stepped back. "And you would make such a bargain?"

"He saved me from witch hunters, my Lord. He treated me kindly and told me his tale as he did you." Agrat began crying angry tears. "You have power, my Lord, to do as you will. According to Satan, he can awaken dormant powers of my ancestors, thus be able to fend for myself. Would you deny me such assurances!" Agrat exclaimed angrily. Jose asked quietly. "At what price"? Concern in his voice. "All he said I had to do was assist him in regaining his seat of power and restore balance," Agrat answered. "Did you ever stop to think he could be lying to you?" Jose asked.

"Do you think me a fool?" she asked hotly. "I had him swear on the cross that no harm would come to me and that my soul would not be damned by assisting him. Please understand, Jose. The only reason I ask is that he will grant me extended life, and I would like to share that time with a master as yourself."

Jose thought Agrat to be the most beautiful woman he's ever seen, and seeing her distressed troubled him. "Allow me to converse with him again, and I shall have an answer," Jose responded.

"Thank you, Jose. I shall summon him and relate our proposal of joining him if you are convinced of his sincerity; I shall await you in my hut by the river." She concluded.

"As you wish," Jose agreed. Later as the night wore on, Jose waited on the mountain, with several thoughts racing in his mind. But *she* kept replacing those thoughts. The image of her long, almost glowing black hair. Her deep golden-brown eyes. Full pouting lips. Jose shook the cobwebs from his head and noticed Satan standing there looking over the plains.

"How long have you been standing there?" Jose demanded.

"I saw you were in deep reflection, and I did not wish to disturb what could have been some very pleasant memories."

Jose considered that for a moment. "They were indeed pleasant," he acquiesced.

"Shall we get down to the matter at hand?" Satan asked. Jose nodded. "Have you asked your master of the things I told you?" Satan inquired. Jose shook his head. "No. They dismissed me."

"What?" Satan said, feigning surprise. "He wouldn't even listen to you"? Jose shook his head in the negative again.

"If you would allow, Satan, I would ask something of you?" Satan smiled. "Please do." "Are all the promises you made to Agrat . . . do you have any intention of honoring them?" Jose asked suspiciously.

Satan looked genuinely hurt. "It used to be that when one made a deal with me, they knew I'd keep my word."

"Yes," agreed Jose. "But they usually paid for your gifts with their soul," he pointed out. "True," Satan admitted. "But it was the only form of payment they could offer me that was of worth to fulfill all their desires. Besides that, it's a good way to separate the good from the evil."

"Ah," grunted Jose. "Hence the question, what would you demand of Agrat?" he asked pointedly.

"Why, nothing, of course." Jose had a look that said, "I caught you in a lie."

"Don Jose, why would you put Agrat in league with mere mortals? She has the bloodline of some of the most powerful witches that ever walked the earth! And if you were to join us, what a marvel that would be!" Satan said with a flourish.

"The price, Satan. What would be the price?" insisted Jose.

"My dear young dark Lord, you misunderstand me. For helping me recover my throne, I will gift both of you with an awakening of power; no one on this plane of existence has my favor to you and the lovely witch for aiding me. Perhaps if you don't mind, I'd drop in on occasion as my duties permit just to hang up the old horns, as it were. To have an earthly place to relax and be welcomed." Jose looked at Satan's sincere face. "And you just expect me to take your word on it"?" he asked tentatively. "I do, Don Jose, and beyond a promise, I give you my word. Help me achieve my goal of returning me to my seat of power and restoring balance, and all I've said shall be fulfilled". Satan claimed.

Jose thought a moment longer. "It is possible we'd join you, but only if you remember your promise to not attempt to seduce or snatch our souls afterward."

"Agreed!" Satan said happily. "Now bring Agrat, and we shall begin the awakening."

Jose leaped down the mountainside, smiling. "*Tonight, I will embrace my love in immortality.*" Jose thought joyfully, not for a moment considering the consequences that were to come.

CHAPTER 21
DIEGO'S PRAYER

Diego sat quietly, looking up at the stars. Thoughts of Jose raced through his mind.

Will the loyal Jose seek power to the point of corruption? He wondered. Diego felt as if it was his fault. If he had only let Jose die instead of being selfish, thinking as if Jose was a living testimony of his previous life. He secretly prayed for Jose's deliverance, not caring that it was not likely that his prayer had any power as he was undead.

"Master," Ishar called out.

Diego's introspection ceased. "Yes, Ishar. What can I do for you?" Diego asked.

"Master, I see that you are deeply concerned for Jose. Allow me to go keep an eye on him for you," Ishar requested.

"Thank you my, little friend, but Master Cain is right. Jose has to make his own choice, for better or worse."

"But, master, I could—" Ishar stopped when Diego held up his hand for silence.

"No, Ishar. We will discuss it no further!" Diego demanded.

Being thus dismissed, Ishar sought Cain out and found him in the reading room, where a sad melody issued forth from an ancient lyre he strummed. Ishar paused at the doorway, awaiting Cain's acknowledgment and permission to enter.

Cain's fingers glided effortlessly from sustained melodic aria to an attacking staccato, giving the impression of extreme aggression. Ishar was taken aback. In all his existence, he had never heard such a transition from angelic to hellish in such a personally interpreted manner. Joy beyond pain and pain beyond joy accompanied Cain's music.

ain turned to see Ishar standing transfixed in the doorway. "I agree with you both, Ishar," Cain said before Ishar could utter anything. "Jose must meet the temptation alone, without assistance. But I understand the difficulties of releasing what one believes brings validation to his own existence. So I would say to you, Ishar, a note, in order to be, a note must play alone. However, the rest of the strings may sit aside silently to see if it maintains its integrity, not wavering or diminishing so that it may join the others to become a chord in accord with the symphony."

"So what I believe you are saying, master, is that I may watch but allow things to transpire as they will with no interference by me?" Ishar asked somewhat tentatively.

Cain smiled. "Ishar," Cain said in warning, "beware of the conductor!"

Ishar nodded in understanding and disappeared in his ritualistic cloud of smoke. Cain wondered if he was becoming accustomed to the little demon, as his stench was becoming less repulsive.

Diego sat in the garden. He had become so fond of reflecting on a memory that became more distant with each passing day.

He remembered Jose's kind and patient father, the good man Enrico the blacksmith. If he remembered correctly, Enrico had forged a fine Toledo Salamanca for his grandfather Rodrigo, which he had named "Astrellia Rey," the King Star sword. It was a beautiful sword. Strong yet flexible.

Diego remembered being reprimanded by the old duke for daring to play with it. He remembered his grandfather sitting him down, explaining why Diego must never draw a sword unless he intended on killing someone and that his ducal sword was incredibly sharp, and unless he planned on going on with the rest of his life minus a few digits, he should repress his desire to handle such a weapon until he was well trained with such instruments. Diego, being the defiant child that he was, took it as a challenge and spent years perfecting his swordsmanship. All these thoughts Diego realized were a poor attempt to take his mind off Jose's ordeal.

Cain walked up behind Diego. "We must have faith in our friends, my son," he admonished.

"I know, but against Satan? I fear Jose's arrogance will get the better of him," Diego answered.

"As do I," admitted Cain.

"Diego," Mulsine called out. "Come, brother, play some guitar for us so that we may be soothed. I would ask Cain, but his music tends to lean to the morbid." Cain looked swiftly at Mulsine. "No insult intended, master. You, in fact, play beautifully, except I always want to kill myself afterward," Mulsine observed.

Diego, to distract himself, acquiesced to Mulsine's request and fetched his guitar. Upon retrieval, Diego sat by the well and began playing a beautiful piece that was both Spanish and Romani, creating magnificent point and contour points that hinted at damnation and redemption.

Cain and Mulsine sat by the garden, enjoying the music while feeling the pain of it.

Cain smiled at Mulsine. "Good idea, Pierre," he simply stated.

Agrat's Reward

At the base of the mountain, Agrat sat in seeming anticipation. The moon hung high with a chilly bite to the air. She turned to the sound of Jose landing lightly on the roof of her hut. Standing from the stump, she was sitting on in her garden, she greeted Jose tentatively. "How is it with you, my lord?"

Jose smiled, enchanted. "It seems well enough. Are you sure you want to go through with this?" Jose asked.

Agrat smiled. "I feel safer knowing you are with me. Will you stay with me, Jose?" she asked demurely.

Jose was stunned and overwhelmed with desire. "For as long as you would have me, senorita," he replied gallantly.

"I must rest before going up the mountain again, my prince, for I tire easily," Agrat said meekly.

Jose smiled, sweeping her up in his arms. "Worry not, my lady, for your passage will be swift and not lacking comfort."

Agrat giggled innocently in direct contradiction to her evil nature. As Jose carried her off, swiftly ascending the mountain.

High above the village, Satan sat in repose as Jose arrived with Agrat. Satan sat on a tree stump. As the pair approached, he rose.

"Satan, will you now give me the power I desire?" Agrat inquired.

"It shall be as promised, a descendant of Endor. You have only to pledge your alliance to me, and you shall be restored to your birthright," Satan intoned. Jose stood feeling dizzy. Satan looked over at him. "What is wrong, dark master?" Satan innocently asked. "Nothing," Jose lied, trying to maintain his balance. Satan sounded off with a friendly chuckle. "Do I amuse you, dark one?" Jose asked defensively.

"Not at all, dark lord. What I find amusing is that you have the gumption to attempt to lie to the father of lies," Satan explained.

Jose smiled. "Forgive my rudeness, dark one," he said apologetically.

"No apologies necessary, young master. It is I that should ask such a courtesy," Satan offered.

"How is that?" Jose asked curiously.

"I have been around your kind long enough to recognize when the hunger is upon them," Satan explained.

"It is generous of you to have such considerations, but I am fine," Jose argued.

"Nonsense!" Satan admonished. "If you would but allow me to Summon four healthy calves so that you may feed," Satan requested. "Really, you do not have to . .," Jose stammered.

"Please, Jose," Satan interjected. "I have never been a poor host to invited guests. I will instruct Agrat as part of her first exercise of power to conjure adult animals. They will have the sins of their life on their souls, so you will not violate Cain's edict of feeding on the innocent," Satan proclaimed., "You know of our ban?" Jose asked, shocked.

"Of course, my son. I know everything there is to know about Cain and his pitiful attempt to seek redemption though, in all honesty, I think him a fool for shying away from his true power." Satan said. "True power?" Jose asked, intrigued.

"Yes, Jose. Forgive me, for I spoke too much on the matter, as it has to do with the end of days, and God has permitted me to have only one disciple and one harbinger. So unless you decided to be that apprentice, it is not something I could share with you. Anyway, where are my manners? Agrat is done with her summoning. Please, my young friend, go eat. I will await you here until you are refreshed and can decide things for yourself clearly," Satan suggested.

Jose, finding himself in an extreme state of hunger, gave a brief bow to Satan. "I shall do as you say and go feed. Thank you, dark lord." Jose bowed and went to where Agrat sat beside four squealing pigs.

Crouched in his cloak of invisibility, Ishar watched with growing dread and concern for Jose. He watched as Jose picked up and began to feed on a small shape that sounded as if it were squealing. Ishar heard the crunch of Jose's bite as he almost tore the head off the now-silent *baby*! Ishar could not believe his eyes as he watched Jose ravaged a healthy baby boy, tossing it aside and reaching for a baby girl; thirst unslaked Ishar stumbled back in shock. Before he could get his bearings, Satan stood in front of him. "Well, hello, little one,"

Satan said menacingly. "How good of you to join us." Ishar looked over at Jose, who was in a mad feeding frenzy, gorging through the children. Satan laughed triumphantly. "Now, Jose, feel the power that is the darkness. Awaken, awaken; the light is forsaken. Awaken, awaken, by the darkness be taken." Satan ended his incantation, clapping his hands together as lightning came from his hands and thunder issued from his clap.

Jose stood tall, roaring with the evil power. Beside him stood Agrat, betrothed witch wife and servant of Satan.

"Noooo!" screamed Ishar. "What shall we do with the traitor, Lord Serrate? As henceforth, shall you be known disciple of the one true God," Satan proclaimed.

"Do as you will with the traitor, my lord," Jose replied with no remorse as he bathed in the power of darkness.

"As you say, so shall it be done, Lord Serrate," Satan said. He gripped Ishar in a psychic grasp; the poor imp shrieked in intolerable pain.

ISHAR'S REDEMPTION

Hearing the scream, Diego jumped to his feet. Cain was instantly beside him, pressing him down forcefully. "Diego, you must stay," he demanded.

Diego struggled against the oldest vampire for a moment before recognizing the futility of the action. "Master," Diego pleaded, "that was not Jose but—"

"Ishar. I know, my son," Cain interjected.

"But why is he . . ."

Cain looked sadly at Diego. "Because I instructed him to do so," Cain explained.

"Why, master? You knew how dangerous, especially for him, it would be to get caught!" Diego shouted.

"I also saw where the path he chose would lead him," Cain explained.

Mulsine came flying out of the villa. "Mon Dieu, what was that scream?"

"Ishar has been seized by Satan, and Cain will not let me go!" Diego exclaimed angrily.

Mulsine looked over at Cain. "Master?" he asked.

Cain shook his head. "This is Ishar's moment. Let us respect the path he has chosen for himself."

Diego ceased struggling. Mulsine sat on the grass, shaking his head sadly for the little demon he had inexplicably become fond of. A mighty roar echoed in the mountains. Cain looked up suddenly. Focusing, he projected his thought. "Shao-sin, where are you?"

The giant cat did not reply as he bounded up the side of the mountain. Cain relaxed his grip on Diego, focusing harder on Shao. "Shao, answer me!" demanded Cain.

The cat responded, "Doing what you taught me to do, master."

In that instant, Diego broke free and bolted to the cliffs. Mulsine looked at Cain for a split second before bolting after Diego. Cain sighed. *Children*, he thought critically before taking flight himself.

Atop the mountain, Ishar writhed under the torment afflicted by Satan.

"Did I not warn you that none escaped my wrath, puny one?" Satan declared. "Did you truly believe some damned blood-sucking younglings could save you from me?"

Through the pain, Ishar muttered, "I never believed they could save me, master of filth. Being saved was never my intention. To know true friendship, to be spoken to directly, without deceit or ulterior motives, this I sought and what I found with my prince Diego."

Satan inflicted greater pain. Ishar screamed. "Still think it's worth it?" Satan asked sarcastically.

Ishar sobbed, choking out, "Father, forgive me," before collapsing in Satan's grip.

At that moment, Shao bounded over the lip of the cliff, heading straight at Satan. Jose leaped between them, knocking Shao aside. Satan threw Ishar's lifeless carcass aside. "Have you come to play, kitty?" Satan mocked. "As you see, I have the noble Dark Lord Serrate as my protector," he said, presenting Jose.

"Have you lost your mind, Jose?" Shao growled. Cain is our master, and Diego is yours!" Shao exclaimed.

"The Dark Lord Serrate has no master, as he is infused with negative aspects," Satan said happily.

"You are insane to trust this piece of sh—"

Shao didn't get to complete his insult, as he was hit by hell fire shooting from Satan's hand. "Bad kitty," Satan admonished. Jose snatched the stunned cat and hurled him off the mountain. Satan laughed loudly.

Agrat walked over to Jose to embrace him. "Well done, my love," she stated as he embraced her.

"Not as well as one would hope," said Shao as he launched himself from Diego's arms. Diego had caught him midway through his plunge. "We must stop meeting like this," said Diego as he caught the cat.

Shao growled, "Very not funny. Now take me back up there."

"Yes, Shao, you are welcome, and I know you meant to squeeze a please somewhere in there," Diego muttered, just as anxious to get to the top and mete out some vengeance. Shao growled. "I'll thank you later.

Shao slammed into Jose/Serrate and Agrat with tremendous force, sending Serrate reeling and snapping a few of Agrat's bones. She screamed in pain. Satan conjured a few demons who engaged Cain and Mulsine as they breached the mountaintop.

Before anyone noticed, Diego hurled himself at Satan, knocking the God of darkness down with a mighty crash.

Mulsine and Cain quickly dispatched their enemies while Serrate snatched up Agrat and launched himself into the air at an incredible speed. Satan, seeing his disciple flee, disentangled himself from a pressing attack from Diego, whispering, "Soon, upstart, soon enough." He vanished in a noxious cloud of putrid vapors.

Upon Satan's disappearance, Diego's attention went immediately to Ishar. "Foolish demon!" shouted Diego as he threw himself beside a fatally wounded Ishar.

"The title of those without wisdom," quipped Ishar in bleak response.

"Ha, still think we're funny, don't we?" Diego asked teasingly, seeing the courage this small imp was displaying. He was torn with a realization that he cared a great deal for this brave and honorable demon.

"What is this we business? You, Diego, are not funny. Morose is more apt. Now me, on the other hand," Ishar coughed out, wincing in pain. Weakly, he said, "Diego, my good master, forgive me for my clumsiness, but I knew how you loved Jose . . . I only wanted to save your friend, mast." Ishar gasped out his last breath with a pool of blood.

Diego fought the dizziness that threatened to envelop him. He sat clutching the demon, rocking back and forth. Shao walked up beside Diego, purring and nuzzling Ishar's hand. Diego roared an ear-shattering scream for his two losses tonight. His friend Jose and his demon friend Ishar. His face was streaked with blood tears.

Cain stood beside Diego. "Come, my son. Let us give our friend a proper burial."

Mulsine, Shao, Cain, and Diego, carrying the limp form of Ishar, glided their way down the mountain to Mulsine's villa.

Diego laid Ishar by the tree where he first spotted the demon spying on him and remembered with vampiric clarity the bonding of two unlikely beings forming the unlikeliest of friendships.

"Master, why didn't Ishar burst into flames as most demons do when they meet their demise?" Diego asked curiously.

"I have been pondering that very notion, my son," Cain replied.

"But is that not unusual, master?" asked Mulsine.

"Most unusual, wise Mulsine. In fact, in my thousands of years as a Vampyre, I have never encountered or read lore that spoke of such a thing," confessed Cain. "You two stay here. I shall return to my library and research this mystery." Cain related. He did possess the most extensive collection of arcane literature in the world.

Shao sat up, staring at Cain. "Yes, my feline friend, you may accompany me if you wish."

Shao growled his pleasure. He walked up and licked Diego's hand. "My heart grieves your loss, brother."

Diego recognized how difficult it was for this giant killer of men to display such compassion. "Your consideration is most appreciated, my brother," Diego responded.

Shao growled and nipped at Mulsine. "Take care of the youngling, brother."

Evading his teeth, Mulsine responded, "Yeah, don't worry about me, mangy cat. I'll be just fine." Mulsine poked, seeking ground of normalcy.

They both stared for a moment before sharing a Bengal growl-laugh.

"Be well, brother," said Shao.

"You as well," responded Mulsine.

Cain shot into the air as Shao let out a mighty roar as he bounded into the night.

Diego let out a sigh. Mulsine spoke, "How are you feeling, Diego?"

"Very angry, Pierre. I can't believe that Jose not only joined Satan but allowed Ishar to be slain. He has much to answer for," Diego growled, sounding like Shao.

"So, what's the plan?" Mulsine asked.

"I plan on wreaking havoc on Satan's minions until Judgment Day. I will bring down his schemes wherever I find them. He will regret the day he made an enemy of me!" Diego declared fiercely.

Mulsine shook his head in pity for the ferocity about to be unleashed. "And what of the innocent caught in his web?" Mulsine asked.

"We shall honor Master Cain's law of protection and offer the guilty a chance to repent. Will you join me, Pierre?" Diego inquired. "Are you kidding, Diego? Try and stop me."

Diego smiled. "Thank you, brother. It is good that I am not alone in this."

"All I ask is that we have a plan of attack, and we seek Cain's blessing," Mulsine added.

CHAPTER 22

FRUITS OF BETRAYAL

Jose flew with Agrat in his arms. He was beside himself with the incredible power he felt flowing in his veins.

Agrat snuggled in his arms. "I feel your power, my prince. Indeed, Satan keeps his promise. I can now summon and cast powerful spells." The moon appeared to be winking at Jose, who pulsated with the negative aspect of creation flowing through him.

Jose, or Lord Serrate, as Satan now called him, tried to focus on his new powers, but the image of the poor little imp Ishar kept jumping in and out of his thoughts. Dawn was making its grand appearance. "I must find somewhere to rest," Serrate said. "Why, my prince?" asked Agrat sarcastically.

"Seriously, woman? Do you not see the rising of the sun?" he asked.

"Of course, dark prince, but the master gave you the power to withstand sunlight," Agrat informed him.

"But Cain told me . . ."

Agrat spoke to Serrate sharply. "Forget Cain. He is a fool and has no idea of the unbridled power of darkness," she intoned. "All the things Cain taught you are for a weaker class of Vampyre. You are no longer Vampyre as Diego, or the effete Frenchman Mulsine, or the ignorant Cain, but you, my love, are a dark prince. Your power far surpasses that of any of your former comrades. Did not the master promise us strength and power? Has he not delivered them to us? And has e not allowed us to set our kingdom as we see fit?"

"Si, mi amor. That and more," Serrate agreed. "Where shall we go, my prince?" Agrat inquired.

Serrate shifted to a more southerly direction. "Home. We go to our new kingdom of Cadiz, the former home of Diego Torrolisimo, and build our nation."

"Will not the Christian kings object?" Agrat teased.

"We can only hope, mi amor," Jose agreed, desiring the opportunity to revel in his newfound powers.

Upon seeing Castle Torro, Serrate soared to the village square. He landed forcefully, touching down like a loud thunderclap.

The villagers that were stirring for their morning work were shaken from their activities to see a dark figure step out of a hole and gently place a beautiful woman down. Being superstitious and suffering incredible hardship, the people were somewhat suspect until seeing Agrat in her beautiful majesty. She bowed to Serrate. The people, seeing this, slowly came out of their miserable shacks to see this majestic pair. They stood there, before Agrat and Serrate, until curiosity overcame their fear, and the villagers slowly presented themselves.

"How may we serve you, Lord?" asked an elderly villager fearfully.

"Who are you, ancient one?" Jose demanded more commanding than request.

"I am Pablo Sanchez de Torro, village elder, my lord."

"Excellent! You may address me as…."

"Jose?" interjected a shocked old man. "Joselito, we thought you were dead! Perished nobly fighting to protect Manuelito, the last Torrolisimo heir against the darkness that came to plague us."

Serrate bellowed, "I know not this Jose you speak of! I am Lord Serrate! And this is my consort, the Lady Agrat!"

Cowering at the ferocity in his voice, the villager retreated. "How may we be of service, my lord?" the elder asked.

"First, you may escort us to the castle atop the mountain."

"My lord," the elder said tentatively, "Castle Torro is abandoned since the massacre of the Torrolisimo family."

"And why should this concern me?" Serrate barked belligerently.

"It is the domain of the honored Rodrigo, duke of the Cadizean highlanders, my lord," the elder explained. "No longer!" exclaimed Serrate.

"The land and all its properties have fallen under the protection of Lord Serrate. The beautiful Agrat stepped forward. "The castle shall be built anew, and its people be known as Serratians," proclaimed Agrat; as she stepped forward, she invoked a spell of submissiveness. Turning, she bowed to Serrate. "My lord, the villagers are so informed," she proclaimed, exuding power.

Serrate smiled a sinister smile, turning his attention back upon the elder. "Do we understand one another, old man, or need I conquer for obedience?"

"Nay, lord. We are a weakened people and would beg your mercy," the old man said fearfully. "Very well then, You and the people shall always address us as milord and milady. Let none conceive of treachery. Obey without question every edict I set. Let none approach the manor or our persons without permission," Serrate ordered.

"But, my Lord, how shall the people?" Pablos' voice trembled.

"You say your name is Pablo?" Serrate interjected.

"Yes, Lord," the elder confirmed.

"Very well. You shall be my chamberlain and see to my need concerning the people. You have only to call out for me. But let me warn you, I have no tolerance for incompetence or frivolities. It would do you well to remember this."

The petrified elder, Pablo, bowed deeply before retreating.

"Well, my lord, is this what you've always desired?" Agrat teased.

"Si, mi amor. We will harness the resources here. It is rich with emeralds," answered Serrate.

"I doubt we'll have such concerns, my love," Agrat cooed.

"What do you mean, Agrat?" Serrate asked curiously.

"I have the power of enchantment. Did you not feel it go forth when I addressed the peasants?" Agrat asked, somewhat surprised.

What a gift if she could spell cast undetected, he mused. "I felt a surge emit from you, but I could not define its purpose," Serrate admitted.

"Be that as it may, I could easily enchant a few royals to pay us a substantial allowance," Agrat proposed.

"An allowance? An allowance for what?" asked a slightly baffled Serrate.

"How charmingly innocent, my prince. For allowing them to continue living, of course," Agrat said maliciously.

"Yes," Serrate agreed, somewhat stung by Agrat. "We could start with the church. They have started the penitential movement in Northern Italy and have come here to España with the Dominicans. That is a movement that would serve us well," he surmised. Agrat threw her hands up, relishing the moment. "And so shall it be," Serrate promised.

Cain and Shao arrived at Cain's villa. The moon was touching the western horizon as the sky grew paler with the approaching dawn. "How many trips have I taken you on, my friend?" asked Cain.

"Too many," answered Shao. Except for leaping, which in the great cat's case was tantamount to a short flight, he was strongly against the idea of cats flying, calling it unnatural. Cain was at odds with this notion, as Shao's present existence as a preternatural immortal feline was about as unnatural as it came. "Call me a purist," Shao would argue. "You know I could have run here." Shao pointed out, somewhat perturbed. Cain smiled. "Yes, brother, but I was in a hurry." Cain apologized, knowing how much Shao hated flying.

Upon landing, Shao excused himself to go hunting. Cain went to his library to check his scrolls to see if there may be some ancient prophecy that might hint at or further explain the odd sequence of events that have been taking place recently.

A day into his reading, Cain found what he believed to be relevant to his particular situation. He found a prophecy in the Book of the Dead written by the wise Egyptian Im-ho-tep. He also found a correlation clause. A passage from the *Book of the Dead*

THE DARK DAYS PROPHECY

"In the days when three points and the cat that guards them are assembled, a great wail shall issue forth from the mouths of the people as the firstborn shall take new brothers unto himself and they upon a steed that is not, shall bear them into combat and the firstborn shall be aided by the wretched, the beast and the twice cursed. They shall battle for the light, though they are bathed in darkness, and they shall make war against him.

Reading the book of Solomon, Cain found another prophecy of interest.

PROPHECY OF THE SEEKING

I Solomon, son of David king of Israel, set forth as so revealed to me by the Lord.

And a day shall come before the end of days when perdition shall set forth upon the earth to test the faith of men.

He shall set forth to further weaken man's link to He that is, was, and always shall be.

And the fallen one of the morning shall seek to raise a dark prince that fills his goblet with the blood of men.

Six shall be their number as the fallen leads the dark prince and the beguiler while planting his seeds of dissension. Deep shall the blood pour forth as the light pierces the darkness, and the shackles of the damned shall shatter as night seeks day.

Cain sat, reflecting on what he had read. Shao strolled into the parlor, where he sat himself down and began cleaning himself.

"Really, Shao, do you have to do that here?" Cain complained.

"You are simply jealous because I can lick myself places you wish you could lick yourself," Shao growled.

"How I wish that were true, then I could enjoy it as much as you appear to," Cain debated. "Yes, it feels good to do so," Shao admitted.

"You are perverse, my feline brother. Now, if you don't mind," Cain responded.

"What! Are you putting me out again!" Shao nearly shrieked.

"Wow!" Complained Cain, covering his ears. "First, that shriek. Please, let's not make a habit of emitting that cowardly wail again. It doesn't suit you. Secondly, I do have work I'm trying to get done, so would you kindly take your sack-licking, perverted kitty, who likes to scream like a frightened kitten and begone with you."

Shao left somewhat testily. "I think you're getting grumpy with age, old man," he quipped.

"At least, I'm not becoming gross and senile, old Cat!" Cain retorted.

"Why won't you share?" Shao whined. not wanting to leave.

"Can you read?" Cain asked.

"Can you lick your sack?" Shao retorted.

Cain considered that for a moment. "Point taken." He laughed. Cain then summarized what he had read.

"And?" Shao asked.

"And what?" Cain asked. "It is bad form to begin an inquiry with an and," he said snidely.

"Oh, my apologies. What is it that has the great and powerful old man so confounded?" Shao asked sarcastically.

"We have to work on your manners," Cain said provokingly.

Shao stared at him. "Are we done?" Shao asked.

Cain read the two prophecies to Shao. "Is that what's confusing you?" Shao teased.

"Oh, I suppose you have an answer," Cain mocked.

"I do," Shao answered condescendingly.

"Might you care to share your wisdom, mouse chaser?" Cain replied sarcastically.

"Fine, old man. First, the Egyptian tablets speak of our coven."

"What!" Cain said disbelievingly. "You think it is us."

"You're sure you're not coming down with an old man's infirmities?" Shao teased.

"What besides sarcasm makes you say that?" Cain asked, feigning hurt feelings.

"Well, I thought that easy enough when the book spoke of the three points guarded by the great cat . . ."

"And Diego, Pierre, and myself are the three points," Cain realized. "Do you then believe as I that Solomon spoke of Satan and Jose, or Serrate, as he now likes to call himself?" he asked.

"I do," agreed Shao. "However, to whom does he refer when he spoke of the beguiler?" he asked, admitting his confusion.

"Let us make haste then to Mulsine's villa. I have a very bad feeling about this," Cain suggested.

"Right now?" Shao asked wearily. "Master, you know how much I hate flying, and we just got here and . . ." Shao's argument lost momentum as he saw how Cain was staring at him.

"You may stay if you wish, but I must see to the safety of my disciples," Cain exclaimed adamantly.

Shao growled. "Fine! Let's go. I just think it unfair that I should be relegated to literal flights of fancy," complained Shao.

Snatching up the great cat, Cain shot into the air for Mulsine's villa. "I hate this crap!" Shao roared over the screaming wind.

"Close your mouth, or you'll catch bugs," Cain instructed.

Shao spat out a mouthful of bugs.

Church of Corruption

Diego walked into the library to find Mulsine hard at work. "What are you working on?" he asked.

"Well, I've been studying a movement by the church that has its roots in Italy. It was started several centuries back and has increased its power dramatically."

"And what has this to do with us?" asked Diego."

Mulsine looked up from his reading. "I believe Master Cain's mission is somehow tied to all this," he proclaimed.

"I still fail to see the connection," stated Diego.

Mulsine retreated from the potential argument as he had no further evidence to support his theory. "I just feel it is so Diego," he simply stated.

"Let it not be said that I am obtuse or rigid in my thinking," said Diego.

"Too late for that," interjected Mulsine sarcastically.

"Nevertheless," Diego said pointedly, "I suggest we be highly aware of anything—"

"Suspicious?" Mulsine again interjected.

"I was going to say out of the ordinary, but yes, *suspicious* as good a word," Diego ended his statement, feeling a bit obtuse. He looked at Mulsine. "What do you suggest, brother?"

Mulsine smiled. "First, brother, I feel we have ignored this movement called the Inquisition. It has spread from Italy to France and Spain. It has gained further influence in your beloved Spain as the *Inquisición Española*. Its current leader holds the office of inquisitor general, and his name is Tomás de Torquemada Francisco Jiménez de Cisneros," Pierre finished.

Diego was astonished. *How could such a thing have occurred without his taking notice?* He wondered.

Reading his expression, Mulsine answered gently, "Brother, you have lost much from Jose to Ishar. The betrayal of Jose and slaying of Ishar left you . . . less than observant," he finished.

Diego looked at Mulsine, hating the truth of his words. Sighing deeply, Diego said, "Forgive me, brother. You are right, but fear not for I am myself and will not allow my fury to replace common sense". Diego concluded. Mulsine smiled. "Welcome back."

CHAPTER 23

INVESTIGATION OF THE PERSECUTORS

Mulsine and Diego started investigating the accusations being hurled at the church. During one of their sorties, they ran into a monk who called himself Brother Raymond of the Agnostic sect of Cathers. Meeting the monk cloaked, and under cover of night, they asked about the rumors circulating about the Inquisition; Brother Raymond was quick to affirm the rumors. "The Pope has decreed that anything but the four Gospels is hearsay and subject to persecution." Raymond also informed them of a noble that was very powerful and aiding the church in identifying the subjects who were disobeying the decrees of the Holy Father.

"He dresses in all black with a beautiful consort by his side. The people are terrified of this noble, and they cater to the consort's every wish," Raymond related.

"Do you know their names?" Diego asked.

"I am sorry, Senor, but I did not stay long enough to find out. Members of our order started disappearing when this lord and his mistress came along. I heard it said that he has a grand castle in the Cadizean highlands."

Diego's interest piqued upon hearing this.

"Is there anything more you can tell us of these two?" asked Diego.

"Only, Senor, that you would do well to stay clear of them. The odor of death is about them. I fear they are agents of the horned one," Raymond concluded.

"What makes you say such a thing?" Diego inquired.

"Señor," the monk answered, "from the things I hear from the villagers, these two appear with great malice, and those that obey seem to exist with no sign of life in their eyes while those that rebel vanishes. And I do mean they vanish. Not taken prisoner, but seem to disappear entirely, as if whisked away from everything, as if they never existed," the monk finished, somewhat exasperated.

Mulsine looked at Diego. "Do you think . . . ?"

"It couldn't be anyone else," Diego finished.

Hearing the sound of rushing wind, Diego and Mulsine looked up to see Cain holding a struggling Shao, dropping down to where they stood.

A few feet from the ground, Shao squirmed loose. "Let me go!" Shao-sin growled. Spitting bugs from his mouth, he roared, "Did you really feel the need to fly so fast!"

"When we're in the air, all you do is complain about flying. When I speed up to quicken the flight, you complain about that," Cain countered.

"I believe you purposely look for patches of bugs to fly through to stuff my face full of those nasty insects," Shao complained.

"If on occasion you could find the opportunity to shut the hell up as opposed to, I don't know, complaint unceasingly, you would find fewer bugs in your mouth," Cain argued.

"I still think you do it purposely," Shao growled. Walking to a nearby shade tree, Shao collapsed to sulk.

Cain walked over to his two disciples, who greeted him. "My, he is ornery, isn't he?" Mulsine observed.

"Master," Diego said, "you don't purposely . . ." Cain held up his hand for silence and looked down at the monk who was kneeling and praying. "Monk," Cain called. "His name is Raymond," Pierre informed Cain. "Raymond." Cain uttered the name softly. Against his will, the monk raised his eyes to look at Cain. "You will awaken in a few moments feeling refreshed from your evening walk. Of what you have seen, you will remember nothing, do you understand"? Cain softly commanded. Raymond nodded in obedience. Cain signaled for his coven to follow him. They flew back to Mulsine's villa. Shao followed, refusing to fly again. "Do you think the suggestion worked, master"? Pierre inquired. The trio arrived before Cain responded to Pierre.

"Of course I do," Cain quibbled. "Regarding Shao and flying, I love giving him a hard time," he said teasingly.

From his spot under the tree where he had sprawled, Shao growled, "I heard that!"

The disciples, along with Cain, laughed at the outburst.

"When you are done sulking, we will be inside deciding what to do," Cain addressed Shao, laughing.

"I'll tell you what, you could go do," Shao managed to grumble.

Inside Mulsine's library, Cain, Diego, and Mulsine swapped information. Diego and Mulsine were likewise amazed at the revelation Cain shared from his research. They were hearing what Mulsine and Diego discovered Cain reflected.

"It would seem that Satan is using Serrate and his consort to manage the Inquisition and reap dissension amongst the faithful for his ends," Cain acknowledged, admiring the devious fashion of Satan's ploy.

"What are we going to do about it?" Diego asked.

"I think we'll find out how powerful we are as we fight the master of evil," Cain said ominously.

"But, master, does not the good book say that it will be the Christ that shall lay him low?" asked Mulsine.

Cain confirmed that was indeed the case.

"Are you then intending to rewrite the word?" Mulsine asked, mortified.

Cain smiled at him and an anxious Diego. "Of course not, my son. I am counting on the literacy of the prophecy," Cain answered.

"I'm sorry, master, but I am confused," Mulsine admitted.

Realization struck Diego. "You mean to say while he bites at your heel, you will step on his head!" Diego exclaimed.

Cain smiled. "Precisely," he agreed.

"But, master, how do Diego and I fit into this?" Mulsine asked.

Cain looked over at him. "Read Revelations."

"I have, master. I do not recall...."

Cain interjected, "'And behold, two shall come as witnesses to the coming of our Lord.'" Read the rest if you want to know it in its entirety," Cain finished.

Just then, Shao stirred. Stretching and briefly cleaning himself, he looked up.

"Well, who do we kill first?" asked a hungry Shao.

"Were you listening the whole time?" Mulsine asked.

"How could I not!" exclaimed Shao. "The three of you going on like an unfed litter. And you, Pierre, I would watch my pitch if I were you when confused or upset."

Mulsine looked hard at the cat. "Meaning what?" he asked.

"Well, since you asked, I mean to say your voice takes on, shall we say, effeminate qualities when upset."

Diego burst out laughing while Mulsine fumed. "I don't know what you're laughing about, Diego! You wait for the clues to be revealed, then say aha as if struck with an epiphany when it was naught but common sense." Shao accused.

Diego abruptly stopped laughing. At that same moment, Mulsine burst into laughter. After a brief moment, he joined Diego in silence. Exchanging evil glances thrown back and forth, Mulsine said, "Look, Diego, the old kitty thinks he is funny."

Diego stared at Shao. "Is that right, gato? You think you're funny?" Diego nearly hissed.

Shao stood where he was. "Okay, this isn't funny anymore. I apologize if I hurt your feelings." The last word brought Shao into a fit of uncontrollable laughter. Rolling and laughing, Shao taunted the disciples. "Have You heard, Master Cain? I hurt their feelings," he roared. Shao, unfamiliar with the joy that derives from honest laughter, was unable to stop. He kept nodding to Diego and Mulsine. "Ssssory, miss."

Before he realized it, Shao was snatched up and thrown into a nearby pond. While in mid-flight, plunging to the pond, Shao shouted, "You guys suck" he almost finished as he hit the water and scrambled to get out. Shao let out a roar of frustration, zeroed in on Mulsine, and shot at him like lightning.

Not to be outdone, Mulsine noticed Shao's intent and bolted away. After a dozen or so steps, Shao altered his direction radically and charged at a still laughing Diego, who immediately stopped laughing and also took to running, though admittedly slower, as he had difficulty running and laughing at the same time. Shao brought Diego down with a bone-crunching tackle.

Still laughing, Diego teased Shao. "Did the kitty not enjoy his much-needed bath?" he prodded.

Shao loosened his grip on Diego to roar. Diego took advantage of the momentary release and got from under the great cat to begin running.

"C'mon, kitty," Diego teased.

Shao tore up the earth, charging at Diego. Turning to run, Diego took one step before spinning back around to grasp Shao, who had leaped at him by the throat. "So predictable," Diego teased.

Not liking being outclassed, Shao struggled against Diego's grip. Mulsine hit Diego with a flying tackle of his own, knocking Diego down, giving Shao a chance to get free and start biting at Diego, whose nearly invulnerable skin made it feel like pinches. It made Diego laugh again.

Almost as if on cue, the disciples stopped and looked up at their master. Cain looked at them calmly. "Are you children done?" he said, fathoming the playful spirit of his disciples.

The three charged at Cain, piling on top of him. Diego grabbed him around the waist while Pierre went for the flying headlock, and Shao went for his ankles. Cain tumbled down and did something he hadn't done in millennia. He laughed. Deeply and with a sound that could be mistaken for genuine happiness. All of his disciples sat stunned. Shao, his eldest. Mulsine and Pierre were shocked to hear mirth escape the truest of immortal's laughter. This was a laugh that knew the joy of speaking to the Almighty.

The three sat back in awe. Cain composed himself. "Okay, ladies, are we done?" he snickered.

"Master." The three bowed.

Cain found himself forever grateful for taking joy from such simple play."

EVIL IN THE HOUSE OF GOD

The tolling of the bells summoned the faithful to Church. The villagers walked under gloomy skies to a once beautiful but now battered building. Peeling paintings and holes riddled the peoples' place of worship.

The church was quiet as parishioners gave their confession. Father Antonio de Ponce sat listening to the droning of a villager when he heard a gasp come from the confessional booth.

"Louis, what is wrong?" Father Antonio asked.

After a moment of silence, a deep, ominous voice responded, "Forgive me, Father, for I have sinned." The priest sat in stunned silence.

"Are you not going to ask of my sins, Father?" the voice teased.

"Serrate!" exclaimed Father Antonio.

"That is Lord Serrate to you, fool. Or have you grown unsatisfied with life, priest?"

"No, my lord. Forgive me," the priest acknowledged.

"Very well. Because my mood is pleasant, I will permit the momentary lapse in respect to be overlooked," Serrate said magnanimously.

"It is kind of you, Lord," the priest acknowledged.

"Of course it is! Have I not given you power through information most valuable for trade and such?"

"Yes, Lord, you have." agreed the terrified priest who wondered whether this was a form of divine retribution for the actions of the church. "Sooo. What have you done for me, my dear padre?" hissed the traitorous dark lord.

"My lord, I have tried to coerce the arch-deacon to join us, but he appears adamant in his principles."

"Really?" asked Serrate. "Let us see how rigid he is when speaking to one of power and beauty."

"My lord?" inquired the priest.

"Never mind. I have a new quest for you."

"What would you have me do, my lord?" asked the frightened priest.

"The ancient festival of witches is approaching. On the thirteenth day of next month, I wish to have a grand festival for my mistress,"

"My lord?" said Father Antonio, not sure if he had heard correctly.

"Yes, I want thirteen virgins for milady to convert or sacrifice, and I wish for myself a male sacrifice to become my disciple."

"But, my lord," Father Antonio stressed, "the Crown shall catch wind of this and…"

"And what, priest!" exclaimed Serrate. Father Antonio stammered. "Silence, fool!" Serrate commanded. "Do you not think if milady and I were any less generous, the entire kingdom would be under our thrall?"

"It is as you say, master," the priest agreed.

Calming himself, Serrate aggressively suggested, "Go now and do this little thing I ask, and perhaps if the good archdeacon decides not to join us, perhaps there will be a new position to fill," he implied.

"Thank you, Lord." Father Antonio grinned, bowing as Serrate departed.

From the shadows stepped Agrat. "What now, my love?" she asked Serrate.

"Now, my lady, you shall pay a visit to this archdeacon and show him the errors of his ways," Serrate ordered.

"As you will, Lord." Agrat stepped into his embrace, placing a gentle kiss on his cheek. Pulling back, she whispered,

"It is as the Lord Satan promised, my love, is it not?"

"It soon shall be, milady. Go now so that our desires may bear fruit."

Agrat bowed and left the church. Serrate walked to the altar and stared at the crucifix. "I believed in you once, but you never listened to my prayers. I was an outcast to you. Now, with the power given me shall I lay waste your beloved church! The people shall see true power! In me, they shall see the reality of things and not some fairy tales told the children to frighten them to your cause! Dark shall be the days before your approach, and I shall blow out the light so that the world is so blackened that your coming shall be reviled!"

"These are bold words of arrogance, Jose de Torrolisimo. Your master's head shall be stepped upon by the firstborn. The bride shall be tossed into the fire by the wise one, and you, dear Jose, shall be ripped asunder by the witness!"

Serrate spun about, trying to locate the source of the disembodied voice. It sounded like it but could not possibly be.

"Ishar!" he shouted in the empty church. Serrate spun around to look at the crucifix again. "Resorting to cheap illusions"? Serrate shouted at the crucifix; he spun, heading back to his castle.

CHAPTER 24
FALLEN PRIEST

Agrat approached the archdeacon's manor. The sky threatened with ominous clouds preparing to unleash its fury. She glided up the steps of the manor. The door opened as she reached the top of the stairs.

A servant greeted her. Bowing, he said, "Lady, his Holiness Archdeacon Morales is expecting you."

Agrat entered, saying, "Tell His Excellency I await him in his rectory."

The servant bowed, running to do as ordered, as he sensed the malice emanating from the strange woman.

After a brief wait, Agrat was joined by the archdeacon. "Milady," he greeted. "How may we be of service to you this evening?"

Agrat gazed at him with a penetrating stare. "We know you, deacon!"

Morales tried to cover his shock at her abruptness. "Whatever do you mean, lady?"

"Agrat! I am the Lady Agrat. Consort of Lord Serrate."

"Of course, of course, milady. How may we be of assistance?" Morales asked, silently questioning his safety, unable to say why he felt a very real threat emanating from this strange woman.

"I will ask why you have not as yet gone to pay homage to the new lord of the region, your Excellency?" Agrat asked with a silky quality to her voice that it sounded both extremely smooth yet incredibly dangerous.

"Forgive me, milady, but I've been quite busy—"

"Yes, yes, we know how busy you've been, especially with those lovely sweet boys that sing so well that you feel you must partake in their . . shall we call them gifts?"

The archdeacon of Leon was shaken to his core hearing his darkest of secrets brought to light in such a flippant manner. "How dare you speak to me in such a sacrilegious manner!" blurted out the deacon. "You dare enter the house of the Lord spouting such heresy."

Agrat tore down the partition that separated Priest from the sinner stared at him with a mesmerizing gaze. "I do because you not only permit it but practice it as well." "How dare you!" Morales shrieked.

Agrat looked deeper into his eyes. "Hypocrite, I dare that and much more. Now you will bow to Lord Serrate publicly. You will recognize his rule as legitimate, or it shall become public knowledge that you prefer the company of young boys." Agrat threatened. The archdeacon tried to muster a sense of pride. "The people will not believe you, so why should I concern myself with empty threats?" he asked, half-afraid.

Agrat smiled an evil smile. "Well then, Father, permit me to introduce your lord to you," Agrat responded, pointing her finger.

The priest's eyes followed her gesture. There emerging from the shadow, stood Serrate with stern continence. "By what arrogance, priest, do you summon me here?" Serrate asked angrily.

The archdeacon of Cordoba and Leon, cousin to the Grand Inquisitor himself—though only cousins four times removed, a fact he intentionally omitted in his attempt to ascend the hierarchy—soiled himself. Never had he seen such malice. He felt as if he were confronting the specter of death, which he was.

"Ahhh, look, our little boy did a boo-boo on himself," crooned Agrat.

The humiliated priest found his voice. "Lord . . . I did not summon you," Morales gasped.

"I'm sorry, did you just contradict me?" Serrate nearly growled.

Morales's eyes widened in fear. "No, lord. Please forgive me," the priest begged.

Serrate bared his fangs. "Listen, fool; if you do not obey as the lady instructed, then I shall turn all your little playthings into vampirelings with but one rule. In all the torture and malice they extend to you as they seek their childlike revenge, they must kill you before becoming one like us, immortal."

The archdeacon was a fly caught in a web of his own making. Agrat and Serrate departed, leaving a disturbed archdeacon sobbing. He could not call to God as he forsook him as power perverted and consumed his soul. "I am damned!" Morales cried out. "Yes, you have condemned yourself, priest."

The deacon spun around. He had thought he was alone.

"But you are alone," came the response to the unspoken thought.

Am I going mad? Wondered Morales.

"No," said the disembodied voice. "It shall not be that simple for you. You have chosen a more treacherous path."

"Who are you?" the priest screamed to no one. Archdeacon Morales, who had scrambled up the ladder of Ecumenical authority through whatever means necessary, including but not limited to bearing false witness, sank to his knees and began crying.

Preparations

Agrat entered what used to serve as the old Torrolisimo reception chamber, which was now turned into a throne room, where Serrate sat awaiting his lady's return.

"I like what you've done with the place."

Serrate looked up to see Satan walking through the entryway. "Lord Satan. I wish I would have known you would be coming, milord. I could have prepared."

Satan held up his hand, signaling that all was well. "I must say, Lord Serrate, that you and your consort have done well. You've cowered the indigents and have nearly usurped that damnable Inquisition. Commendable. Quite commendable," Satan said in a rare compliment. "I must say that you have come further than I thought you would."

Serrate bowed. "I am content that you are pleased, lord, but I admit to having difficulty with the Grand Inquisitor himself," he reported.

Satan leered. "Yes, him. He is not evil in the ways you've exploited others. However, leave him to me. His vanity shall be his undoing."

Serrate snickered with delight. "Excellent, lord. Then they will be ours, and their kingdoms shall crumble before your might."

"Not so quickly, my dark prince. First, we must deal with the immortal, his disciple, your former master, and his snobbish Frenchman," Satan reminded him.

Rally Point

Mulsine stepped into the cool evening, joining Shao, Diego, and Cain, who were already gathered.

"I thought you might sleep this one out, Shao," Pierre said snidely.

"Not a chance. I owe the horned one," Shao growled.

"We know what he did to Cain, but why are you so angry with him, Shao?" asked Mulsine.

Shao growled, "When I was still young to our ways, Satan tried to persuade me that I was evil and naturally belonged to him."

"And what did you say?" Diego asked.

Shao bore his fangs in a way that their small coven recognized as an attempt to smile. "I remembered what the master told me," he proclaimed.

After a moment of silence, Mulsine asked, "Do you care to share?"

"The master explained that nature is not inherently evil as opposed to necessary. That evil came from the conscious application of committing an act of selfishness when none is required." "Such as?" asked Diego.

"Such as killing when one did not hunger. This is an unnecessary act based on selfishness."

"What did Satan say to that?" asked Diego.

"He called me a foolish beast."

"Tell them what you did, Shao," Cain added.

"Well," Shao said, showing his toothy grin, "I showed him how much a beast I was." He fell into silence, envisioning the incident.

"And!" spat out an exasperated Mulsine.

"And what?" Shao teased.

"All right, Shao, stop teasing the lads and tell them already," Cain insisted.

"You take the fun out of everything, old man!" Shao complained.

"That may be so, but stop teasing the boys and tell them," Cain admonished.

Diego and Mulsine detested being called boys and lads, but how could they argue that fact when compared to a being over six thousand years old? They were, in fact, by the way, he measured time, young.

"Fine," growled Shao, pausing for a dramatic effect. "I . . . peed on his leg," he said triumphantly.

"You what?" roared Mulsine in laughter.

Diego was laughing so hard his sides began to ache. "That is priceless," Diego gasped.

"I thought so," Shao agreed, purring.

"Shao," Mulsine added, "I will never accuse you of having bad taste or no sense of humor again."

Shao beamed, looking pleased with himself.

The moon rose, giving off its silvery light. Cain gathered his disciples. "My children, you do realize that we go to battle whose outcome looks bleak. We go to battle against the master of evil and his cohorts. Remember, you have proven your inherent goodness by keeping to my edicts of doing no harm to the innocent. I cannot promise you redemption, but my faith, except for a small part of my life, has always been to the Lord. If you, my sons, maintain this faith, then I invite you as comrades in the hope it pleases God." Mulsine spoke first. "Master, where you go, so go I. To the very pits of hell if need be."

Cain looked at Diego, who nodded. "Master, as our brother has said, we do pledge undying loyalty," Diego looked over at Shao, who, in approval, released a deafening roar.

Cain smiled at his disciples. "I have chosen well with you three. Come. Diego, fetch your family sword so that your victory may have significance; as your villagers see the sword of the Torrolisimo clan return in glory, Diego's face lit as he dashed to his quarters to retrieve his sword.

CHAPTER 25

CASTLE TORROLISIMO– THE GATHERING

Agrat stood atop the tower of Castle Torrolisimo, overlooking the moon-draped landscape. Serrate approached her from behind. "What is it, milady?" he asked.

Agrat turned to face him. "The priest has brought forth the women I requested," she replied.

"Excellent!" responded Serrate.

Agrat reached up and touched Serrate's hair. "I have come for your permission to take my students to a nearby cave I've prepared to begin their training," Agrat said. "Go then, milady, and train me a fine brood of witches," Serrate answered in dismissal.

Agrat bowed, taking her leave. She summoned her new trainees and departed the castle.

The servant Pablo entered the balcony where his master stood. "Master, the Lord Natas is here," Pablo announced.

"Natas? I don't know." Serrate paused. "Show him to the reception room. Tell him I shall join him momentarily," Serrate ordered.

"As you command, master," Pablo said, bowing and exiting the balcony.

"He's turning into a fine servant. Perhaps I should make him my majordomo," pondered Serrate, who then chuckled thinking of Lord Natas.

Entering the reception room, Serrate greeted Natas, "My lord, greetings. I am impressed by the simple anadrome exemplified by your name."

"Yes, yes. I find it fascinating how men accept things at face value." Natas quipped.

"Yes, Lord, but why Natas?" Serrate asked.

"It was complex enough for your servants, but I knew you would consider. Shall we call it my backward nature? Besides, I did not wish to frighten your servants," Natas explained.

Serrate nodded understanding. "I'd imagine you might receive a bit of trepidation announcing yourself as Lord Satan."

"True," Satan responded. "Now tell me," he continued, "how are things proceeding?"

"Well, my lord, Agrat has taken her new novices to her cave to begin their studies, and the priest shall be bringing me my new disciples in time for the festival of the hollows," reported Serrate.

"Excellent!" exclaimed Satan. "And the Inquisitions?" he asked.

"They move forward, lord," Serrate answered.

"Very well," Satan responded. "I shall go forth and fetch an item or two we shall require for the feast." With a triumphant laugh and a cloud of sulfurous smoke, Satan vanished.

Serrate smiled in glee. "All goes accordingly. My witch shall have her brood, I shall soon control the empire, and the master shall soon drive the world to its knees to an uncaring God and be lost forever," Serrate quietly snickered.

"You are wrong, old friend."

Serrate whirled at the sound of the voice. "Who's there?" he shouted.

"From greed was born betrayal, and from the betrayal was born your downfall," said the disembodied voice.

"Show yourself, coward! Face me if you dare!" challenged Serrate.

"Poor Jose, scared little vampire. Only now has your fear been justified," said the voice.

"Are you spirit? Demon? Angel or damned soul wandering the earth? Cursed, unable to find peace!" screamed Serrate.

"How sad that you do not realize that you are the one cursed. By your own words and by your own deeds have you brought everlasting damnation upon yourself. Poor Jose," said the voice, fading away.

Serrate would have thought he was going insane, except that the comings and goings of this entity were practicably palatable. Tasting fear for the first time since becoming immortal, Serrate screamed for his servants to attend to him.

Pablo rushed in, dropping to his knees in front of Serrate. "Master, how may I serve you?"

Serrate looked at his servant with a ferocity that made the aging servant flinch. "A few days now until the feast of hollows, old man."

"Yes, master," a frightened Pablo agreed.

Serrate glared with murder in his eyes. "Know you well, old man, that all needs to be perfect in every way! Succeed, and you shall be well rewarded. Fail me, and there awaits you a punishment worse than death. Do you understand me?" threatened Serrate.

"Yes, master." Pablo trembled. "I have done as instructed. The initiates await their trails, and the latest word from the Lady Agrat is that her students, one in particular, learns quickly and already is becoming more powerful than her sisters," Pablo reported.

"Really?" asked Serrate. "And what is the name of the stellar student?"

"Her name is Anna, lord. It is whispered she is of the Torrolisimo bloodline," Pablo said, quietly fearing the reaction of Serrate.

"What?" roared the vampire. "That is impossible! That line was extinguished when Manuel, the last living heir, was slain in this very courtyard by the master himself".

"This is true, master; however, he had a cousin, removed a few times but still of the line." Pablo waited for the reaction this piece of news would make illicit, as Serrate was known for his brutality.

"This is perfect!" Serrate beamed. "If the accursed Diego wishes to make an uninvited appearance, then we shall present his witch cousin to him as a hostage ad demand his servitude," Serrate said with pleasure. "Begone now and see that all is prepared, for the night comes upon us." Pablo bowed out of the evil presence.

THE CAVE

In the great cave under the mountain of Castle Torrolisimo, Agrat drilled her witches in the dark arts.

"Lady Agrat," said one of her initiates, "a rider approaches." Agrat looked up to see a rider approaching the entrance of the cave. "Who is it?" demanded Agrat.

"It is one of the lord's men, begging audience."

"See him in," Agrat ordered.

The messenger approached the witch with great trepidation. "Milady," he said, bowing. "the Lord Serrate wishes to know if your sisterhood is prepared for the ceremony?"

Agrat enjoyed watching the man tremble in fear. "Tell me, do I frighten you?" she asked. The messenger thought quickly. "How does one not fear such magnificence, milady?" Agrat smiled a beguiling smile. "Well said. Now tell us your name," Agrat cooed.

"My name is Rueben, my lady," answered the fearful servant.

"Very well, Rueben. I am taken by your courtly manners. Thank my lord for sending one such as you." Rueben stayed kneeling, head bowed. "Request of him from me that you be set as my personal envoy. Does this not please you?" Agrat asked menacingly.

"Well beyond my worth, milady," Rueben quickly answered.

"Just so," agreed Agrat. "Go now and tell our Lord that all will be ready, then make haste in your return to me," she commanded.

Rueben quickly mounted his horse and rode off.

"Gather to me, sisters, for tonight we prepare for our return to our castle for the great feast of the hollow."

The witches shared a look of anticipation; as most were chosen from the teachings of Agrat, they would return with power.

Celebration of Witches

The event was in full motion as Pablo ran to and fro, making sure all was ready for Lord Serrate's celebration.

While the peasants were unsure of what they prepared, they were made aware that extremely powerful lords were taking part in this celebration. There were rumors that even the arch-deacon would sanctify the ceremony.

At the chiming of the great clock, the procession would begin with the newly developed sisterhood of the hollows, followed by the nobles. Then Serrate would ascend his throne to greet his visiting dignitaries. It was even whispered that the king might attend.

Only during the grand days of old Duke Rodrigo had Torrolisimo had the honor of hosting the king. For the simple peasants of Torrolisimo, it was as if the days of prestige were returning, if not for the constant threat of the new nobility formed by Serrate and Agrat.

As the village clock struck midnight, a great braying of horns announced the beginnings of the proceedings with fanfare. The sisterhood looked resplendent in their scarlet robes, led by Agrat in a red robe trimmed in gold. The sisterhood indeed appeared powerful, with an aura of mystery shrouding them. The nobles in their gear of war, fine armor, and shining swords were followed by dour priests in black robes. They were led by the archdeacon holding a crucifix while a friar swung a censer, filling the air with the pungency of incense.

After the dignitaries filed in, there was a moment of silence that was broken by the horns blasting out a triumphant chord and filling the air with impressive authority as a gold-clad individual stepped from a horse-drawn chariot trimmed in more gold than most in attendance had ever seen in their lives. When the men exited the carriage, Serrate stood from his seated position as Lady Agrat joined him in front of the throne.

The peasants kneeled as Lord "Natas" walked with an air of grandiosity toward the throne.

"My Lord Natas, the city of Torrolisimo, welcomes you and prays our reception is pleasing," Serrate said, bowing.

Natas lifted his hand in acquiescence. "A lovely reception indeed, my Lord Serrate. I am looking forward to the festivities," he said eagerly.

"May I present the Lady Agrat, mother superior to the sisterhood of the hollow," Serrate said by way of introduction.

"My lord." Agrat bowed. "We are most fortunate to be graced by your presence, as my lord and master have spoken of you in the highest regard."

"It is well of him to do so, lady. I have heard a great deal of the Lord Serrate and how he came to lead your people." Natas smiled.

"Shall we begin then, milord?" Serrate asked.

"By all means, let it be so." Natas agreed. They were being led to the grand hall, followed by their retinue and celebrants.

Evil Confronted

Cain flew alongside Diego and Mulsine. Keeping pace not far below was Shao, who had rather adamantly refused to be carried across the French countryside. He complained with a vicious growl that he was not a kitten to be carried. Cain knew that although a killer beyond measure, Shao didn't really hate anything, well, except, of course, Satan, but the recent sojourns have added flying to the shortlist.

"Will he not tire, master?" asked Diego, catching and spitting out the occasional bug unfortunate enough to be caught in his flight path. *A bizarre trait shared between Diego and Pierre, talking while flying, perhaps it is a trait of Crusaders to do the ill-advised. Mused* Cain. Smiling, he projected telepathically. *"Diego, are you hungry?"*
Mulsine fought the impulse to laugh aloud.
"Quite humorous, jesters, are we now?" Diego projected to Cain.

Cain smiled. "Shao will not tire, my son," he projected.
"Once, he chased me from the province of Cambay in India, across the Himalayas, all the way to Baghdad," Mulsine projected.
"What the hell did you do to him?" projected Diego.
"Well, I don't recall exactly," Mulsine thought, evading the answer.

"As I recall," Cain interrupted, *"you two were out in one of your, what did you like to call them, ah yes, exploratory expeditions when Shao began courting a young tiger and Pierre interrupted the courtship by descending on nearby prey, which frightened the poor young tigress to no end. So she bolted in a desperate attempt to escape the savage and strange creature that flew like the eagle, as vicious as a lion, yet walked like a man. She leaped a ravine she had no hope of making. She plunged to her death, and Shao became so angry with Pierre that he chased him across the continents,"* Cain finished.

Diego looked over at Mulsine with a disapproving glare. "What!" he exclaimed.

"I didn't see him. I saw a prey and attacked! It wasn't my fault!" Mulsine argued.

"Have you finally convinced yourself of that?" asked Diego, forgetting his present situation, catching more bugs for his neglect.

"Listen," Mulsine projected, *"I apologized to Shao a thousand times over."*

"We're entering the province of Torrolisimo," Cain interrupted. *"Let us descend to that tree-filled hillside there,"* he instructed, pointing at the spot.

"Shao," Cain projected, *"to the hillside, brother."*

"Yes, master." Shao projected in response, altering his course for the hill.

Upon landing, Diego looked in the distance at his ancestral home. "It is about ten miles from us," observed Mulsine.

"It would appear we've arrived just in time for the feast," Cain noted as Shao crested the hilltop.

"Excellent! I'm famished and would love to suck on some demon marrow," purred Shao in response.

"You do realize just how terrifying that sounds when you purr like that, don't you?" Mulsine asked Shao, who responded with a toothy grin. "Creepy," Mulsine said, shaking his head.

"All right, children, we shall await the dismissal of the peasants and nobles before we make our entrance. Until then, be on your guard, for much evil is afoot tonight," Cain warned.

The ceremony lasted late into the night. With a signal from Natas, Serrate motioned for Pablo to start seeing people out.

"Honored nobles, the Lord Serrate thanks you for attending the graduating ceremonies of the sisterhood. He looks forward to your continued support and prays that you are pleased with the security he provides. He wishes you all a pleasant night and begs to be excused while he and our dignitaries attend to the matters of state. Thank you." Pablo intoned while escorting them to the tall doors. With the slow dispersal of the dignitaries, the villagers and servants streamed out of the entryway, gossiping among themselves.

"Did you see the great lord clad in gold?" quipped one villager. "That was enough gold to feed us for generations." He complained jealously.

"He was impressive," said another. "But the sisterhood was amazing. All that power! Can you imagine?"

"I'm going to find what one needs to qualify for such training," said another villager. "In case you didn't notice, they were all women," teased a neighbor. "Enrique do you want to dress like a senorita"?! he teased.

"Are you stupid?" Enrique snapped. "Not for me, for my daughter. Idiot."

And so the conversation drifted back and forth as the guests exited the castle, with Pablo eavesdropping so he could report the response of the people regarding the party.

Upon the closing of the great gates, as the last guest exited, Serrate ordered Pablo to bring forth the initiates. Side doors opened, and several young initiates walked into the great hall. Serrate then dismissed Pablo with strict instructions. "See that we are not disturbed, do you understand." He demanded with an evil glare. Pablo nodded his understanding in mute terror. Turning to Natas, Serrate spoke softly. "My Lord, the castle is clear if you wish to dispel of your guise." The gold-clad Natas nodded and resumed his normal form.

"I thought you would have had more than these few who would wish for immortality Lord Serrate," observed Satan.

"I did, my lord, but our training was vigorous, and many could not achieve the goals I set forth," answered Serrate. "Pity that," Satan added sarcastically.

"Not at all, my lord. There was significant corruption acquired to assure their damnation and subsequent enslavement to your cause," Serrate reported proudly.

"Well done, Lord Serrate." Satan responded.

"My lord," uttered Agrat, who had stood with her sisterhood, awaiting to speak, "my lord, what would you have of us?" she inquired.

Satan signaled to Serrate. The dark prince took his cue from Satan. "First, Lady Agrat," Serrate began, "in accordance with our lord's will, your sisterhood shall be henceforth known as the 'Order of Endor.'

Your title shall be 'Mother Most Reviled,' and you shall assign a first disciple as your personal attache. You shall focus your study on mesmerization, conjuration, possession, and illusion. You shall retire your coven to the ancient sands of mankind's ascendancy and incite the people there through your witchery. Our Lord Satan shall lend us the power to nourish the greed that will redevelop in a faraway land in a future era.

"You shall prepare your disciple to assist you in fulfilling your role in a new yet ancient land. In this land shall the unholy make himself known and be a self-proclaimed god! And we, his servants, shall have dominion over his slaves. As commanded, you shall set forth immediately. This is his bidding," proclaimed Serrate.

The Mother Most Reviled bowed, accepting the charge. Gliding to the remaining initiates, Serrate began, "You among your brothers have shown the required perseverance, dedication, and spirit for the next step from initiate to disciple. Do you so agree, and do you wish to do so of your own free will?" inquired Serrate.

The disciples nodded their heads in unison as they had practiced. "We do, master."

"Pledge you. Heart, mind, and soul to us, those that would grant you immortality, that all of our commands are to be obeyed without question and in full commitment to obeying your lords' decree"? Demanded Serrate.

"We do so pledge, master," the initiates responded.

Serrate looked at Satan, who stood at the throne and nodded his head. With a flash, Serrate grabbed the first initiate, sank his fangs into his neck, and drank deeply.

The exchange of blood occurred a few more times as Serrate drank from each initiate while a revealed Satan stood at the throne. He chanted while reddish mists gathered at the foot of the throne. "Mortis sangre viva Diablos et victor." The initiates, now turned disciples, heard the echoing chants of demonic hordes in the shadows. "Blood of the dead in the devil rise victorious."

The new initiates drank deeply of sacrificed peasants' blood. Those of no consequence, as these peasants were kidnapped from nearby provinces to avoid suspicion and thereby go unnoticed by the local populace.

"Let the newly formed minions; the turn of the new disciples be as soldiers to the disciple, who in turn shall act as captains to the dark prince Serrate, who rules in my absence. In my name. So be it," proclaimed Satan.

The witches filed out of the room to prepare for their transport. Satan sat with a smile on his face on the gilded throne. Serrate kneeled at its foot. "What would you have of me, milord?" he asked.

Petting Cerebus, the three-headed dog of the pit, Satan answered, "I have a concern, Lord Serrate, that I believe you should take care of for me."

"How, Lord, may I serve thee?" Serrate inquired.

"I think it is time you confronted your former master and removed the last obstacle to our full power. I have empowered you to slay Cain and finally destroy the damnable line of Adam," Satan proclaimed.

"And what of Diego and the Frenchman, milord?" Serrate asked.

Satan smiled. "You have your disciples to aid you," he answered.

"I will keep Cain preoccupied while you handle his bastard disciples. Once finished with them, you shall end Cain."

"And the great cat Shao-sin?" asked Serrate.

Satan smiled, petting the hell hound. "This is why Cerebus is among us. He's been begging for an opportunity to kill him for nearly a millennium."

"Kill cat. Kill, rip, shred," growled the hollow-voiced dog. Serrate had to repress a shiver as he heard the moans of the damned in the beast's growl. "I lead my pack," he growled. "We tear cat," he nearly howled.

At the hillside, where Cain and his disciples scouted, they took notice of the celebrants departing the castle.

"I think perhaps I'll pay that corrupt archdeacon a quick visit," Diego said quietly.

"Let Shao go instead," ordered Cain. "We need you to breach the castle," he added.

"Hell dog in the castle," Shao pointed out.

"How do you know?" asked Mulsine.

"Can smell foul dog," growled Shao. "Smell hate, death, foul," he coughed out.

"That may be so, Shao, but we need you to stop that caravan before the deacon gets back to his diocese to legitimize Serrate's claim getting the pope and the church inextricably involved."

Shao snorted but bolted after the caravan.

"Okay, let's go." Cain and his disciples ascended the mountain to face the master of evil and his fallen followers.

The moon hung low as the festivities lasted late into the night; a chilly breeze blew.

The horsemen leading the caravan of dignitaries from both church and castle had their horses walk together for safety precautions. In the lead carriage, the archdeacon and his priests discussed the events of the evening.

"Father," said one of the priests, worry in his voice, "this is a very dangerous game we are playing."

"You think so, Father? Tell me, do you have the fortitude to withstand these powerful dark lords?" the archdeacon asked sarcastically. "If so, why didn't you voice your objections at the gathering?" The complaining priest fell silent. "That is exactly as I thought," finished the archdeacon.

Suddenly, without warning, the horses whinnied in protest, thrashing violently then falling silent. A moment followed with the slaughtering of all the horses in the caravan. The priests inside their carriages crossed themselves vehemently, praying for assistance. A deep, ferocious growl issued forth from the shadows. "Praying will be of no avail to you, fallen priests."

The priests looked around frantically as Shao swooped in, snatching them one by one and disappearing into the shadows with their bodies mangled by Shao's crushing jaws. The priest heard the moans of agony from the priests Shao left alive but suffering.

The archdeacon trembled in panic. "Kill me already, foul beast!" shouted the archdeacon.

"Momentarily, disgraced one. I wish for you to fully appreciate the terror being visited upon you, and I thought the pitiful moans and screams of your apostate priests would be the appropriate music to accompany you to hell!" Shao growled."

The tactic was proving effective, as the deacon began whimpering as he listened to his dying followers. The deacon heard a loud crunch as Shao chased, bit into, and tore away the neck of a suddenly silent priest. The arch-deacon screamed, turned, and ran screaming, "Nooo!"

Shao kept pace, nipping at his heels. Each nip took away a scrap of flesh, followed by a scream by the deacon. This continued until they were in sight of a church. The deacon, seeing this, screamed loudly for help. Shao tripped him, and the deacon slammed into the ground. Looking up, he saw the great cat stand above him, opening his great mouth, revealing his enormous fangs. The scream the deacon was going to emit was cut short as Shao, with his razor-like fangs, crunched and tore the face of the deacon completely off. Shao's ears perked up as he heard the howl of the hell hound baying. *They've made the breach,* Shao *t*hought. Bunching powerful muscles, he sprang toward the castle.

CHAPTER 26

BELLUM TORRIS (BRAND OF WAR)

The path was clear as Cain, Diego, and Mulsine cleared the lip of the mountain.

"Odd that the dark one has not set a watch," observed Mulsine.

"Not at all," Cain said aloud.

"Master, had we not best keep our voices down so as not to ruin the element of surprise?" asked Mulsine.

"I am not inclined to believe we are fortunate enough to have that element as an ally, Pierre," Cain pointed out.

"Excuse me?" Mulsine asked.

"What he means is that Satan already knows we're coming," clarified Diego.

"Really? Do you think so? Shame that!" Mulsine muttered sarcastically. Just as the three began their gauntlet, Shao joined them. "What did I miss"? he growled.

"Nothing yet." Pierre responded.

The three, accompanied by the great Bengal, approached the gate, unmolested.

"Really?" asked Mulsine. "Not even a warm-up?" he shouted aloud.

"He wants us relaxed with our guard down," Cain declared as he stepped up to the gate and politely knocked.

"What the hell was that!" declared Mulsine.

Cain glanced at him. "Grace. We will always act accordingly."

"But, master, what if he doesn't answer?" Mulsine said loudly.

"Then we knock again, Harder!" Cain replied.

"To what end, master?" Mulsine asked, exasperated.

"To the end that we either annoy the hell out of him, pardon the expression, or we terrorize him as the doors are smashed from their hinges and wood becomes splinters," finished Cain.

"I can live with that," Mulsine said, smiling.

Upon the fifth knock, the gates splintered open, flying off its hinges. The hallway leading to the main reception room was bereft of everything except grotesque statuary. Diego glanced at them with disdain.

"Oh my!" Mulsine exclaimed between revulsion and macabre amusement. "How would one categorize this . . . exhibit?" he finished.

In the blink of an eye, Diego tore through the room, smashing everything. Looking back at his handiwork, he glanced over at Mulsine. "Well, Pierre, from my perspective, I'd categorize it as broken," he said.

The large doors at the end of the room swung open, noisily belching out the odor of brimstone, sulfur, and noxious fumes of decay. Diego spoke to Shao telepathically. *"Brother, outflank the beast"* Shao backed away and, with great stealth, snuck along the right side of the throne room. Within the mists issued forth a beastly growl as Cerebus took post beside Satan, who sat upon a throne. At the foot of the throne stood Serrate. "You dare enter the presence of the eternal Satan!" declared Serrate. "Firstborn of angels. Rightful lord of Earth!" proclaimed Serrate.

"He does go on, does he not?" asked Pierre snidely.

"That he does," conceded Diego. "A bit flowery to suit me," he observed sarcastically.

"Where cat!" growled Cerebus. "Me wants destroy cat!"

Diego smiled at the hound. "You really should work on that syntax thing you got going on there. Where cat? Cat says dog too small. The cat might break dog," Diego teased, infuriating Cerebus.

As one, Satan charged at Diego. Serrate, Cerebus, and his remaining disciples attacked Cain and Mulsine.

The mountain shook as the titanic forces engaged in battle on the mountain top. Far below on the docks, Agrat and her sisterhood prepared to board their ship.

"Madam?" one of the sisters called Anna inquired of Agrat.

"Yes, sister," responded Agrat.

"What is it that we flee from with such haste?"

"It is not for us to question our lord's command, sister, but to obey!" declared Agrat. "Of course, Mother, I meant no disrespect," declared Anna.

"Be sure of that at all times. We set sail for the ancient city. Now be about your duties," Agrat commanded.

The sister bowed, retreating.

The roof of the castle exploded outward as the ship set sail. Agrat felt dread as she looked back. Her flock left her alone for fear of the volatile temper of the Mother Inferior. Anna quietly slipped over to the side of the boat, swimming beneath the surface as the boat pulled away from shore. She quietly swam to shore, watching the boat depart. She turned around, looking at the Castle again, and sought the entrance to the cave they had just departed.

BATTLE

The disciple called Zutha hurled himself at Cain, who caught him by the throat just as the disciple Angor crashed into his exposed side. Cain reached with his free hand, grabbing Angor by his collar.

Lamiel, the third disciple, seeing Cain exposed, dove in for a killing blow. His flight was interrupted just as he reached its target as Mulsine snatched him by the neck, stopping him cold in mid-flight. Lamiel thrashed as Mulsine, using him as a club, swatted the hell hound, who had hurled himself at Mulsine, sending the beast crashing into a wall.

Diego and Satan flew into each other, colliding with titanic force, causing the roof to explode.

Mulsine stopped using the battered disciple as a club, flipped him around, then hit Lamiel so hard as to partially decapitate him. Angor, seeing this, screamed, struggled loose, and swung at Cain again, striking him with a powerful blow.

Satan reached for Diego. Diego caught his hand and, to Satan's amazement, bit his fingers off. Howling, Satan pulled his hand back.

With Satan's shriek, Angor looked up to make sure his Lord was still in the battle. He looked back at Cain and was shocked to see a smiling Cain standing where Angor had just landed a blow that would have felled a giant tree. "My turn." Cain smiled. He snatched the supposed disciple. "This is a poor excuse for a disciple, Serrate! Did we not teach you better?" Cain said as he shook the frightened vampire and began pounding him on the head and body, breaking bones quicker than they could heal.

Cerebus had struggled to his feet. Seeing Cain battling Angor with his back exposed to the beast, charged him. The roar that followed his movement brought fear to the hell hound. He felt the hot breath that warned him of an imminent bite as the mighty Bengal Shao-sin attacking from his flanking position bore down on him.

Satan, in the meantime, struggled with Diego, surprised that this youngling could be giving him so much trouble. As they engaged again, Satan tried to distract Diego. "The last of your bloodline is destroyed, fool. Your servant is now mine, and your cousin is now one of my witches!"

Satan mocked. Diego stared, shocked about the news of a cousin. He snapped out of his reverie as the hell hound yelped. Shaos' fangs were firmly embedded in one of the necks of the three-headed dog. He straddled his back and, with his powerful hind legs, began shredding the other two heads of the foul hound, who let out blood-curdling yelps.

Satan took advantage of the distraction and bore his claws as he dove to impale Diego. Seeing this, Cain ripped the head off the disciple Angor. Diving into the fray, Cain caught the blow meant for Diego full in the chest. Satan was repelled by an indescribable force hurling him backward. All the combatants were also thrown to the ground by the power of the force.

Recovering quickly, Mulsine hurled himself at Serrate and began steadily pounding on Serrate when he saw his master fall. Hurling Serrate at a far wall where he crashed, Mulsine rushed to Cain's side, where Diego was already kneeling beside him.

"Master, master!" Diego screamed. "Diego," Cain whispered. "Please stop shouting, Diego." Looking down at his brother, friend, and mentor, Diego spoke softly. "I am here, master," Cain whispered. "You must not continue this fight." Diego's face showed fury. "But, master," protested Diego. "No, no buts. Obey me, Diego."

Satan had gotten to his feet. "Yes, Diego, obey him or die! Your master foolishly sacrificed himself. Join me now or die!" he threatened.

Before Diego could think, he had flung himself at Satan. The impact was like a thunderclap as Diego landed atop Satan, pummeling him furiously. Serrate jumped on Diego's back in an attempt to yank the enraged Diego off his master. Mulsine came up behind Serrate, kicking him in the back. Just then, Satan struck Diego, sending him sprawling and unconscious. Satan then knelt over Diego, raising his hand to strike when Shao jumped on Satan, knocking him off Diego.

He stood guard between Satan and Diego. Satan, satisfied with the results, called to Serrate, "Let us depart!" The hell hound limped to his master, back shredded, foul flesh oozing slime.

"I kill you next time, cat," threatened the hound.

"Come play, puppy," Shao invited.

"Your master is dying. Your time is at an end. You should have joined me when you had the chance. The next time we meet we will finish our business"! Satan exclaimed. Embracing his disciples and vanishing in a cloud of sulfuric smoke.

WITCHES DEPARTURE/ CAINS REDEMPTION

The fleeing ship containing the witches sliced through the waves as the castle became smaller and smaller in the distance. A stiff breeze made for choppy waters that slapped the hull of the boat. Upon hearing the explosion of the collapsing roof and the din of battle even out this far, Agrat collected her witches and realized that one was missing. "Where is Anna"? Agrat demanded. The sisters looked among one another before Sister Dalia spoke. "Mother Reviled, we can only guess that the Disciple Anna has snuck off the boat." Agrat, back-handed Dalia knocking her to the floor. The other sisters looked on in silence. "Mother," Dalia begged. "She is only one sister and the timidest amongst us, and she is weak and no great loss to us." Agrat glared at Dalia with barely contained fury. "Fool! are you blind? Can you not see that she came in a manner that drew no attention and left just as quietly?" Agrat whispered harshly. Dalia looked at Agrat with a blank stare. Agrat growled. "Stupidity stares back at me through your eyes, child." Agrat spat condescendingly; looking around, she gestured to the other sisters. "Come, let this be a lesson. The one we call Anna is of the Torrolisimo bloodline; we are interested in her because of her relationship with the master's enemy Diego Torrolisimo". "The one that made master Serrate?" Sister Magdalena asked unwisely. Agrat slapped Magdalena across the face, shouting. "Blasphemy! The lord Serrate was born when the dark aspect was awakened in him". Agrat declared. "Now consider all that I have shared with you. Learn from it. I will deal with the traitor later; right now, we have a job to do. They went below decks, where they immediately set up a witches' circle. Burning various items of evil potency, they began chanting spells of protection and deflection, attempting to aid their evil master.

If one could view the spiritual, they would have seen the effects of their incantations gathering around the boat as red and green tendrils wrapped themselves around it and began to head toward the castle, where the witches were directing the hellish spells.

A bright light seemed to intercept the evil vapors. They appeared to entwine with each other until the sick-looking tendrils retreated, settling over the boat it came from. It seemed to pulsate then spew forth its contents upon the boat. The Sisters now found themselves fighting off a cohort of Ravagers who were summoned to aid their master but were somehow deflected back at them. A short battle ensued. Sister Theresa and Magdalena caught the worst of it as they were beaten and scratched. Dalia was bitten before Agrat wove a spell of teleportation and dropped the Ravagers in the ocean. The boat continued to its destination with a very angry Mother reviled and a badly beaten coven of witches. Agrat aimed her anger at the traitor Anna. Thinking, the young witch spied to learn their secrets to aid her damnable cousin. The Mother most reviled swore an oath of vengeance. The bright vapor that intercepted the boat hovered a moment then made its way to the castle, settling gently between the grieving trio of Diego, Mulsine, and Shao-sin. Lying prone, breathing shallowly, was Cain.

"Well done, my sons," Cain gasped.

"Father," Mulsine gasped. "How could you say that? We have failed you," he cried, blood tears streaming down his face.

"No, my son, you have done well. the three of you have managed to foil Satan's plot of total control of the church, and he has brought his judgment upon himself". Cain informed them.

Still not understanding, Diego asked, "How did we accomplish that, master?"

Cain smiled. "Satan has foolishly burdened himself with the curse that has inflicted me; only his weight is sevenfold as deemed by the Lord during his judgment of my slaying beloved Abel." Cain coughed.

"But why master? Why sacrifice yourself this way?" Diego asked.

"The Son revealed to all that through self-sacrifice, heaven could be attained. From the moment I struck Abel, a lamented knowing the evil, I in part had awakened in man. I waited many thousands of years for one with your particular qualities Diego, The stubbornness of a bull, the heart of a lion, and the compassion of a priest. I knew such a combination was going to be difficult to find, but here you are. Cain expelled softly.

"It is as you say, Cain, son of Adam and Eve. First of the flesh touched by God," a voice said, filling the room. It was authoritative powerful. "So as a messenger sent from the beloved Son, and in his name I proclaim, so is the firstborn of a man forgiven of his transgressions. In his name, let him join from that which he was separated." The voice began to center itself in the room as vaporous tendrils of the rainbow, brilliant in its spectacle, began to coalesce into a form.

As the brilliance faded, a beautiful yet familiar man stood before them. The man smiled. "My dear friends," he greeted warmly.

All but Cain were confused with their inability to identify the familiar man.

"Forgive me," said Mulsine, "are we aquatinted, monsieur?"

The spirit said gently. "You once threatened to rip my arms off," the shining being replied, snickering.

Mulsine seemed to grow pale. "Mon dieu," he proclaimed. "Monsieur, I assure you I have no recollection of ever . . ." Mulsine paused as Diego smiled, recognition in his eyes.

"Ishar!" Diego proclaimed.

Mulsine looked shocked. "Is this possible?" he asked.

The brilliant being said, "I was he you knew as Ishar, but thanks to you, Masters Cain and Diego, and of course the merciful Son, who interceded on my behalf, I was redeemed, surpassed my nature and was thus reborn," the being reported. "Who then are you, brother?" Mulsine inquired.

"I have been restored. I am now Rasha-el," The gently shining being said by way of introduction.

Cain sat up, which instantly set Diego and Mulsine to fuss over him. "Master, you must rest," claimed Diego.

Cain slapped their caring hands away and called to Shao, who had found a quiet corner to lie down, appearing to pout. "Shao, my friend, why are you not beside me?" Cain asked.

Shao turned his head away as if perturbed by Cain. Diego and Mulsine were stunned by Shao's behavior, as he was undoubtedly the most protective of Cain's disciples. "Shao, what troubles you? Did you not hear the master request his beloved disciple beside him?"

Shao growled, "If I am his beloved, ask him why he would leave me!"

Confused, Diego and Mulsine turned to Cain for clarification. "Master?" Diego asked.

Cain looked to Rasha-el, who nodded. "Children, I have been redeemed. With his hand, Satan drew my curse unto himself. Diego, you and Pierre must drink of me so that my demon within may join with you since he has of yet attained redemption and is still counted among the fallen. Adremalach will join with you and aid you in punishing those that would harm the innocent in his bid for forgiveness. Shao, you will guard Mulsine and Diego, for their destiny is prophesied, and they shall have the honor to be two witnesses of The holy sons' righteousness. One shall come you thought was lost, Diego, and she will aid you and your family shall be restored. Cain offered his wrists to his disciples. "Drink my sons and take the fire lord into yourselves, and he will aid you as he aided me." Diego and Pierre looked at one another and as one drank from their maker. The spirit of the fire-lord entered Diego, who sat absorbing the memories of Cain; Pierre, however, heard the voice of Cain in his head. *My son Adramalech will reside with Diego; something awaits you that would not abide the dread fire lord, so I ask this of you.* Cain spoke aloud.

"Pierre, I ask that you watch over these two rather temperamental disciples of mine, for though Diego is strong and fast and Shao powerful, you, Monsieur Pierre du Mulsine, are wise and patient. You all must sleep now, for a time comes that shall signal the end of times. Then you three shall waken and set straight the path for his coming.

"As for myself, it is through you, my disciples, that I have found my redemption and earned The holy Son's forgiveness. I am forever in your debt. Now I join my father, mother, and beloved little brother, who have prayed for me since my fall. I join them now with the forgiving Son and loving Father of us all. Fare thee well, my children. Know that I will always be watching."

Cain turned to Rasha-el. "I am ready, old friend." He turned and smiled at his three disciples, that wept for both joy for Cain and sadness at their selfishness, knowing they would not see the great being again. Rasha-el and Cain were enveloped in a great bright and warm glow that appeared to surround them; they watched Cain and Ra-sha-el walk toward glorious colors and shapes beyond their comprehension as they slowly disappeared. The disciples sat there for a time motionless and stunned at the turn of the nights' events. The sky began to pale, announcing the coming dawn; Diego snapped out of the reverie.

"Let us be about the masters last commanded," Diego said coldly, suppressing his feelings. "I shall go to my ancestral home that we have regained to sleep until the time of awakening."

"I shall retire in my villa," proclaimed Mulsine.

"I shall go to the Pyrenees to be close to both of you, my brothers," Shao growled.

"Until that time then, Diego." The great cat nuzzled Diego, who roughly grabbed his ears. "Now, don't go spending the time chasing mice Gato" Diego whispered affectionately. Shao laid a gentle paw alongside Diego's head, then pushed it. "As long as you don't try bull riding." Shao joked, bringing Diego back to his first attempt at feeding as a Vampyre. Shao then turned to Mulsine. "Frenchman," Shao growled. Pierre looked at Shao coldly. "Cat." They both slowly grinned. "Still creepy." Pierre pointed out. Shao tilted his head and bolted off to the Pyrenees Mountains to guard over his two Vampiric brothers until the prophesied end of days. Pierre turned to Diego. "Much has occurred upon our meeting, young brother," Pierre observed. Diego nodded. "With much yet to unfold, dear elder," Diego replied affectionately. "We shall mourn the loss of our master." Pierre intoned sadly. "Yes, brother, but we should also rejoice; not only has our master achieved heaven, but our dear Ishar- Ra-sha-el also has a place among the blessed. Diego observed. Mulsine nodded. "Agreed." He responded simply. The Vampyres of the firstborn embraced. "Until the summoning, brother." Whispered Pierre. separating Diego grinned. "Always so dramatic," he laughed.

Upon returning to their respective lairs, each set private chambers deep in the earth. Pierre found a beautiful spot close to his villa, while Diego returned to the caves beneath his beloved homeland. He did not rest immediately, as one thing Cain had mentioned kept him preoccupied, and that was of the one thought to be lost but shall be found. As perplexing as the thought was, Diego shut his eyes for his sleep, not knowing it would be centuries before reawakening.

In the Pyrenees, the great cat looked over his last kill. *Better than waking up starving*, the cat thought. The wonderful thing about the Basque Pyrenees was the limitless amount of caves. Upon finding the one most suiting his taste, Shao prepared for his rest. He was impatient to see his friends again and anxious for the time when they would be reunited.

Quietly, shrouded by a spell of negative space, deep in the caves of Torrolisimo, a witch prepared a spell of suspended animation. The sleep period could be very long, so she filled herself with slow dissolving herbs coated in honey. Her last thought before sleep was, *"I shall fight beside you, cousin, and avenge our family."*

EPILOGUE

Revelation 11:3–7

(v. 3) And I shall give power to my two witnesses, and they will prophesy for one thousand and sixty days clothed in sackcloth.

(v. 4) These are the two olive trees. The lamp stands before God.

(v. 5) If anyone seeks to harm them, fire proceeds from their mouth and devours their enemies.

(v. 6) They have the power to shut the heavens, so there are no rainfalls. They have the power to turn water into blood and strike the earth with plagues as they desire. I rise to make war against them that would quench their flame

FIN
Written by J.E. Serrano